She was getting ready to go back upstairs when she heard the storm door open. Tensing, she waited for a knock. But there was only the whoosh of the door closing again.

''Kirsten?'' she called as she peered through the sidelight.

There was no answer, and nobody to be seen. Slowly she opened the door, and a fat manilla envelope fell inside. Picking it up, she looked at the address. Her name was printed across the front. Instead of a stamp in the upper right-hand corner, there was a block of four old Christmas seals. Across them someone had drawn wavy cancel lines. **But it was the postmark that made the hair on the back of her neck stand up.** It wasn't the usual circle with the name of the post office around the inside edge. It was an infinity mark. Just like the signature at the bottom of the last few letters.

SAMANTHA CHASE'S

POSTMARK

Tudor Publishing Company
New York and Los Angeles

Tudor Publishing Company

ISBN: 0-944276-11-3

Printed in the United States of America

First Tudor printing—July 1988

Dedication:

To Linda, Kate, and Lydia
for their aid, comfort, and insights

Acknowledgements:

We are greatly indebted to Captain James A. Taylor, Commander Rockville District, Montgomery County Police, and Captain John F. Miller, Deputy Police Chief, Rockville City Department, for answering our many questions about police procedures; to Sergeant Roy P. Hudson, Jr., Tactical Enforcement Unit, Fort Pierce, Florida, for providing information on drug trafficking; to Dr. Frank T. Barranco, Sr., Orthopedic Surgery Staff, Johns Hopkins Hospital, for help on medical procedures; to the Ambassador and Mrs. Petrignani of the Italian Embassy, for graciously inviting us to their National Day Celebration; and to Tom Clancy for being brave enough to teach us how to shoot.

Prologue

Sunday, May 8

As they drew near the edge of the field, the leather strap suddenly dug into Marian Lewis's hand.

"Baron! Heel!"

The ninety-pound Labrador at the other end of the chain came to a reluctant but abrupt halt.

"Good boy." Marian patted the dog's dark flank before moving. He was used to a half-hour walk, and the thing he liked most was romping in the field between Orchard Brook and Potomac Manor. But today, with sixteen people coming for Mother's Day brunch, Marian had a million things to do.

When she and Baron turned the corner that would take them away from the field, the big dog swiveled his head and fixed her with a mournful look.

Marian hesitated and then made a decision. Screw the vacuuming! Her sister-in-law's kids were going to drop more food on the floor than they ate. She might as well clean the whole mess up along with the dog hairs later.

As she reached down to release the catch on the leash, Baron quivered with excitement. In a flash he was off across the field. Marian watched as he headed for the stand of pines where some elementary-schoolers had built a play fort.

She gave him five minutes to enjoy himself before calling him back. "Barrrr—ron."

He didn't emerge from the trees. Served her right for letting him off the chain, she thought as she started across the field. He must have found some kids to play with, and he wasn't going to come.

But as she stepped under the branches, there was no sound of high-pitched laughter.

"Baron. Where are you?"

The dog responded with a low growl that raised the hair on the back of Marian's neck.

He was pulling at something just out of view beyond the weathered boards of the rickety playhouse. As she watched, a scuffed red sneaker incongruously matched with a lace-edged sock emerged. They were attached to a thin white leg.

My God. One of the kids was hurt, and Baron had found her.

Marian sprinted forward. It took several seconds, after she'd rounded the corner of the little building, to take in what she saw. Then her throat constricted in a soundless spasm, and her heart slammed against the inside of her chest.

A chalk-white face wreathed with blond curls. Slashes in the tee shirt. Dried blood that stained the white fabric a dirty rust. Lifeless fingers clasped around the waist of a Victorian doll. And the smell of death.

A little girl. Butchered.

The scream that had been frozen inside ripped from Marian's lungs.

Chapter 1

Tuesday, October 18

The biting October wind closed the heavy front door with a decisive slam. Johanna Hamilton was still shivering as she hung her leather raincoat on the antique rack in the corner. After the gray drizzle outside, the office, located on the ground floor of her home, felt like a haven of warmth and light.

Johanna's middle-aged assistant, Betty Cumberland, looked up from the word-processor screen. "How'd the meeting go?"

"It almost didn't. You know how it is in D.C. when it rains. I got stuck in a traffic jam at Dupont Circle and was fifteen minutes late to the Mayflower."

"But you made it."

"Um hum," Johanna turned to give her appearance a quick check in the mirror. "I wasn't ready for weather like this," she mused as she finger-combed the thick, dark curls that framed her oval face. Except for the slightly wind-blown hair and pale skin, the young woman who stared back with wide-set blue eyes looked very professional and in control. It hadn't always been that way, she thought as she absentmindedly rubbed the aching chill out of her left wrist. But that just made success all the sweeter.

Betty caught the satisfied expression on her face. "I take it you got another contract."

"Yes. And it's a big one. I'll tell you about it at lunch." Johanna crossed to her honey-colored oak desk, sat down, and began to shuffle through pink message slips. There were lots of calls to return, but that was simply testimony to how well her public relations business was going. Her client list included a senator who had his sights set on the White House, half a dozen authors, and a select group of businesses and public service organizations.

Two years ago, after her marriage had come apart at the seams, she'd put her career on hold while she struggled to pull her personal life back together. Then she'd literally fled the city—giving up her condo in Bethesda and her office in the National Press Building and moving herself and her daughter Kirsten into the old farmhouse in Potomac, Maryland, that her grandfather had partially restored.

Some days she'd almost been afraid to leave the house. The fact that she was making regular appointments downtown again was a measure of how far she'd come.

"Mitch Johnson is anxious to tell you about his interview with *Sixty Minutes*," Betty noted.

"Then I'll call him first," Johanna said, reaching for the phone.

Mitch was a Vietnam vet confined to a

wheelchair. He hadn't made her a lot of money, but working with him had helped put her own problems in perspective. Through her efforts, he'd become a focal point for national concern on dignity for the disabled.

Johanna beamed as she hung up the phone. "Sounds as if he had Ed Bradley eating out of his hand."

Betty nodded with satisfaction and got up to bring some folders from the walk-in closet. With the files and supplies hidden, the rest of the office had a spacious look. Two velvet couches flanked the wood stove set in the old fireplace, and twin desks faced each other across an Oriental rug.

While Johanna returned calls, Betty assembled press kits. They broke for lunch and then put in another hour on routine tasks.

"I need to stretch my varicose veins before I do the labels," she finally said.

Johanna laughed. "Want to get the mail?"

"Sure."

"Bundle up. And take the umbrella."

When Betty returned from the end of the driveway, she set a pile of mailers and envelopes on her employer's desk before she hung up her coat.

Johanna thumbed through the usual assortment of bills, junk, and business correspondence. But her fingers stopped when they encountered a square envelope tucked between her American Express bill and a confirmation letter from the producer of the *Larry King Show*. It could have been a greeting card. Johanna knew it wasn't.

Her pulse rate accelerated as she scanned the careful printing on the front. There was no return address. There never was.

It had been two months since she'd gotten a letter from her ex-husband, and she'd dared to hope he had finally decided to leave her alone. She should have known better.

Quickly she checked the postmark and let out the breath she'd been holding. Pittsburgh, Pennsylvania. The last time he'd written, he'd been in Richmond, Virginia, a lot closer. At least that was something.

"From Rick?" Betty's question was edged with alarm.

"Afraid so." Johanna tried to sound nonchalant, but the pitch of her voice gave her away. She forced herself to slide the piece of yellow lined paper out of the envelope. As her eyes scanned quickly down the page, she felt her mended wrist begin to throb. This time it was more than the cold weather.

Her ex-husband had started off printing. But control had quickly become too much of an effort. As the words marched across the lines, his handwriting degenerated into a wavy scrawl.

> You have no right to keep Kirsten to yourself. I'm her father, for Christ's sake. I want her back. I want you back. And if you're too high and mighty to see things my way, you're going to be sorry. I can take her away from you any time I want, and there's not a damn thing you can do

about it. We need to be together.
And don't you ever dare think that
some other man can take my place
with either one of you.

The rest of the text degenerated into a
series of threats. Johanna blanched. She could
picture Rick's hand shaking as he wrote.

God, what had happened to the man she'd
married, she asked herself for the thousandth
time. At first she'd tried to hold the marriage
together. She'd given him the benefit of the
doubt, and she'd bent over backwards to see
things from his perspective. But the night
she'd ended up in an emergency room, lying
about why she was there, she'd known the
time for excuses was over.

After tossing the letter on the desk, she
stared unseeing at the gray sky out the window.

Betty was leaning forward anxiously. "Bad?"
she murmured.

Johanna closed her eyes for a moment and
then nodded. Betty knew what bad really was,
she thought. A widow almost ten years, she'd
come to work for the Hamilton Agency when
it was so small that the two of them had had
to share one temperamental electric typewriter.
And she'd stuck with Johanna through the
worst of it.

"Rick's back on his 'togetherness' kick."

"Want to call the police again?"

Johanna sighed. "You know what they
think—that it's just harrassment. Rick's in
Pennsylvania, and the police aren't going to
do anything unless he shows up around here.

Besides, he's so whacked out now, I can't picture him carrying out any constructive plan of action," she added, as much to reassure herself as for anything else. It was a ritual. Listing all the reasons why Rick couldn't hurt her or Kirsten again. Like when she'd been a kid and afraid of the dark. She'd protected herself by going to bed with a bunch of stuffed animals that all had to be in a certain place on her bed. There was hardly room to sleep. But as long as the menagerie was surrounding her, she wouldn't be grabbed by the nameless monsters out in the darkness.

Her monster had a name and face now. But he hadn't dared come near her in over a year. Her lawyer, Sam Fontino, had made sure Rick Hamilton would be arrested if he set foot in Maryland. And she could only pray that Sam's restraining order would continue to keep him away.

Detective Dan Whitmore, Montgomery County Police Department, pressed the handkerchief over his nose and mouth and tried not to breathe too deeply.

God, what a stench.

Unfortunately for the Morgensterns, they'd left a dozen eggs in the refrigerator when they'd taken off for a week at their condo in Ocean City. They'd also left fifteen pounds of prime steak and two gallons of ice cream in the freezer compartment. Butter Pecan and Strawberry.

The ice cream now made a congealed brown and pink lake in front of the open refrigerator. On top, the expensive steak had been turned to dead meat by the heat of the compressor. The broken eggs lay where they had landed, in random sulfurous splotches on the floor and counters—interspered with scattered crackers and the contents of cereal boxes.

The Morgensterns had taken a quick look at the mess in the kitchen and the rest of the house and had retreated to the Marriott in Rockville.

Dan wished he had that sort of option. No longer able to fight the foul odor, he backed out of the kitchen and shut the door. The dining room wasn't in much better shape. There was broken china and crystal all over the faux-marble floor. At least they didn't smell.

He'd already looked at the rest of the house. Living-room upholstery slashed with a knife from the kitchen. Bedrooms a wreck. The Morgenstern daughter had had a doll collection. Now it was reduced to a hurricane debris of tiny arms and legs and smashed porcelain faces.

His partner, Nicolas Jackson, came down the stairs shaking his head. "Worse than Brenton Village. Only the stuff there wasn't worth anything to start with," he added, his café-au-lait face carefully emotionless. Nico's father had been black, his mother Puerto Rican.

Dan knew he was referring to the D.C. housing project where he'd lived as a kid. There weren't many guys on the force he'd talked to about his childhood. But skin color notwithstanding, the two of them had discovered they had a lot of things in common growing up: second-hand clothes, drug dealers trashing the hallways of vacant apartment buildings, mayonnaise sandwiches for dinner.

They'd been partners for three years, and they made a good team, although you wouldn't know it to look at them. The only physical resemblance was their short-cropped, dark hair. Short was coming back into fashion now—but neither of them cared.

Nico was slight and wiry with deceptively smooth, rounded features. He could duck under a punch with a dancer's grace and give as good as he got. Impulsive, he was given to blinding flashes of insight that were right almost as often as not.

Dan was tall and rangy, with a quiet, hidden strength patiently acquired. His face was angular and roughly sculpted. Deep-set gray eyes fringed with thick lashes softened the effect a bit. His nose had been broken in a street fight. And once, his jutting chin had gotten in the way of a switchblade, which left an inch-long white scar. His mind was logical and analytical. No one could beat him for collecting information, sorting through facts, and poring over them until he'd solved a problem.

"Man, this is crazy. Think it was dopers?" Nico asked.

Dan shook his head. "Whoever it was left the Sony Profield, and Mrs. Morgenstern ran upstairs to check her jewelry box. Her diamonds are still there."

The team from the lab arrived, and the detectives stepped outside, glad to get away from the senseless destruction.

"This remind you of anything?" Dan asked, turning up his collar against the wind.

"You mean Jack Daniels? This isn't exactly his M.O."

"Except for the half-empty bottle on the table and the wiped-clean glass in the sink."

"Yeah. I'll bet the lab isn't going to find any prints."

For the past year there had been a series of peculiar break-ins in several of the expensive developments off Falls Road. The pattern was always the same. Residents out of town. Forced entry. No fingerprints. Nothing of value taken. But the perpetrator usually fixed a sandwich and poured himself a generous glass of his absent host's liquor. Preferably Jack Daniels.

"Jack's always been so neat and tidy. If it's him, what made him go berserk this time?"

"No cold cuts in the fridge."

Dan groaned. The smart-ass remark defused the odd sensation of tightness that had spread across his chest. There was nothing he could put down on paper right now to prove the thesis, but this wasn't ordinary vandalism. It was something pathological. "I think the guy's a sicko."

"Yeah. It was spooky in there."

"You felt it too?"

Nicolas nodded.

They had reached the sidewalk. A cover of dark clouds still hung in the sky like wet cotton batting. Thrusting his hands in his pockets, Dan surveyed the quiet neighborhood of three-hundred-thousand-dollar homes with their trimmed hedges and manicured lawns. He could bet the residents were going to be pissed off about the piles of raked leaves that had been scattered again by the storm.

The Morgensterns' four-bedroom, stone and half-timber house was on a large corner lot. "Let's see if the neighbors heard anything," Dan suggested.

"If we're lucky enough to find anyone home."

Nico had pegged the subdivision right. It was the kind of place where most of the wives worked along with their husbands to support the upscale lifestyle. Although they started with the house next door, there was nobody home in the block except a mother with three preschoolers. She hadn't heard anything.

"We're going to have to come back in the evening," Nicolas predicted.

"There's a Buick in the driveway next door that wasn't there before," Dan pointed out. "Let's try that house again."

"Okay."

This time when they knocked, an old woman wearing a stained chenille bathrobe answered. Her hair was a white bird's nest; her blue eyes were cloudy.

"Did you knock before?"

"Yes, ma'am."

"I was on the pot." Moving aside with a slow shuffle, she gestured for them to come in.

The front hall smelled like Lysol.

"Mom, who is it, Mom? I've told you a thousand times not to open the door to strangers." A short, balding man wearing a sport coat that wouldn't have buttoned across his paunch came down the hall from the kitchen. He was holding a spatula.

"Police," Dan explained, flipping open his identification.

"Mom?" There was a pinched expression on his face as he looked from the policeman to the old woman.

She glanced down at her wet bedroom slippers and shrugged. "Can't get there as fast as I used to."

"No. No. We're just here to ask some questions about the house next door," Nico hurried to explain. "There was a break-in. Probably about four or five days ago."

"The Morgensterns? I think they're out of town, but I don't know where they went," the man said.

Dan nodded.

"They haven't been real friendly since my mother picked all the tulips in their yard last spring." A flash of pain flared in his eyes and his lips thinned for a minute. "She came to take care of me when Carol packed up the kids and moved out. And now—" He sighed and inclined his head toward his mother.

"Did either of you hear anything over at the Morgensterns late last week? It would have been at night."

"No."

"Yup."

It was the old lady who had answered affirmatively. Both officers turned in her direction. "Can we have your name, ma'am?"

"Why—uh—let me think. Muriel Beckett," she finally crowed triumphantly.

They exchanged glances. Nico shrugged and got out his notebook. "Can you tell us anything about the break-in?"

Her eyes took on a glint of excitement and words tumbled out in a rush. "Breaking glass. Woke me up. Three in the morning."

Officer Jackson was taking it down on the off chance it was going to be useful. "Are you sure about the time?"

"Of course I am! The clock struck."

"Did you see anything?"

"In the moonlight. It was him. It was him. I'd know him anywhere. Even dressed like that."

Dan could see the balding man tense and wondered what was coming.

"What did you see?" Nicolas asked.

"My father," the younger Beckett jumped in to answer the question.

"Tommy, go pick up your toys. It makes him angry when they're all over the floor," Muriel continued.

Nico raised his pencil. Dan shot the son a questioning look over his mother's head.

Tom Beckett shrugged. "My father was killed in Korea. She never got over it. Lately she's been positive she's seen him everywhere." He took the old lady's arm. "Your eggs are getting cold, Mom. Come on and have your lunch so I can get back to the Treasure Chest."

"He's not dead!"

"Mom, I'm sorry."

Muriel Beckett blinked in confusion and looked from her son to the police officers and back again. "You don't understand what I mean. You never understand what I mean." She shook her head and her gaze seemed to turn inward. "He didn't have his uniform," she mused. "I guess it couldn't have been him."

"No, Mom. It wasn't."

Her jaw jutted up. "You never believe me. You never believe anything I say." The words slurred into a childish whine. "I want Mrs. Wilson. Mrs. Wilson is nice to me. And he's nice to me. Not like you."

Tom Beckett had run out of patience. "Christ, Mom. Don't you remember? Mrs. Wilson is sick today. That's why I came home for lunch. Remember she called this morning? Remember we talked about it?"

"Maybe we should come back—" Dan began.

He didn't finish because Muriel's clawlike hand shot out and with surprising strength snatched the spatula from her son's grasp. He just managed to deflect the blow as she swung the metal cooking implement in the direction of his face. "Oh shit. Now see what you've done." He was looking at Dan and Nicolas.

"Listen—we didn't realize."

"Just get out of here. Okay?" As he spoke he seized his mother's hands roughly and held them in front of her.

"Okay. Sorry."

When they'd closed the door, the two men looked at each other.

Nicolas let out a breath. "Jesus."

"If she saw something, maybe we can get it out of her later."

"I doubt it."

"Yeah, for a moment there I thought we'd gotten lucky."

"Not us, man. Jack Daniels."

Chapter 2

Betty had just left for the day when Johanna picked up the phone.

"Are you in the mood for someone else's cooking?" her friend Susan Randolph asked. "Bob called to say he's working late, and I've just fixed a big casserole of stuffed shells. I need someone to help me out."

"What about Kirsten?"

"Brenda's volunteered to sit for her."

"Well—"

"When's the last time you were out of the house in the evening?"

Johanna grimaced, glad that her friend couldn't see her face over the phone.

"I know how you feel about being Super Mom," Susan continued.

"I'm not feeling super anything."

"What's wrong?"

"Another letter from Rick."

"Oh, Johanna, I'm sorry. You can tell me about it at dinner. And I'll cheer you up with the estimate from Kevin's orthodontist."

"Sure."

"Say yes and I'll throw in a glass of Chablis."

From upstairs came the high-pitched screech of a bow being torturously dragged across the strings of a rented violin. As per instructions, Kirsten was practicing. Did it ever get any better, or did you just go deaf, she wondered.

"Do I hear you wavering?"

"I do need some adult conversation this evening," Johanna admitted.

"Good. You'll be thrilled to know that the community safety meeting you've forgotten about is still at my house at eight."

"Ambushed. And I walked right into it."

Susan laughed, obviously pleased with herself. Then she grew serious again. "Johanna, I know you're busy. And I promise you don't have to be part of the committee if you don't want to. But we need someone with publicity experience to get us started."

"Okay. But those shells better be good. What time shall I come?"

"I'll send Brenda over around six. That'll give us at least an hour and a half before the meeting."

After getting her daughter's dinner started, Johanna went upstairs to change into a burgundy wool dress with a softly pleated skirt. As she was putting on some blusher, Kirsten came into the bedroom carrying her violin. "Do you want to hear me play 'Mary had—' " The blond-haired little girl broke off the question and stared at her mother. "Where are you going?"

"Mrs. Randolph invited me to dinner and a meeting."

"I don't like you to go out at night."

"I know, honey. And I don't do it very often. But I've already told her I'll come. Brenda is going to sit with you."

"Mom—"

"You can make brownies in the microwave."

"We can?"

"Uh hum."

The eight-year-old pursed her lips. "I need some dolls to sleep with me." She paused. "To keep me safe while you're not here."

Johanna's chest tightened as she remembered her own childhood need to fill her bed with stuffed animals when she was feeling scared. But with Kirsten there was more to it than just normal childhood fears. She'd seen her daddy's rages and his out of control behavior. She'd heard him vow that he was going to take her away with him.

Reaching out, Johanna put her arm around the narrow shoulder and squeezed reassuringly. "You know I wouldn't let anything bad happen to you." But even as she murmured the promise, she couldn't help thinking about Rick's letter. Damn him! Why couldn't he just leave them alone?

Kirsten turned serious blue eyes up toward her. "I know, Mommy. But my dolls make me feel better. Help me put them out."

"All right, sweetheart," she agreed.

The tired floorboards squeaked as mother and daughter made their way down the hall.

Sometimes this old place sounds like a haunted house, Johanna thought. The next time Hecht's had a sale, she was going to put in carpeting. That would cut down on the creaks and groans—which always seemed louder at night than during the day.

Johanna had decorated her daughter's room in quiet colors—soft peach and mauve. The furniture was the cherry set she'd had as a girl. But she'd added shelves against one wall to hold Kirsten's collection of dolls. Every time they went to White Flint Mall, Johanna let Kirsten drag her into Treasure Chest Toys. Even when she'd been pinching pennies, she'd found the money to surprise her daughter with the dolls she'd been admiring.

Johanna silently admitted she was trying to overcompensate. But sometimes she couldn't help herself. She understood how hard the past few years had been on Kirsten. And even though she knew most of it hadn't been her fault, she wanted to make it up to her daughter.

"Which ones do you want?" Johanna asked.

"Annabel and Victoria and Princess Leia. And my Cabbage Patch twins." Kirsten looked up at her mother. "And I want my bride doll and my ballerina."

The last two were part of an expensive collector series. "I thought we agreed those were just to look at—not play with."

"Oh, Mom. Carrie gets to play with hers. She even gets to give them a bath."

Johanna ignored the comparison. Instead, she turned down the covers on the frilly canopy bed while Kirsten brought the dolls from the shelves. As they had done many times before, they arranged the nighttime company against the headboard and along the sides of the bed.

Hands on hips, Kirsten surveyed the result. "And I want Julie, too," she announced.

"Any more and you'll have to sleep in the bathtub. Come on, let's have dinner."

"Can I have Coke?"

"Milk. Don't push your luck, my girl," Johanna said firmly.

Before going off to his important job at the National Bureau of Standards, Señor Hempsted had asked Juanita to make vegetable soup. Like everything else Mr. Hempsted wanted, it had to be done a certain way: with leeks and parsnips and plenty of barley and dried lima beans. You had to brown the bones to make the stock rich and cook it a day ahead of time so you could cool it in the refrigerator overnight and take the grease off the top. He had been very specific about that.

Juanita was just turning the bones in the hot oil when a flash of memory made her fingers clench convulsively around the plastic handle of the big spoon.

The bad dream she'd had last night. *Madre de Dios,* she didn't want to think about it. Resolutely she concentrated on scraping brown bits of meat from the bottom of the stock pot. But even when she squeezed her eyes closed, she couldn't shut the images out of her head.

They were bright and sharp and confusing—like bits of colored glass turning in a kaleidoscope. But the pattern didn't make any sense. The past? The future? Some muddled mixture of the two?

She had had dreams like this before. Back home. Never since she'd come to *Los Estados Unidos*. That was what had given her chills when she'd woken up.

Sometimes they had been nothing. Sometimes when they kept coming back they told the truth. If she could figure out what they meant.

In this dream she had seen a woman, her face framed by dark curls. *Hermosa*—pretty. *Delgada*—slender. *Miedosa*—afraid. Part of the time she had been in an office. Part of the time she had been standing in the middle of a room—a kitchen. Someone had made a mess of the place. Food from the freezer lay in a putrefying heap on the floor. Raw eggs were splattered around the kitchen counter. The woman's breath was shallow, her eyes wide as she surveyed the mess.

Where was the daughter? *Un hombre muy mal* had brought them here. A bad man. A crazy man. Or maybe he was going to bring them. Juanita had strained to see the bad man's face. It was important. But even as she had tried to bring it into focus, the features had melted and run like hot candle wax. And then they had reformed into another face.

There was a spitting sound in the pot and drops of hot oil exploded upward, hitting

Juanita's hand. She gasped and jumped back before reaching to turn down the heat.

Billy Hempsted looked up from the kitchen table where he was doing his homework. "Juanita, are you okay?"

"Si. Solo aceite caliente."

"I hate Dad's stupid vegetable soup. He makes every maid we get fix it."

"The soup is for tomorrow. I cook Esloppy Joes tonight."

"Esloppy Joes," Billy repeated. "Yeah. Esloppy Joes."

Juanita took a deep breath and turned back to the stove. Keep Señor Hempsted happy. Keep Señora Hempsted happy. Keep *los niños* happy. She wanted to stay here. It was a good job. And the Hempsteds were putting through the paperwork so she'd be legal.

It didn't cost much to live in their basement, so she could send a lot of money to her mother and brothers and sisters in Guatemala. If the immigration people didn't catch her before she got her green card. If she didn't call any attention to herself.

Forget the dream. It's none of your business. That woman is nothing to you, she told herself. You don't even know her name. Maybe the dream won't even come back. Then it'll be nothing. But she couldn't fool herself. Please God, make it just a dream.

Johanna kept her daughter company while she ate.

As the little girl bit down on a carrot, she gave an exaggerated grimace.

"What's wrong?"

"My loose tooth."

"Want me to wiggle it off?"

"It's not ready yet." She switched the food to the other side of her mouth and chewed contemplatively for a moment. "Terri says the tooth fairy brought her a dollar last time."

"Maybe she didn't have any change."

Kirsten gave her mother a suspicious look, but didn't press the issue.

Johanna was just putting the plates in the dishwasher when the phone rang.

Did Susan want her to bring something? She wondered as she picked up the extension on the kitchen desk. "Hello."

There was no response, yet she could hear the sound of breathing on the other end of the line.

"Hello?"

No answer. And no click. She knew someone was there. And it wasn't the office line. It was her personal number, which was now unlisted.

"Who is it?"

Still no answer. Johanna waited for a moment, her fingers turning icy and tightening on the receiver until the knuckles whitened.

"Rick?" She strained her ears again. "Is that you?" There might have been a change in the breathing pattern. Or maybe it was her own hollow breath echoing on the line. In the months after she'd first left him, her ex-husband had delighted in this particular kind of intimidation. How had he gotten hold of her new number?

Well, it didn't matter. She'd had enough. Anger made her features rigid, her voice hard and cold. "Rick, I don't care where you are or what kind of shape you're in tonight; I won't stand for this kind of harassment."

After what seemed like an eternity but was probably only a few seconds, she heard a click and then the dial tone. It should have brought relief. Instead she had to clasp her hands together to keep them from shaking. Rick had badgered her once today. Wasn't that enough? Maybe she really should call the police. Then she shook her head. She knew what they would say.

She glanced at the phone, half afraid it would ring again. Maybe she should cancel out on this evening after all. Then she firmed her lips. There was no proof the phone call was from Rick. And the postmark on his letter had told her he was in Pittsburgh. He didn't usually call long distance. No, letters had become his chief way of harassing her. It was probably a wrong number, and her own nervous tension had stretched the few seconds before the caller realized his mistake into an eternity. If there weren't any more calls by the time Brenda came, she'd go to Susan's.

As Johanna unloaded the dishwasher, her eyes kept darting to the phone. It seemed to stare silently back at her. To work off her nervous energy, she took a Brillo pad to the frying pan. She hadn't scrubbed the copper bottom in months. Now she attacked its black coating with the zeal of a sandblaster restoring a historic monument. When the doorbell rang, she jumped.

"Brenda's here." Kirsten's shout echoed through the high-ceilinged hall. "And she's got Amy with her. Can I open the door?" Susan's younger daughter, Amy, was in Kirsten's class.

To Johanna's delight, the two little girls had become friends. Kirsten wasn't going to mind staying home at all now. What a good idea of Susan's to send Amy along, Johanna thought. Kirsten had a playmate. Amy was out of her mother's hair. And there wasn't any problem about staying up late because school was closed tomorrow for a teachers' meeting.

"Go ahead and open the door," she called out.

As she came into the front hall, the two third-graders were already giggling about the gym teacher's stepping on her glasses. Johanna smiled as the small blond and carrot-top heads bent together. It was wonderful to see Kirsten forgetting about her fears and acting like a normal eight-year-old.

She glanced at her watch. It had been half an hour since the phone call. So it had just been a wrong number after all. She wasn't going to be far away. And Brenda was a freshman at the community college and a very capable young woman. There was no reason to stay home.

After instructions for Brenda and a hug

for Kirsten, Johanna took her leather coat out of the closet. There was a time not so long ago when Kirsten would have thrown a fit just as her mother tried to step out the door. Instead she'd led her guest down the hall to the kitchen.

Perhaps the worst was behind them after all, she told herself. As she closed the door and turned the dead-bolt, she could still feel a barbed wire knot of tension twisting in her stomach.

Chapter 3

The leaden gray of the sky had faded into a navy blue twilight. Johanna could have driven to Susan's but she felt the need to stretch her legs. Probably there would be someone at the meeting who could give her a ride home.

Halfway down the driveway she stopped to toss a small dead branch onto the grass. Then she looked back at the old house—all that remained of Orchard Brook Farm. Through the kitchen window she could see Kirsten and Brenda standing in front of the pantry. Evidently her daughter wasn't wasting any time getting to the brownies.

Johanna smiled. Years ago when she'd come for visits, she and Grandma had made brownies there, too. Grandma's old gas stove was just a memory now, along with the lace curtains in the living room window and the barn out back.

After Grandma had died, Grandpa sold off the land piece by piece. Now there were only two acres surrounding the house and a development of modern colonials and ranch houses where the cow pastures had been. The subdivision was called Orchard Brook after the farm.

But that couldn't erase Johanna's recollections of the past. She'd played with her own dolls in the old carriage house she now used for a garage. And she'd picked an orange striped kitten from one of the litters born in the barn to take home with her. She'd grown up loving this old place.

So it had been natural to think of moving out here after leaving Rick. The farmstead was a haven, a retreat. It was a place where she could lick her wounds and get back in touch with herself. Rick had almost made her lose her own grip on reality. But she'd fought back. And she was all the stronger for having battled her way free.

She turned for one more look at the house, clenching her fist as she remembered how she'd come so close to selling the place when Rick had been desperate for money. Thank God she'd insisted on renting it out instead.

At the end of the drive Johanna turned right, down the hill toward Susan's. Her friend's red brick colonial over on the next street was one of the houses she'd once thought of as invaders. Now she appreciated having neighbors.

The development had no streetlights and no sidewalks. The shadows had deepened. As Johanna walked along beside the curb, she wished more of the homeowners had turned on the ornamental lamps beside each driveway.

Her footsteps echoed on the damp black-top. Johanna turned up the collar of her leather coat and thrust her hands into the pockets. She couldn't hear anyone behind her. Yet she couldn't shake the sensation that there was someone out there in the night—following.

Somewhere behind her, gravel crunched. It sounded like car tires, but she couldn't hear a motor.

Maybe she should get out of the street and onto the wet grass. She glanced over her shoulder. No headlights. No engine sounds. Only darkness. Yet she still half felt something moving behind her.

Nerves, she told herself. But it was impossible to quiet the thudding of her heart. Her steps quickened as though trying to keep pace with the pounding in her chest.

Glancing to her right, she saw the Donovans' Cape Cod. Kirsten sometimes played with their daughter. She could knock on the door and go in there. But that was ridiculous. What would she tell the Donovans? Susan's was only down at the end of the block, she reminded herself.

Four houses away. Her stacked heels echoed on the wet street. Three houses away. Two houses. The feeling of a car drifting down the hill behind her was almost overwhelming. By the time she reached her friend's driveway, she was practically running and almost out of breath.

Susan didn't answer the bell until the second ring. She was a tall redhead with an animated face and a generous mouth that always made Johanna think of Carol Burnett.

"Come in. I was beginning to wonder where you were."

As Johanna stepped into the hall, the pounding rhythm of a loud rock album assaulted her ears.

"Kevin, turn that down," Susan called up the stairs. "Immediately." The volume was lowered a couple of decibels, but it didn't improve the sound of the music. Susan shrugged. "Sorry. Thirteen is impossible—for boys. With girls, you have another year's grace." Then she took in her friend's flushed face. "What's wrong?"

"I walked over." She hesitated. "I know it sounds silly, but I felt like someone was following me."

Susan turned to stare at her.

"It was probably just my overactive imagination."

"I guess that letter from Rick shook you up."

Johanna nodded. "And there was a phone call that made me jumpy."

Susan found a hanger and wedged her friend's coat into the over-stuffed front closet. "Rick *called* you too?"

"I don't know. I couldn't be sure it was him. Whoever was on the other end of the line didn't say anything. Probably they were embarrassed about getting a wrong number."

"I've done that," Susan agreed as she led the way to the kitchen. Stacked in the corner were half a dozen grocery cartons of assorted canned and packaged foods. This year, Susan was the chairman of the food drive for the underprivileged. In fact, every time Johanna came over, her friend was involved in at least two or three community projects. The child safety meeting tonight was another example.

A long time ago Susan had given in to Bob's insistence that his wife's place was at home. The energy she might have put into a career went into volunteer work. She got as much satisfaction from seeing fifty needy families fed on Thanksgiving day as Johanna did from getting one of her clients on the *Donahue* show. But no matter how busy she was, she always made time for her family and her friends.

Johanna noted that the table was already set for two. "Anything I can do to help?" she asked.

"Toss the dressing with the salad." After bringing the casserole to the table, Susan poured two glasses of wine. "Have you been out to the new outlet mall in Gaithersburg?" she asked.

Johanna shook her head.

"Alice Goodwin said they've got Ralph Lauren for kids—and Anne Klein for us. Want to check it out next week?"

"Sounds good."

"Did you hear that Alice's husband won another sales contest and they're both taking off in November for a ten-day Caribbean cruise?"

"Some people have all the luck. Didn't they go to Paris last summer?"

"No. Rome."

"I think we'll just have to settle for the outlet mall."

The meal was a pleasant interlude for Johanna. In her friend's sunny yellow kitchen, chatting about shopping and the Hamilton Agency's latest coups, it was easy to convince herself that there had been no one out there in the dark stalking her. She was wrong.

Out in the darkness he started the car, went down to the end of the street, and made a U-turn. Johanna had talked to him on the phone this evening. He'd taped the conversation with one of those special attachments you could buy at Radio Shack in the mall. They were having a red tag sale. He was glad he'd bought it. Now he could listen to her whenever he wanted.

Reaching for the cheap recorder beside him on the car's bench seat, he pressed the "play" button.

"Hello."

The only answer was the echo of his own breathing on the tape.

"Hello?" Johanna's voice was strained, tense.

There was a five-second pause.

"Who is it?" He knew it was dangerous to take the chance. But he'd wanted to hear her voice—and to make sure she was home. She'd done so much for so many people. Gotten them publicity. Changed their image. She'd even turned a helpless cripple like Mitch Johnson into a national hero. If she could do that for someone like poor old Johnson, she could do it for him. She already liked him. It was just a matter of getting her to understand his problems. And he could do something for

her, too. Her personal life was a mess. She'd be very grateful when he'd straightened that out for her.

"Rick is that you?" The question had sounded fearful. But she'd firmed her voice when she delivered the ultimatum. *"Rick, I don't care where you are or what kind of shape you're in tonight. I won't stand for this kind of harassment."*

He'd wanted to set her straight. Instead he'd hung up before he succumbed to the pressure of the words building up in his chest.

A few months ago he'd found the perfect place to watch Johanna's house. It was at the top of the hill where her grandfather had planted a stand of white pines. They were big trees now, with branches that overhung the road. At night, you wouldn't spot a small car parked under them. But with his high-powered binoculars, he could see inside both floors on one side of the house, the side with Johanna's and Kirsten's bedrooms. People didn't realize how much you could see through the windows at night.

He'd just gotten settled for the evening when Johanna had come out the front door and headed down the drive. She wasn't going to be home after all. Anger had boiled up inside him, and his hand came down on the steering wheel, barely missing the Goddamned horn. How dare she mess up his plans! He needed to be sure about her. He needed to know everything.

With a hand that trembled slightly, he reached into his pocket for a lemon ball. Rolling them between his finger and thumb like marbles always calmed him down. When his hand had stopped shaking, he took one of the candies out, stripped off the wrapper, and tossed it out the window. Then he pressed the candy into his mouth and started to suck.

The familiar lemon taste soothed his tight throat. There was nothing to worry about. Everything would work out the way he wanted it to. He pictured Johanna's face and the times her eyes had lit up when she saw him. He needed her. But she needed him, too. The letters would make her see that.

He let his quarry get halfway down the hill before shifting into neutral, letting out the brake and coasting down the street after her. He followed her all the way to the Randolphs' house. She was going to her friend Susan's. For how long? he wondered. It didn't matter. He could get by with hardly any sleep. That was one of the things that gave him an advantage over ordinary people. He could wait all night if he had to.

"You get the door while I put out the coffee and cookies," Susan said. "And make Kevin turn that music down some more, or the meeting's going to be blasted into the next galaxy by the Jefferson Starship."

"All right."

After passing the word to Kevin, Johanna greeted the first two arrivals. One was Ted Theologus, the president of the P.T.A. The other was Anne Waterford who was on the program committee. Johanna had met both of them at the school book fair last year.

Anne looked pale and drawn. "If I leave early, don't take it personally," she told Ted. "I've been sick."

Others drifted in over the next fifteen minutes. As the ten parents talked quietly in the Edwardian-style living room, Susan set out an electric coffee urn on the sideboard and a plate of bakery cookies on the low table in front of the tapestry-covered sofa.

The voices might be quiet, but Johanna could sense a feeling of tension in the room. In the spring, the community had been shocked by the rape and murder of eight-year-old Heather Morrison, whose body had been found in a field next to one of the neighboring developments. In the next few weeks, there had been considerable pressure to "do something." But it had been impossible to get a child safety program going over the summer. Now that the group was finally getting organized, everyone was feeling a bit guilty that it had taken so long.

After the coffee had been served, Ted checked his list. "I think everyone's here except the representative from the police department."

"I'm not surprised," somebody quipped.

The remark was followed by nervous laughter. It was a sore point with the community that the Morrison murder had never been solved.

"We're not here to critique the police," Ted reminded them. "We're here to find ways of keeping our kids safe."

There were murmurs of agreement.

As Ted went on to outline some of the problems they faced, Johanna glanced up to see Anne Waterford pleating her napkin. She didn't know the woman well, but she recognized the look. Was she also worried about an ex-husband who had threatened to snatch their daughter? Or was it just the idea of losing your child for a few minutes at the mall and never seeing her again?

Ted had just wound up his opening remarks when the doorbell rang, and the hostess got up to answer it.

There was a brief conversation in the hall. Then all eyes turned to the door as Susan ushered a tall, dark-haired man into the room. She introduced him as Detective Dan Whitmore from the Montgomery County police force.

Johanna could tell that Whitmore didn't like being the center of attention. He was a bit rough around the edges, she mused, wondering if he had been the right choice for the committee. But she concluded silently that she probably wouldn't have felt comfortable with any cop who showed up. Not after the way she'd been handled by the police department when she'd complained about Rick.

This guy was wearing a rumpled corduroy jacket. He obviously hadn't shaved since early in the morning. Beneath the stubble she could see the white slash of a scar. Working street patrol was a lot more dangerous than community relations, she thought. But he didn't look exactly at ease as he lowered his rangy body into the straight-backed chair that no one else had wanted.

"Can I get you something?" Susan asked.

"Coffee." Dan hadn't had any supper, and the cookies looked pretty good, too. But the hostess might raise her eyebrows if he went for the whole plate. In this decorator setting he felt like a cube of Spam on a plate of fancy hors d'oeuvres. He'd put in fourteen hours already today. If there hadn't been a robbery at Montgomery Mall a couple of hours ago, at least he would have had time to shower and shave before the meeting. But those were the breaks.

The hostess handed him the coffee, and he took a sip. He didn't have a lot of practice with community relations and hadn't exactly volunteered for this assignment. But when the guy who's going to write up your promotion recommendation thinks it would be good experience, it isn't smart to refuse.

"We'll ask Detective Whitmore for an update in a few minutes," the stockbroker type running the meeting said. Ted Theologus, Dan realized. They'd talked on the phone.

"Perhaps Johanna Hamilton could give us some ideas on the publicity angle," he went on.

A thirtyish brunette on the couch sat up straighter. Her clear blue eyes scanned the room for a moment. As her gaze passed over him, she stiffened slightly. He was a quick study when it came to body language. She had something against him, and they didn't even know each other.

What? His interest was piqued, and right now he had the perfect excuse to focus on her. From a strictly male perspective, he liked what he saw, he admitted. Pretty, well-dressed, nice breasts, good legs. But way out of his league. Dan could picture her living with her doctor or lawyer husband in one of the upscale houses in the development. She probably spent her days shuffling between the country club and White Flint Mall. Maybe she'd gotten too many speeding tickets on Rockville Pike.

When she spoke, her voice surprised him. It was pitched low for a woman, and was easy on the ears. Yet it carried a note of authority.

"I think the most important thing is getting the message out to as wide an audience as possible," she began. "What we need to do is emphasize the positive approach with the media."

She went on to talk about a contact at the *Washington Post* who would be receptive to a story on child safety in the *Style* section. And she was sure that at least one of the local news programs would be interested in an interview on the subject.

Ms. Hamilton knew a lot about public relations, Dan conceded. And he owed her one. By the time Ted turned the meeting over to him, the assembled parents seemed optimistic about preventive measures. To his relief no one put him on the spot by asking why the police still hadn't found out who'd murdered Heather Morrison five months ago.

He had just finished telling them about the department's child fingerprinting and school lecture programs when the phone rang.

The hostess excused herself, but she was

back in a minute and motioning to Johanna
Hamilton.

As the PR lady went to answer the phone,
Susan appealed to the group. "I think Johanna's going to need to get right home. She
walked over here. Can someone give her a
ride?"

Dan stood up and went over to Susan.
"What's the problem?"

"Kirsten—Johanna's daughter—thinks she
saw someone outside the window," she related in a low voice.

"Is she a jumpy kid?"

"Sometimes. This may just be her imagination." Susan paused. "But I don't know. Johanna's ex-husband has been threatening them
both." Dan filed the information.

"Is she there alone?"

"My daughters are with her. But they didn't
see anything."

"Maybe I'd better take her back."

He turned to the parents. "Sorry to cut
things short, but I was about finished anyway."

Ted nodded. "Thanks for coming."

Johanna's eyes were wide as she rushed
back into the hall. She'd definitely lost the
cool, unruffled look.

"Detective Whitmore's going to take you
home," Susan said, helping her into her coat.

"I—uh—" She'd been hoping Ted would
drive her.

Whitmore put a hand on her arm. "Let's
go."

Bowing to the inevitable, she let him steer
her to his unmarked Chevy sedan. Maybe she

should look on the bright side. If Rick was lurking in the bushes, this was the kind of help she needed.

After Whitmore closed the door, she automatically fastened her safety belt. But she couldn't relax. God what a day. First that letter. Then a phone call. And now this.

Dan slid behind the wheel and started the engine. "Where to?"

"To the left and just up the hill."

"Has your ex-husband done this sort of thing before?"

She shot him a questioning look.

"Mrs. Randolph told me."

"He hasn't been in Maryland since my lawyer got a restraining order. The police department has it all on file."

"From the tone of your voice, it sounds as if we weren't much help."

She shrugged in the darkness. "They told me to try and work it out."

Dan understood her frustration. But there was another side to the issue. Last year the department had received over eight thousand calls involving domestic problems. It was hard to deal with that kind of volume effectively and still handle the thousands of cases that affected the general public.

"Have you heard from your ex-husband since you stopped reporting the harassment?" he asked.

"Every now and then he sends me threatening letters. I got one today." She didn't want to talk about it. She just wanted to tell him to drive faster. Instead she massaged her wrist.

They were halfway there.

"Did you tell your daughter about the letter?"

Her head snapped around. "Of course not." Johanna pointed to the driveway. "Up there."

Dan was surprised to see an old farmhouse at the top of the hill. Most of the lights downstairs were on, drawing their attention to the interior.

Before the sedan came to a halt, Johanna opened the door and scrambled out. As her trembling fingers fumbled for the house key, Kirsten threw the door open. In the next moment, she wrapped her gangly arms around her mother's waist and pressed her face into her midsection. For several minutes they rocked back and forth.

In the darkness none of them saw the figure dressed in black who crouched under the pine trees along the road.

His fists were clenched, his face screwed up in a mask of self-disgust. Before he could stop himself, he kicked his sneaker into the pine needles that blanketed the ground under the trees. Stupid. Stupid. Stupid. Now he'd really fucked up. He'd thought he was being so smart. He shouldn't have taken the chance on getting so close.

When people had started arriving at the Randolph house, he'd figured Johanna was going to be there for a while. But he'd been too worked up to go home. Then he'd remembered the girl. Pretty little Kirsten and her friend. He could watch them. Especially

Kirsten. He had a soft spot for little girls with blond hair and blue eyes.

He could even get close to the house. That was more exciting than watching through binoculars.

He'd thought it would be safe, because they were just kids, and they wouldn't notice anything. It would have been all right, too. Except for Kirsten. If she hadn't been looking out the window just when he'd slipped from one bush to the next . . .

For the first time he noticed that Johanna was with a man. Bloody hell!

All the anger that had been directed at himself suddenly found a better focus as it surged outward toward the man with Johanna and Kirsten.

His hands clenched around the binoculars as he lifted them to his eyes and trained them on the trio. Johanna had knelt down and was hugging Kirsten. But who in the name of God was that guy with the rumpled corduroy jacket and the five o'clock shadow? He wasn't one of Johanna's friends as far as he knew. He wasn't even her type.

Violent possessiveness rose in his chest like gas bubbling up through the muck of a polluted swamp.

That guy had no right to be in the house with her. *He* should be the one!

The door closed, and his view was cut off. They must be in the hall. He stood clenching and unclenching his fists, his heart slamming against the inside of his chest.

He could feel the need to do something

pulsing through his veins like molten lava. A red mist rose before his eyes. He teetered on the brink of insane fury.

Like a man on a wire, caught in a briar, a soul on fire.

The rhythm of the words set up a vibration in his head, and he clamped his hands over his ears to shut it out. He had taken several stumbling steps down the hill when a slicing gust of wind shook the tree branches, spattering raindrops across his flushed skin. The cold water was like a slap in the face. The shock snatched him back from the edge.

He shook his head, disoriented for a moment. Then he took a deep, steadying breath of the crisp air. What was he thinking about, for Christ's sake? If he did something stupid now, it would ruin his plans for Emily's birthday.

Like a Catholic reaching for a rosary, he slipped his hand into his pocket and let his fingers slide reassuringly over the cellophane wrapped candies. The familiar touch was soothing. Slowly he got hold of himself.

He had just sighed deeply when he remembered something that made his heart leap into his throat again. For a moment Kirsten's frightened eyes had seemed to meet his through the window. Oh God, had she seen his face? He hoped for her sake she hadn't.

Chapter 4

"Kirsten, I know you're upset," Johanna soothed. "But we need to know what happened."

The little girl only pressed her face tighter against her mother.

Dan watched quietly. After giving the pair a few moments together, he laid a hand on Johanna's shoulder.

She looked up.

"Let me talk to her."

Brenda and Amy had been hovering in the background. "I can tell you, Mrs. Hamilton," Amy piped up.

Kirsten raised her head. "No. I will."

Dan knelt down beside her. "Kirsten, I was at the meeting with your mom. My name is Dan, and I'm a policeman."

Kirsten's eyes grew round. "A policeman."

"It's all right. I'm just here to help you. Can you tell me what happened?" His voice was low and reassuring and encouraged trust.

Kirsten licked her lips. "I was scared."

"It's all right to be scared. I'm scared sometimes, too."

"You are?"

He nodded gravely. "It's scary to see some-one peeking in the window at night. Which window was it?"

"The kitchen. We cut the brownies, and I took the pan to the sink." She paused. "I was standing on a chair the way I do when I help Mommy. There was this flash of light like on a mirror. I looked hard to see what it was. Then I saw this man."

"Was it your daddy?"

She buried her face in Johanna's stomach again. "I don't know. I hope not." She made a sound that was half hiccup, half gulp. "He ran away."

"Calling your mom was the right thing to do," Dan soothed. He squeezed her shoulder and then looked over at the other girls. "Is there anything you can add?"

"Kirsten screamed," Brenda said. "But by the time I got over there, I couldn't see anything."

"Do you remember what time it happened?"

"I looked at the clock on the stove. It was eight forty six."

It was now a little after nine. "You proba-bly scared him off," Dan said. "But I'll have a look around outside anyway."

"Can I send Brenda and Amy home?" Johanna asked.

"Yes." He turned to the girls. "Did you walk over?"

"No. We drove."

"Good. Then I'll see you to the car."

Kirsten turned to her friend. "Amy, prom-ise you won't tell anybody at school."

Amy looked crestfallen.

"Please!"

"All right. I promise."

After Johanna paid the sitter, Dan escorted the sisters outside.

Alone in the hall with her mom, Kirsten looked down at the pine floorboards. "Do you think I'm a scaredy cat?" she asked in a low voice.

"Of course not, honey. Why don't you help me turn off some of the lights." Arm in arm they began to walk around the first floor, flipping switches. Still in a tight embrace, they climbed the stairs. As Kirsten was brushing her teeth, Johanna heard the front door open and tensed.

"It's Whitmore," Dan called.

Some of the tightness went out of her muscles—leaving a dull ache. "I'll be down in a few minutes."

Kirsten came back into her room and made a beeline for the doll shelves against the wall. "I need Christianna and Melinda, too."

Johanna wasn't about to protest. If the dolls made her daughter feel safer, great. She wished there was something as simple for herself. Something that would make all her problems go away. Like a pill you could take, and it would be better in the morning.

The thought of drugs made her shudder. God knows *that* wasn't a solution.

Ten minutes and a half dozen hugs later, Johanna finally got her daughter tucked under the covers.

When she came back downstairs, she found

Dan Whitmore at the table, a half-eaten brownie in his hand.

He glanced up with an endearingly guilty expression. "Hope you don't mind."

"Of course not. How about some milk to go with it?"

"Thanks. I'd like that."

"It must have been a long time since dinner," Johanna observed.

"I had a robbery investigation for dinner."

She turned from the refrigerator to look at him. At Susan's she'd been put off by the rumpled jacket. Now she noticed the fatigue lines around his gray eyes. Earlier she would have described their color as gun metal. Now they reminded her of smoke. "And then you had to go right to the meeting after putting in a full day."

"Yeah."

"Why don't you let me get you some real food?"

"I wouldn't want to put you to any trouble." The look on his face told her he was lying.

"It's no trouble. I have a leftover Spanish chicken and rice casserole."

"That sounds great."

Johanna got out the baking dish and spooned out a man-sized portion, which she put in the microwave.

"How's your daughter doing?" Dan asked.

"She's in bed—protected by a battalion of dolls. They're her security blanket."

"Every kid's entitled."

Johanna took a deep breath. "Did you find anything outside?"

"Maybe a footprint in the flower bed. It's hard to tell in the dark."

"I know Kirsten. She wouldn't make up a story about seeing something. But it could have been anything—like a car's headlights."

"You're pretty far from the road. But maybe."

The bell on the microwave rang, and Johanna brought the chicken to the table.

"Smells delicious."

As Dan began to eat, Johanna filled the kettle and set it on the stove. "Coffee or tea?"

"Coffee, if you have decaf," he said between mouthfuls.

Such a typical domestic scene, she thought. After the day she'd had, the normality made her feel secure. Or perhaps it was the man. Back in Susan's living room she'd let her prejudices against cops color her reaction to him. He wasn't the kind of man she usually met socially. Now she admitted to herself that he had a rugged masculinity she found appealing.

"You and your daughter look like you have a good relationship."

"Mostly. But being a single parent has its ups and downs."

"How long have the two of you been on your own?"

Johanna brought a pair of coffee mugs to the table along with milk and sugar. "I left Rick over two years ago. But the divorce only became final in March."

"It's rough to go through it."

"Are you just being philosophical? Or are you speaking from personal experience?"

"The latter. My ex-wife didn't like having to reheat dinner. And just about everything else that goes with my line of work." He shifted in his seat. "But I'm not going to bore you with my life story."

Johanna suspected she wouldn't be bored. There was a lot more to Dan Whitmore than she would have guessed at first.

"You were wonderful with Kirsten," she said softly.

He looked embarrassed. "Part of the training."

"I guess it isn't macho to admit you're sensitive."

Dan laughed again. But that didn't cover the sudden flash of vulnerability on his face. "I owed you one, you know."

"What do you mean?"

"I came into the meeting sure they were going to use me for target practice. But you got them thinking along constructive lines. How do you know so much about PR?"

"It's my job. I have my own agency."

When he expressed interest, she told him a bit about some of her D.C. clients while he finished the chicken and rice. After his plate was clean except for a couple of bones, he eyed the brownies.

"Help yourself."

He took two. "This was the best meal I've had in ages."

The compliment—even over something so simple—made her feel good. With her clients and with Kirsten, she was the one who usually did the stroking, and it was nice to get some of that back. Suddenly she didn't want him to simply get up and walk out of her life. "You could come back for a real dinner," Johanna suggested impulsively.

"I wasn't fishing for an invitation."

"I know." Automatically the fingers of her right hand curled around her left wrist, massaging the familiar ache.

"You did that in the car, too. What's wrong with your wrist?"

The fingers paused in mid-stroke. He saw too much. Maybe she shouldn't have asked him back. "It's nothing."

"I'm off duty Saturday night."

She couldn't tell him she'd changed her mind. Maybe she hadn't. "How does six-thirty sound?"

"Good. Do you like wine?"

"Yes."

"Then tell me what you're having for dinner so I can ask the guy at the liquor store what kind to bring."

Wednesday, October 19

He should be feeling good, Tom Beckett thought the next afternoon as he punched the price of a deluxe edition Monopoly game into the cash register. School was out for a teachers' meeting today, and business was brisk.

After handing back change from a fifty and bagging the purchase, he wiped a bead of perspiration off his upper lip. He just couldn't stop thinking about what had happened at the Morgensterns' house.

When he'd walked into the hall and seen those two policemen talking to Mom, he'd almost crapped in his pants. A picture of what was hidden in the back of his closet had flashed into his mind. What if they'd gone upstairs and found them? It would have been all over for him right there.

After he'd realized they hadn't come to search the house, he'd concentrated on trying to keep Mom on the right track. God knows what she could have told them if he hadn't been there. Jesus! The last thing he needed was the police snooping around.

"Where can I find the G. I. Joes, mister?"

Tommy stared at the kid as if he'd requested directions to Mars. He knew every aisle and section of his store. But today he could hardly remember where to find the combat action figures.

"Over there on the wall," he finally muttered and pointed to the last row on the left.

"Thanks."

When the boy had disappeared from view, Tommy looked around the toy store. Usually the neatly stacked shelves cheered him. He wished he could muster up that sense of satisfaction now.

In today's market, it was hard to compete with the big discount chains. He had to carry the popular stuff too. But where he really made his money was in personal service and with the high-priced specialty items. The train layouts and rolling stock. The educational toys. The dollhouses and furniture. And the collector dolls.

He'd learned the toy business from his uncle. And he loved it. He'd spent fourteen hours a day making the Treasure Chest a success. But this was one of those days when he couldn't stop thinking how easily it would all come crashing down around his head if somebody started digging into his background.

Christ! There were so many things he had to worry about: whether he was going to have to put Mom in a nursing home; getting decent help in the store; and the self-destructive need that ruled his life. He'd tried to stop so many times. But his good intentions never lasted more than a few months—even when he'd been married to Carol. Even after Tommy, Jr., and Mandy had been born.

He ground his teeth. There was an unnatural craving deep inside him. Every time he tried to deny it, he felt the pressure building up until he knew he had to do it or explode into a million pieces.

He preferred them young and blond . . . But so many of the ones he'd been with were dead now. The thought made him shudder.

"Mr. Beckett!"

Tom's attention snapped back to the shop. For a moment it was hard to focus, and then he saw Kirsten Hamilton. She was standing on the other side of the counter, breathing hard. "Mom's outside talking to a lady. She said I could come in and look at the dolls if it was all right with you."

He mustered a weak smile.

"Are you okay, Mr. Beckett? You look sick."

"I'm fine." He straightened. "Let's see, you got the bride doll last time and the ballerina in August. I've gotten in a few you haven't seen. Let me show them to you." He put his hand on her shoulder and led her back to the far corner of the store.

Johanna nosed her gray Cougar up the hill. Since there hadn't been any school today, she'd left Betty in charge of the office and taken Kirsten to White Flint Mall for a desperately needed new pair of sneakers.

At dawn Kirsten had crawled into bed with her. She'd still been shaky from the night before. But some warm cuddling and the promise of a stop at the toy store had done wonders.

From over the crest of the hill came a red, white, and blue mail truck. As it stopped by her drive, the broccoli quiche Johanna had eaten for lunch suddenly seemed to congeal in her stomach.

Then she squared her shoulders. She couldn't make herself sick every time she saw the mailman. Beside, Rick didn't usually send letters two days in a row.

Johanna pulled into the driveway and stopped. Before she could say anything, Kirsten was out of the car and running toward Cliff Fuller, their wiry, sandy-haired mail carrier.

Kirsten was showing Cliff her new doll as her mother drew abreast of the pair.

He gave her a boyish smile.

"Mr. Fuller has the rest of the development to do," Johanna said.

"Oh, I can always spare a minute for a pretty young lady."

Johanna breathed a sign of relief as Cliff handed the mail to Kirsten. Once when he'd seen she was upset about a letter from Rick, she'd told him her ex-husband was sending threatening correspondence. So they'd made an arrangement; he didn't give the mail to Kirsten if there was anything from Rick.

The little girl beamed and clasped her doll along with the pile of mail.

"Don't drop her."

"Oh, Mom. I'm being careful. As soon as I give the mail to Aunt Betty, I'll take her right upstairs."

Both Cliff and Johanna watched the little girl hurry up the drive.

"I remember how she was when I took over this route a year ago," the mailman observed. "I'm glad she's doing so much better."

Johanna nodded. "Me too." If Cliff had seen Kirsten last night, he wouldn't have been so sure.

As she got back in the car and followed her daughter up to the house, she was thinking she had a lot to be thankful for: the way Kirsten had recovered this morning—and, now, the relief of not having to worry about another crazy letter from Rick.

There was a pile of phone messages on Johanna's desk again. But that was the price of being out of the office for a few hours.

"Anything that needs my immediate attention?" she asked.

"Maurizia called from the Italian Embassy.

RSVPs for the Gino Dinelli reception are running twenty per cent ahead of projections."

The party was in honor of the popular opera singer's current American tour, and Johanna was delighted that the Ambassador had offered the use of his beautiful mansion, the Villa Forenza.

"Did she seem to be coping?"

"Yes. But the reception hall isn't going to be big enough. She wants to talk to you about opening it up to the terrace."

"They may need heaters." Johanna reached for the phone. She was put right through to the Ambassador's secretary. "Maurizia—yes—I understand this party has become the hot ticket of the fall season."

The two women conferred over alternative arrangements. Fifteen minutes later, Johanna signed off with a smile and reached for the mail again.

"Before you get to that, I ought to mention that Colonel Jennings is on his way over." There was a tinge of pink on Betty's cheeks. "He's bringing you the new publicity photo and some copies of his book to send out with his press kits." Norton Jennings was a retired colonel whose real-life exploits in the intelligence business had become good PR when he'd started writing spy thrillers.

Johanna grinned at her assistant. "He's as dashing as one of his heroes, isn't he?"

"And—thanks to you—half the middle-aged women in the country think so, too."

"Yes, but he does seem to find excuses to come over and see my assistant, doesn't he?"

Betty made a dismissive gesture with her hand. But Johanna could see that she'd combed her hair and touched up her makeup.

Johanna began to open the mail. Near the bottom of the stack was a square envelope very much like the one she'd gotten the day before.

Reflexively her stomach clenched. But instead of Rick's printing, the address was typed. Automatically she checked the upper right hand corner. Although the stamp had been canceled, the postmark hadn't gone through properly. It was too blurry to read, and there was no return address at the upper left.

Cautiously she opened the envelope. Inside was a folded piece of thin white paper. Not the yellow lined paper Rick usually sent. So why did she have the jitters? she asked herself. But her hand still shook as she unfolded the slightly wrinkled sheet.

Chapter 5

Dear Johanna:
I haven't ever told you how much I admire what you've accomplished on your own, and that has been a major oversight on my part. I know you have been going through a difficult time. But I think the two of us could help each other. More than you know. We need to be together. And I need you to change my image—the way you've done for so many other people. If you could do it for a cripple and a has-been colonel, you can do it for me.

Johanna's brow wrinkled. What in the name of God was this? The letter was typed—on an old portable, it looked like. Rick could have picked one up at a secondhand shop, she supposed. But he'd never learned to type properly and had made her do all his business correspondence when they'd been married. Perhaps that was why some of the letters had struck above the line and some were fainter than others.

A few of the phrases leaped out at her. They were the same ones Rick had used before. But so far the tone of the letter was less intimidating. Maybe that was why it just didn't sound like him. Admire her? Change his image? What in the world was he talking about? Or was she crazy to be looking for rationality in Rick?

She read on.

> There are things I need to do, and the world has to understand why. I'm not very good with words the way you are, Johanna. That's why I'm counting on you to make them see it.
>
> I have looked to the children for my salvation and found no peace. My help must come from you and the arrogant bastards who control the media.
>
> She was a little girl with blond hair and blue eyes. I keep trying to tell her I'm sorry. But she doesn't understand. You are the key that unlocks the seventh circle of torment and frees the captive from the river of blood. A doomed soul caught in a trap. A man who's gotten a bum rap. On a trip through hell without a map.
>
> Think about it and I'll be back in touch.

At the bottom was typed "Very truly yours." There was no signature, only a figure eight turned on its side. Infinity? There was nothing grotesque in the mark itself, yet it and the last paragraph made the hair on the back of Johanna's neck prickle. A little girl with blond hair and blue eyes. Kirsten. My God, he wasn't going to hurt Kirsten, was he? Quickly she read the words again. But they didn't make any more sense than they had before.

"You look as white as a sheet," Betty observed.

At that moment there was a sharp rap at the door. Both women's heads jerked toward the sound. Then Betty laughed nervously. "Probably Norton."

Johanna's assistant got up. After a quick stop at the mirror, she went to answer the door.

From the hall Johanna could hear a warm exchange of greetings, and then Betty's voice dropped. Her hushed murmur alternated with Norton Jennings's authoritative tones. A few moments later, he strode into the room. At sixty-one he was still very fit, with the ramrod bearing of a military man. His steel-gray hair was regulation length, and he wore his tweed sport jacket and dark slacks like a dress uniform.

"I understand you've been having some problems with your ex-husband," he clipped out.

If she hadn't known Jennings, Johanna might have been put off by the brusqueness. Instead, there was something comforting about his take-charge manner. Johanna handed him the letter and waited while he perused it.

When he got to the part about the "has-been colonel," he laughed. "I guess Hamilton wishes he had my six-figure income." But as he read further, his expression sobered. "This fellow doesn't sound as if he's dealing from a full deck."

Johanna nodded.

"Does he just like to flap his mouth, or do you think he's dangerous?"

She considered the question. There had been a time when Rick had definitely been dangerous. Now she suspected he was too strung out. But would she bet her life and Kirsten's on it? "I don't think so. But with Rick, you never know."

"Well, if he comes around, you just give me a call, and I'll take care of him for you."

"Thanks for the offer, but let's hope it won't be necessary." Deftly she steered the conversation back to Jennings's reason for coming, and in a few moments he was showing her the new publicity photo. As the business drew to a close, she detected a surprising nervousness about his manner.

Stuffing his hands in the pockets of his jacket, he turned to Betty. "I happen to have two tickets for the National Symphony at the Kennedy Center this evening. I know it's short notice, but if you're free, I was wondering if you'd like to go."

Betty's eyes lit up. "Why—uh—yes. I'd love that."

"You would?"

"Of course." She looked down at her skirt and blouse. "But I'm not exactly dressed for the Kennedy Center."

"You could go home and change first."

Unable to disguise the eagerness on her face, Betty glanced over at her employer.

"It's already almost four. Why don't the two of you just take off?"

"Are you sure you can manage?"

"Don't worry. Just have a good time."

Jennings sat down on one of the couches by the fireplace and thumbed through *Publishers Weekly* while Betty took care of a few last details.

Just as she was about to reach for her coat, she turned back to Johanna, a guilty look in her eyes. "What do you want me to do about the letter?" she asked.

"Do you still have the one from yesterday?"

"Yes."

"Then I might as well put them in a file and take them to Sam Fontino the next time I see him."

Betty looked from Johanna to the colonel and back again.

A few minutes later, Jennings was escorting Betty out of the office with a possessive hand on her elbow. Johanna smiled and wished them a good evening.

Betty's life hadn't been easy since her husband had died. She deserved some happiness, and Norton Jennings was basically a nice guy, even if he did come across a little like George C. Scott playing General Patton.

But once she was alone, Johanna's eyes

flicked to the letter on her desk, and her smile faded.

Reaching for the phone, she dialed the number of the Montgomery County Police. As she had suspected, they said they couldn't do anything unless Rick showed up. But at least the latest incidents were on record.

Thursday, October 20

Juanita lifted the iron and set it on its heel while she reached for the can of spray starch. Señor Hempsted liked his shirts done in a particular way. Starch on the collar and the cuffs, but the rest of the shirt had to be soft as *las nalgas de un bebe*. But she didn't mind ironing because she could watch T.V.

Her gaze lifted to the thirteen-inch screen on the other side of the room as the haunting strains of the *Live for Tomorrow* theme song started to play. She'd been waiting all week to find out what was going to happen when Maria, a Mexican-American maid, told the heir to the Gallagher oil fortune that she was carrying his child. Maria was a little like her— short and dark—only not quite so heavy. Yesterday the mother of the family had discovered that her lover was romancing her to revenge the murder of his brother ten years ago. Was she going to confront him?

She couldn't wait to find out. The story almost made her forget about the dream she'd had last night. Not like the one before. A blond little girl with a pink ribbon—screaming, pleading for the man not to hurt her. Begging him to let her go.

Juanita squeezed her eyes shut, as if that could block out a picture that only existed in her mind. He hadn't let her go. He had hurt her. And then he'd killed her.

Madre de Dios. Why was she being tortured with this? Her eyes had snapped open, and she'd sat up in bed, her body covered with a film of perspiration.

Now she pressed her lips together and made a savage swipe with the iron across the shirt front. It was just a nightmare. No more real than *Live for Tomorrow.*

Her eyes focused on the T.V. screen. Maria had just sobbed out her secret and thrown her arms around Miles.

Juanita caught her breath as she waited through the commercial for denture adhesive for his answer. Then with a sigh she realized she'd have to wait a day longer. Nothing ever happened on the soaps on Thursday.

Anne Waterford turned off *Live for Tomorrow* and glanced toward the front door. She hadn't been paying much attention to the episode because she was wondering where Jeanie was. She didn't worry so much about the boys. They were older and could take care of themselves. But Jeanie was only in third grade. She was usually home by now. But sometimes she stopped off at a friend's house. She was supposed to call, but you couldn't expect an eight-year-old to remember all the time.

She glanced at the clock one more time. It

wasn't four yet. No reason to panic. She hated to be a nervous mother, but that child safety meeting last night had made her start thinking about all the things that could happen to a little kid these days.

Jeanie was probably at Laura Dunlop's or Amy Randolph's.

Damn her for being so thoughtless! She knew her mother had been sick. She knew she wasn't supposed to worry her. When she came home she was going to be grounded.

Pulling out the school directory, she looked up the Randolphs's number.

"Hello."

"Susan. This is Anne Waterford. I hate to bother you, but I'm looking for Jeanie. Is she there?"

"I don't think so, but I'll check with Amy." When she came on the line a few minutes later, the answer was negative.

"Well, then I guess I'll have to keep looking." Anne forced a lightness she didn't feel into her voice.

When she called the Dunlops the results were the same. By five, she'd called a dozen houses in the development. Annie Simmons remembered that Jeanie had stayed to help Mrs. Kenyon put up the Halloween bulletin board.

Maybe she was still there. Anne grabbed her coat. This was only the second time she'd been out of the house since she'd come down with that viral pneumonia. She was supposed to rest. But she had to find Jeanie. If she took the car, she could get to the school faster, but that wasn't the way Jeanie walked. She liked to take the path because it was shorter. If she went that way, she'd probably run into her.

By the time she came to the clump of big junipers where the path crossed Orchard Hill Run, a sheen of perspiration filmed her face. The county ought to do something about those bushes. The kids had to get halfway out in the street to see if a car was coming.

Then her gaze riveted to a narrow strand of pink fabric clinging to one of the prickly branches. It looked like one of the ribbons Jeanie had been wearing on her pigtails this morning.

Anne's fingers closed shakily around the narrow strip of material. Her heart started to thump. Air wheezing painfully in and out of her lungs, she got down on her hands and knees. She was heedless of the juniper needles digging into her face and fingers as she searched the ground and bushes for something else. There was no other sign of her daughter.

Hardly able to breathe, Anne frantically looked in the direction of the school. In her imagination she could see Jeanie skipping toward her along the path. But there was no one there. She had simply willed the image of her daughter into existence.

Let her be at school. Please, God, let her be at school.

Her lips moved as she murmured that prayer over and over. Her breath was coming in short gasps now. Dizzy with effort, she clutched the ribbon like a talisman and started running awkwardly toward the playground.

"Baron, heel!"

Beside Marian Lewis the big dog growled deep in his throat, but he stopped pulling on the leash.

"What's the matter with you?" Marian asked, her voice soothing as she leaned down to stroke Baron's coarse, thick hair. He was an intelligent dog, Marian thought. Perhaps he understood what had happened. Or maybe he just felt the tension. Baron was sensitive that way.

She glanced toward the Waterford house. Parked along the curb were a police cruiser, an ambulance, and a mail truck. The temperature had dropped sharply, but more than a dozen people were milling around on the lawn. Friends. Neighbors. Even the mailman.

Bad news travels fast, Marian thought. By now everyone in the development probably knew that Jeanie Waterford was missing and that her mother had collapsed.

Johanna Hamilton drew abreast of the woman and the dog. Her face was pale, her features tense. "It's going to be dark soon. And it's so cold. I hope Jeanie is dressed warmly." Then she seemed to notice who she was talking to and blinked. "You and Baron—you found Heather Morrison last spring."

"Yes."

"Oh God. I hope—" She couldn't finish the sentence.

They had almost reached the crowd. The big dog bared his teeth and snarled.

"Baron!"

Several of the people on the Waterford lawn backed away from the Labrador. Marian pulled sharply on the leash and issued another command. He was a huge dog and people were sometimes afraid of him. But he was really very gentle. "I'm sorry," she apologized. "I don't know what's gotten into him. I thought he could help search. But I guess he's too wound up."

Ted Theologus had come out of the house and onto the walk. "Maybe you'd better take him home, Marian," he suggested.

"I guess I'll have to."

Chapter 6

Friday, October 21

He reached out and pressed his fingers gently against her cold cheek.

"Good-bye, Emily," he whispered.

In the moonlight, her pale hair was a white wreath around her head. A lock had fallen across her brow. Carefully he brushed it back from her chalky skin.

She didn't answer. She never did.

For a moment he clenched his fists and squeezed his eyes shut. Then he took a deep, shuddering breath. *Control. Hold it together for just a little longer. Don't let the mist close in.*

He had laid her on her side the way she was supposed to be, her pink corduroy jumper arranged just so, her hands loosely clasped and stretched out in front. Now he decided she looked uncomfortable. Scooping up a little pile of pine needles, he made them into a pillow for her head.

Yes, that was better. She could rest in peace now.

"Don't hate me too much," he whispered. If only she could understand. He'd bought her a new doll and a bright pink ribbon. He'd tried to tell her about the path that had been ordained for him, the burden he was carrying. There had only been panic in her eyes. It was always in their eyes. That had made him angry.

As he knelt there, twin shafts of illumination suddenly cut through the darkness. Headlights.

Bloody hell! He'd known they were out to get him. Why did it have to be now? Not daring to breathe, he flattened his shoulders against the rough bark of a tree. If he faded into the shadows, the bastards wouldn't see him.

For a heart-stopping moment he thought they had found him. Then the lights swung past. It was all right. He had known it would be all along.

When he turned back to the lifeless body huddled on the ground, he had to fight a wave of dizziness. My God, it wasn't Emily. *She'd* been dead for twenty years. And twenty thousand tears. And fears—and jeers—and leers. The syllables vibrated in his head like a swarm of bees the way they always did when his mind started putting things in rhyme. He clamped his hands over his ears to shut the buzzing out. But it didn't help. It was coming from inside.

He tried to focus on the still figure crumpled lifelessly at his feet. The same and not the same. Blond hair. Rosebud mouth. A doll in her arms. But it wasn't Emily. Not anymore. Jeanie! Her name was Jeanie. And she had trusted him.

Despite the chill in the air, sweat beaded on his forehead and ran together along the creases of his brow. The rhythm started to pound in his head again. It was louder this time. He sank his fingers into his hair, pulling in frustration. There was a time for every season under heaven—or in hell. Every detail would count for or against him in the balance. He must get it right. But it hurt to think.

He had to get out of here. Away from Jeanie. Jeanie—meanie—miney—mo. It didn't matter which one—just so he grabbed her—by the toe. Just so she looked like Emily. Just so he stabbed her with the knife—again and again.

He took one more frantic look at the body. Had he done everything the way it should be? Yes, the doll's eyes were closed.

No! The mark—he'd almost forgotten the mark. Kneeling down, he turned over her right wrist and penned a quick signature. Then, without a backward glance, he abandoned the small pitiful figure to the night.

Chapter 7

Saturday, October 22

Johanna stood back and gave the kitchen table a critical inspection. It was set for three. Was Dan going to mind eating with an eight-year-old? she wondered.

As promised, he'd called Friday.

Instead of discussing dinner, they'd started with Jeanie Waterford. "I suppose you'd tell me if there were a break in the case," she said.

"I wish there were something to tell."

Johanna closed her eyes and took a shaky breath. "This waiting to hear something is terrible." But if it was bad for her, what about poor Anne Waterford?

"I know how you feel. The department's been following every lead—no matter how farfetched." Dan paused and cleared his throat. "I'll understand if you want to cancel for tomorrow night."

If she was still looking for an excuse to withdraw the invitation, he'd just handed her the perfect opportunity. "No. I'd like some company."

"Yeah. So would I."

"I've been thinking about the menu. How does beef stew sound?"

"I think you've got me pegged."

For the first time all day Johanna laughed. "Then I'll see you at six-thirty."

He'll be here any minute now, she thought. She straightened one of the blue-and-white checked napkins before starting to fill the water glasses with ice. Should she have set the table in the dining room? No. They'd be more comfortable in here. And she didn't want to make the evening into a big deal—even though this was the first time she'd had a man to dinner since she'd left Rick. So she'd just put on a simple cabled sweater and a green skirt. She hoped he wasn't dressed up.

The doorbell rang, and Johanna headed for the hallway. She could hear Kirsten clattering down the stairs.

Johanna opened the door. "Hi. Come on in."

Dan stepped inside and handed her a bottle of red wine. "This is for you."

"Thanks." He'd dressed casually, too, in a wool sport jacket over a navy V-neck and a plaid shirt, and he'd shaved for the occasion. Neither the clothes nor the grooming quite canceled out her first impression of underlying toughness, but tonight she didn't find it intimidating.

Balanced incongruously in the crook of his other arm was an orange pumpkin.

"Is that for me?" Kirsten asked.

"Um hum."

Suddenly shy, Kirsten moved behind her mother.

"Thank you," Johanna answered for her daughter. Then she looked down at the bottle of wine. "For this, too."

Dan gave her a wry smile. "It's got a real cork instead of a cap that unscrews. Hope it's a good year."

"Let's open it and find out."

The wine was good, and so was the meal.

Kirsten wasn't quite sure how to behave with Dan, partly because he'd come over when she'd been so scared. But instead of talking about the incident, he asked her what she was going to be for Halloween.

"Mommy is making me a dress like my princess doll."

"You're lucky. I usually ended up with an old sheet."

"Didn't your mom help you with your costume?"

"I lived with my grandma." He sounded sorry that he'd brought up the subject.

"Where was your mother?"

Dan shifted in his seat.

"Kirsten," Johanna broke in. "It's not polite to ask personal questions like that." But even as she issued the admonition, she felt torn between good manners and her own curiosity about Dan's background.

Kirsten got more talkative as the meal progressed. She even insisted on showing him her loose tooth. But before the adults were finished, she asked to be excused to watch a movie on the Disney Channel.

"The stew was even better than the chicken," Dan said as he helped Johanna clear the table.

"Thank you. I enjoy cooking." She put the kettle on the stove. "We can have our coffee and cake in the den."

"Cake too? I didn't mean for you to go to all this trouble." He grinned. "What kind is it?"

"Chocolate with chocolate icing."

"Are you sure you're not psychic?"

"No. I just remember you liked the brownies."

Johanna carried a tray into the den.

While she set it down on the coffee table in front of the sofa, Dan turned and looked out the window into the darkness. As he'd pulled into the drive, he'd been thinking how isolated the house was. There were neighbors. But they wouldn't hear a woman scream if she were being attacked. He shook his head to clear away the morbid thought.

"What is it?"

He shrugged. "Just a feeling—" He stopped abruptly. "You know, you really should keep the curtains closed at night."

She knew he was thinking about the intruder who might have been there the other evening. He hadn't turned his back to her before. Now she was conscious of a bulge near his waist under his sport jacket. His gun. It was another reminder that he was never entirely off duty—even when he was relaxing.

He drew the drapes, and the room suddenly seemed smaller and more intimate. When he settled next to her on the corduroy-covered couch, she couldn't help feeling a bit self-conscious.

Dan started to prop his feet up on the polished oak coffee table and changed his mind.

When she'd sat down, she'd automatically slipped off her pumps. "Go ahead. I do that in the evening, too."

He looked from her stocking-clad feet to his size-eleven boots. "I'll take you up on it when I'm wearing loafers."

The casual remark implied he'd be seeing her again. Was that what he'd meant? Johanna wondered.

He looked around the den with its low-slung plum-colored furniture and blue wool rug. "This is a comfortable room."

"I wanted a place where I could unwind in the evening." She served him a piece of cake. "That pumpkin was a great idea."

"I used to like carving them when I was a kid."

"You don't have any kids of your own, do you?"

"No." There was regret in his voice. "But maybe it's for the best," he added. "Kids wouldn't have held my marriage together. And if Erin and I had had any, they'd be in the middle of a tug of war."

She looked down into her coffee cup. "That's what Rick and I are having—a tug of war. And I never know when he's going to jerk on the rope."

"Would it help to talk about it?"

"Maybe. I don't know whether Rick really

cares about Kirsten, or whether he just wants to hurt me."

"How do you mean?"

Johanna sighed and instinctively began to rub her wrist. "I try not to think about my life with Rick much. And I don't like to talk about it. But I guess if you're going to understand what happened—"

She was suddenly reluctant to go on. However, as she lifted her eyes to Dan's, the concern she saw made her want to tear aside at least part of the barrier that separated her from other people. When she began to speak again, it was quickly and in a low voice. "I met Rick the year after my parents died. I was a senior at College Park, and he'd already started his construction business. He seemed so—so mature and solid. Not like the guys in school. Something I could cling to. He was almost six years older than I was, and I didn't realize he wanted someone he could feel superior to."

Her expression took on a faraway quality as she remembered. "At first we each got what we wanted from the relationship. He'd come home at night and unload his problems on me. I'd listen and reassure him that he was wonderful. But I was bored staying home all day and just taking care of the house and cooking. So I started my publicity agency, and it turned out I had a flare for placing articles about clients in the local papers and getting them on T.V. I started small and worked my way up. I guess Rick resented my success. I think he insisted on having Kirsten because he was hoping I'd give up the business."

"That isn't all, is it?"

"No. I could have dealt with that. But he's the kind of man who lashes out when he's angry." She clamped her fingers tighter around her wrist. "Right from the first, there were times when he got mad enough to hit me. But he was always so apologetic afterward. He'd promise it would never happen again."

"But it got worse?"

"Yes."

Dan reached out to gently encircle the fingers wrapped around her wrist. "He broke it, didn't he?"

Her head jerked up in surprise. "No one but Betty knows about that."

"I figured there was a good reason you didn't want to talk about it."

Suddenly Johanna felt drained. All at once it was too much effort to hold her head up, and she let it drop against the soft wool of Dan's sweater. He smelled good. Like soap and subtle aftershave.

When he moved a few inches closer and eased his arm around her shoulder, she closed her eyes and gave in to the luxury of feeling protected. For a moment, neither of them spoke.

"He can be so violent," she finally whispered. "That's why I'm so terrified when he writes me those letters about snatching Kirsten away."

His fingers smoothed reassuringly across her back. "What does he say?"

Haltingly she told him about the letters with the postmarks from neighboring states.

"Just letters?"

Johanna raised her head and pulled away slightly. He moved his hand from her shoulder.

"You don't really want to hear all this."

"Yes I do."

"I got a strange call that night of the meeting. It could have been him. It could have been a wrong number. I don't know."

And it could have been him outside that night, Johanna thought. But neither one of them wanted to mention that.

There was more Johanna could say; suddenly she felt self-conscious. She'd only met this man a few days ago, and here she was telling him details of her life that she'd hardly discussed with anyone.

She drew herself erect.

Instead of pressing her, he reached for his coffee cup.

"That's probably cold. Let me warm it for you in the microwave."

"All right."

The small task gave her a chance to break the confessional atmosphere. When she returned to the den, her composure was restored.

Dan finished the coffee and the cake. "That was a great dinner. But I probably should let you get to bed. I'll bet Kirsten gets up early on Sunday."

"Sometimes."

"Well, good night, then."

"I enjoyed the company. I'm sorry I dumped all that on you, Dan."

"I asked, remember."

He stood up, and she did too. He seemed to hesitate, and she wondered whether he'd been more embarrassed by her disclosures than he was letting on. What would he think if she told him the rest of the mess? she wondered.

"Well—thanks again for dinner." He wanted to see her again. On the other hand, she had a lot of problems. He wasn't sure how much he wanted to get involved. Where could the relationship go anyway? Was she really interested in him, or did she just need a friend?

"I'm glad you came."

"I'm glad you invited me."

As she watched him climb into his car, Johanna admitted she had mixed feelings about Dan Whitmore. The way he'd gotten her to open up so fast was unsettling. Was this the start of a real relationship? Or was it just a combination of his professional training and her need to confide in someone? She didn't know.

Outside in the night, the man who'd been watching was a lot more certain. That bastard had pulled the curtains so no one could spy on them. That meant he'd been doing something in there with Johanna he didn't want people to see. Probably more than eating that chocolate cake she'd fixed. Chocolate cake! She knew it was *his* favorite. Where did she get off fixing it for someone else?

As the man walked down the drive, the watcher faded into the shadows beneath the pines. Stooping, he picked up a sharp-edged rock and tested its weight in his hand. How he'd like to throw it at the guy's head—splitting it open like a melon.

As if sensing the hatred radiating out from under the pines, the man by the car turned and stared out into the darkness. The watcher drew in a sharp breath and pressed himself against the rough tree bark.

That bastard kept messing up his plans. He'd wanted to go have a look at his Chevy while he'd been in the house. But he'd been afraid the guy might somehow pop out the front door and catch him snooping. So he'd stayed back in the shadows. And he didn't like that.

Finally the car drove away.

Upstairs a light went on. Johanna's bedroom. Sometimes she didn't pull the shade all the way when she got undressed, and he could see her moving around. But tonight she pulled it down with a decisive tug.

Bloody hell. Nothing was going the way he wanted tonight—or last night either. But soon, very soon, everything was going to go his way.

Chapter 8

Sunday, October 23

Johanna usually tried to make Sunday breakfast special. This morning Kirsten had asked to help make French toast. They had just browned the last piece of egg-and-milk-dipped bread when the doorbell rang.

Who could that be? Johanna wondered, looking down to make sure the front of her velour robe was securely fastened. There was a dab of egg on the collar. Damn. After swiping at it with a paper towel, she headed for the front door.

"You go ahead and start eating," she told Kirsten. "I'll be right back."

When Johanna peered out through the glass panel beside the front door, she was surprised to see Dan Whitmore. She wondered if he might have forgotten something last night. From the grim look on his face, it could have been his gun.

She opened the door. "I didn't expect to see you again so soon."

He stepped in and looked at her slightly tousled hair and floor-length robe, liking what he saw. In a moment he was going to shatter the peacefulness of her morning. Maybe this was a mistake. "Did I get you up?"

"No. We were just fixing—"

Kirsten popped her head around the corner of the hall. "Mom and me made French toast. Did you come for breakfast?"

Dan shook his head. "You go back and finish yours. I need to talk to your mom for a minute."

The tone of his voice made her obey.

When the adults were alone again, Johanna's eyes searched his. "What is it?"

"I'm afraid I have some bad news, and I didn't want you to just hear about it on the radio."

He'd sent Kirsten out of the room. Deep down she knew what he was going to tell her. "Jeanie—she—" Johanna had to dredge air from the bottom of her lungs to get the syllables out.

"Yes. I'm sorry. They've just found her body in the woods."

His voice was controlled, but the words were like rocks hitting her chest, and she sagged back against the wall.

When he reached out and pulled her against the solidity of his body, she leaned into his strength.

"Oh God, Dan. It's not fair." Then the tears started to flow.

One arm circled her waist. His other hand stroked her shoulders, her hair. He didn't have much experience with comforting people, either on the giving or the receiving end.

But he murmured words he hoped were soothing. He wanted to tell her everything was
going to be all right. But how could he? Jeanie
Waterford was dead. Raped and stabbed just
like the eight-year-old in Potomac Manor. And
if they couldn't figure out who the sicko was,
it was a good bet he was going to do it again.

By small degrees Johanna regained her control. She sniffed. "Thanks for coming over.
You're right; I didn't want to hear it on the
news." She fumbled in the pocket of her robe
for a tissue. "I'm sorry I broke down. I've
been praying they'd find her and she'd be
okay."

"We all were."

"Can you tell me about it?"

"It's a lot like that little girl in May. They'll
have more details than you want to know on
T.V. tonight."

He wanted to take the tissue and wipe away
the tears on her cheeks. He let her do it.

Johanna blew her nose. "I don't want Kirsten to see me like this."

"I'll go in there and keep her company for
a few minutes. But I think it would be better
if you told her."

Johanna nodded.

"Do you mind if I have a cup of coffee?"

"Of course not. And you can have my
French toast. I don't feel much like eating."

Johanna went into the powder room and
splashed cold water on her face. At least her
eyes weren't very red.

When she came back to the kitchen, Kirsten was explaining how they'd made the toast.

Dan managed to look impressed. "You're as good a cook as your mom."

Kirsten puffed out her chest.

Johanna poured herself a cup of coffee and slipped back into her seat. Long after the sugar was dissolved, she kept stirring. God, what a world, she thought. Where you had to give this kind of news to your kid. Last time Kirsten had heard about it before she had. But this was different. Jeanie had gone to her school. Finally she cleared her throat. "Kirsten, Dan came over this morning to tell us something sad."

"What?"

"You know about Jeanie Waterford being missing."

"Yeah. Everybody was talking about it at school on Friday. I hope they find her before the Halloween parade."

"Honey, I'm afraid there's bad news. They did find her. But she's dead."

"But she was just in school on Thursday."

Johanna's eyes started to water again. "I know."

Kirsten scrambled out of her seat and climbed onto her mother's lap. Johanna wrapped her arms around her small shoulders and rocked back and forth.

"It's not something that happens very often," Dan murmured. "But your mom and I want to talk to you about the kind of things kids need to know to protect themselves."

"You mean like about stranger danger?"

"Yes."

They went over the precautions Johanna had talked to her daughter about before.

"And if I do that, nobody will hurt me," Kirsten said, looking from one adult to the other.

The vulnerability on her daughter's face made Johanna's throat tighten. If only there *were* a magic formula that would keep children safe from all harm. But how could she promise that?

Dan came to her rescue with just the right combination of reassurance and reality. "That's why we're reminding you about all of these things even though they're a little scary to talk about."

"And the police will get whoever hurt Jeanie—just like on T.V.," Kirsten added.

"Yes," Dan promised. They would get the child killer, he told himself. The question was—when.

With the tip of his finger, Rick Hamilton bent the dusty venetian blind slat a quarter of an inch and peered outside. The watery sunlight stung his eyes, and he blinked. But he had to check the parking lot. You couldn't trust anyone. That motel clerk had looked at him funny last night when he'd checked in. Maybe he'd called the feds.

He glanced back at the carton sitting by the rumpled bed. The bright green plastic bottles inside were labeled industrial cleaner. And he had all the paper work to prove that he was making a delivery from the Chemway Company. If you opened the bottles from the top, you'd find the industrial cleaner. But under that was star dust—powdered cocaine. Wholesale value 100K. On the street it was worth three times that much. He'd hate to see anyone pour that investment down the toilet.

He'd cut the stuff a little with powdered milk—just enough to take out what he needed for himself. It would keep him going for another few weeks. Plus he'd get five K when he brought the cash for the shipment back to New York. But first he had to make his delivery on Route 1. It was close enough to the University of Maryland to be convenient, but out of range of campus security.

Ohio State. Pitt. U. Va. West Virginia State. He'd been to all the big local schools in the past few months. And it wasn't to attend the football games.

Things had been tight at Maryland for a while after the Len Bias fiasco. You couldn't have a runny nose without being pulled in by the campus cops. But the market had opened up again. It always did.

As his eyes darted around the cheap motel room, he focused on the bottle beside the bed. Last night he'd put himself to sleep with half a fifth of bourbon. With shaky hands he pulled his dirty undershirt off over his head. He needed a shower. But he needed a hit more.

Christ! What if he couldn't hold it together? He'd botched one job, and the organization had been very, very displeased.

But once you got in with these guys, you couldn't just quit. Unless they terminated the employment—along with the employee.

And he couldn't turn himself in to the cops. The guys he worked for would get you even if you were behind bars.

He looked over at the bottles of industrial cleaner. They were another reason he couldn't quit. When you had a thousand-dollar-a-week habit, you had to find some way to pay for it. It was like being in bondage. Unless . . .

He closed his eyes for a minute. Don't even think about it. But his heart had started to pound. Three hundred thousand dollars—if he sold it himself on the street. You could hide for a long time on that.

He sat down on the bed and cradled his throbbing head in his hands. A long time ago, everything had been normal. He'd had a wife and a child and a business. His good life had slipped away so gradually he hadn't even known it was happening.

But it wasn't his fault. It was Johanna's.

After he dropped the stuff off, he was going to head for her house . . . have it out with her this time, if he could keep from wringing her neck, that bitch. She hadn't been willing to sell that damn farmhouse when he'd needed money to save his construction business. She'd left him just because he'd knocked her around a little bit. When he'd tried to patch things up, she had him arrested. Humiliated. And she'd shut him out of Kirsten's life like he had some disease the kid was going to catch. He was never going to forgive her for any of it. For a long time, he hadn't dared get anywhere near her. But that had changed. If she was too high and mighty to see things his way, she was going to be sorry.

He looked over at the bottles again. He'd been thinking about getting Kirsten away from her. Before, he hadn't really been sure he could pull it off. But now there was a way—if he could think straight enough to plan it all really carefully.

After sending Kirsten upstairs to get dressed, Johanna turned to Dan. "When do you think this will hit the news?"

"It'll be on the radio soon. But the T.V. won't air it till this evening. Before I came over here, I called your friend Susan Randolph —and Ted Theologus—because they're heading that committee."

"I wonder why Susan didn't call me."

"I told her I'd tell you."

"I do appreciate that." Then she shook her head. "It seems like the only time we see each other is when I'm falling apart."

Dan cleared his throat. "We could fix that. I know you're going to be busy for the next few days. But maybe we could get together after that."

"I'd like to."

"Then I'll call you later in the week."

"Thanks again for coming over—and helping me with Kirsten."

"She's a great kid."

Their eyes met. *And I wouldn't want her to end up like Jeanie Waterford.* But neither one of them said it.

* * *

It was eleven before Rick made it around the Beltway to Potomac. But when he swung by the entrance to Orchard Brook, there was a cop cruising down the street. Five minutes later, when he turned into the development, he passed two more. Damn! The place was crawling with cops. Maybe they were looking for him. It was all he could do to keep from gunning the engine. With great effort he managed to chug out of there at a sedate twenty-five miles per hour. Man, he'd better come back later. A couple days later.

Chapter 9

Monday, October 24

Phil Hanover from WUSA called first thing in the morning. "Johanna. Heard about the little girl in your neighborhood. I'm sorry."

"It's really got everybody around here upset."

"I want to run a spot on the twelve o'clock news—"

"Phil, I think—"

"I don't mean just rehashing the crime. I've got a couple of kids myself. I want to go for something positive. Something hopeful."

"You mean—like what can parents do to protect their children?"

"Yeah. Got anybody articulate who could be down here in a couple hours?"

"I think so. Let me get back to you."

As soon as Johanna hung up, she dialed Susan's number. They'd seen each other the evening before at the Waterfords'. Both of them had gone over with covered dishes for the grieving family.

"I know you're as numb as I am," Johanna told Susan when she answered. "But we have an opportunity to do something more constructive than just making chicken casseroles for the Waterford family."

"What?"

"Telling a whole bunch of people about some of the precautions they ought to be taking."

Susan was enthusiastic about the idea—until she found out that as co-chairman of the Child Safety Committee, she was the one Johanna had in mind for the T.V. interview.

"I'm a behind-the-scenes person," she protested. "When you talked at the meeting the other night about getting T.V. coverage, I wasn't thinking about myself."

"You're a good speaker. You can handle it. It'll be just like talking to a P.T.A. group."

It took some fast footwork and a promise to come along and lend moral support, but Johanna finally persuaded her friend to accept the offer.

"I suppose you've gathered that I'll be gone till this afternoon," she told Betty as she put down the phone.

"Um hum. Don't worry about anything here. I'll be fine." She stacked up a pile of letters for the outgoing mail and carefully straightened the edges. "You know, I feel guilty—"

"About what?"

"About having a good time with Norton when someone like Anne Waterford has lost her little girl—in such a tragic way. I didn't want to tell you, but we have another date tonight."

Johanna crossed the room and laid her hand

on the older woman's shoulder. "Oh Betty, that's great. You of all people deserve some happiness."

"But—"

"Don't let this put a damper on your relationship."

"I know you're right. I just can't help thinking about that poor little girl. A person has to be sick to do something like that. God, I hope they catch him."

"I do, too. But until they do, we've got to protect the kids." She stopped and closed her eyes for a moment, trying to will away a sudden picture of Kirsten being hustled into a car by a strange man—or even one she knew. "That's why I'm taking Susan down to D.C. this morning."

"Well, good luck. I'll tape it for you."

"Thanks." Her brow wrinkled. "If it turns out well, maybe we can make an arrangement to have it shown on some of the local cable channels."

It did go well, Johanna thought several hours later. In fact, it was amazing what Phil Hanover had pulled together on short notice. In addition to Susan, he'd had an interview with a spokesperson from the Missing Children's Network and a local psychiatrist who had suggestions for dealing with children's anxieties.

"You were great," Johanna told Susan as they left the studio.

"I was nervous."

"It didn't show much—just at the beginning. Once you started answering questions, you sounded very authoritative."

"Thanks to your coaching on the way down."

Johanna grinned. "That's what I get paid for."

"Yes, but I've never seen you in action before—I mean except at something local like the meeting the other night. You really know your way around a T.V. studio. If you hadn't told me, I wouldn't have known where to look—at the host or the camera."

They stopped for lunch at the American Cafe on Wisconsin Avenue and critiqued the show over asparagus soup and pasta salad with sun-dried tomatoes.

"This could be the start of your T.V. career," Johanna teased her friend.

"Once my knees stopped shaking, it wasn't so bad."

"So if I can get you some other spots, will you take them?"

"I want to look at that tape before I make up my mind."

By the time she'd dropped Susan off at home, Johanna was feeling tired—but good. They really had accomplished something important.

As she pulled into her drive, Johanna stopped at the mailbox. Cliff Fuller was only a few houses down the street. He turned and watched her open the box. As she pulled out a stack of envelopes, he waved. She waved back.

Johanna began to thumb through the letters. A confirmation from the Larry King show. A reminder Kirsten was due at the dentist. A note from her Vietnam vet client, Mitch Johnson. In the middle of the pile was a square white envelope that made her stomach lurch.

The wind caught it and tore it out of her hand. She was tempted to let it go.

But Cliff came running back and caught it as it skipped along the ground. "I wouldn't want you to lose something important."

"Thanks."

Johanna hugged the pile of mail against her chest and got back in the car at the bottom of the driveway. Cliff closed the door for her, but she waited till he'd turned away before looking at the postmark on the envelope.

This time it wasn't something that had been mailed from West Virginia or Pennsylvania. It was from right here in Maryland. Less than a half-hour away. With shaky fingers she opened the flap and pulled out the folded sheet of paper.

As her eyes scanned the erratically typed text, her blood ran cold. It was sprinkled with references to the night Kirsten had called her home from the meeting and the night Dan had come to dinner. He'd been watching. Rick? It sounded like him. But instead of his signature at the bottom of the letter, there was another one of those infinity marks.

"I thought the show was fab—" Betty began as soon as Johanna entered the office. She broke off abruptly when she saw her employer's bloodless face. "My God—what is it?"

Johanna held up the letter.

Four blocks away, Dan and Nico pulled into the driveway at 12703 Apple Blossom Way. A break-in. The phone report mentioned another bottle of expensive bourbon on the table and half a frozen pizza sitting on the kitchen counter. But nothing else was missing, and the house hadn't been trashed. Jack Daniels. At least it looked as if he was back to his old M.O.

A middle-aged woman answered the door. She was tall and thin, with square shoulders and erect posture.

"Miss Pearson?"

"Yes."

They introduced themselves, and she asked them in. "I'm lucky he didn't take anything," she began. "But I live here alone, and I just feel so funny about someone's having been in the house."

"He? You sound sure it was a man."

She reddened. "He—you know—left the toilet seat up."

Nico bit back a grin as he consulted the phone report. "You were away for a week?"

"Yes. At an executive seminar in Denver. I'm a division chief at NIH."

Dan nodded. The type of woman who let you know right away who was boss. Like old Miss McClure back in fifth grade. "And who knew you were out of town?" he asked.

"Just the neighbor who was bringing in my mail and papers and watering my plants." She gave them the name.

"Do you mind if we look around?"

"Go right ahead."

They checked upstairs first, with Miss Pearson leading the way and pointing out the antique pieces she'd inherited from various members of her family. How often did she get to give the grand tour like this? Dan wondered.

She gestured toward a carefully polished filigreed brush, comb, and mirror set. "The silver alone is worth over a thousand dollars. If robbery had been the motive, he certainly would have taken it."

"Um hum." Like the other Jack Daniels break-ins, this one didn't make any particular sense.

The family room off the kitchen was their last stop. It was in back of the garage and a step below the main level. Wall-to-wall gray shag carpet over heavy padding covered the floor. Dan looked at the furniture. It was in a precise arrangement, with two wing chairs facing a coffee table in front of a camelback sofa. But as he walked in back of the chairs, he could see castor marks in the carpet.

"Have you rearranged the furniture recently?" he asked.

"Why, yes I did. The man who was here pushed the chairs and table out of the center of the room. I put them back."

Dan pointed toward the rectangular indentations. "So the chairs were back here and the table was against the wall?"

"Yes."

Nico had already begun to inspect the area where the furniture had been cleared. As he walked, he swept his foot along the shag of the carpet.

Dan was pretty sure Miss Pearson was going to vacuum it as soon as they left.

The light caught a flash of silver as Nico's foot dislodged a dime. He picked it up and handed it to the woman.

"Thank you." She turned it over in her hand. "Why, this isn't mine."

Dan cocked his head to one side. "How can you tell?"

"Because it was minted in 1961."

"So?"

"So, the last year the Treasury minted silver coins was 1964. You just don't get them in change."

"Do you have a coin collection?" Nico asked.

"Yes. But I keep it in a safety deposit box."

"And you haven't had any visitors who might have dropped this?"

"I suppose it's possible. But I don't entertain much."

"Then you won't mind if we keep the dime?"

"Go right ahead."

Nico slipped it into a small envelope and labeled it. "So what do you think?" he asked Dan when they got back in the car. "Does Jack Daniels collect coins?"

"Could be. *Somebody* dropped the dime. On the other hand, I don't remember any coins being reported missing from any of the other houses."

"Yeah." Nico started the engine. "But what I'm wondering about is why Jack pushed the furniture out of the middle of the room."

"Maybe he wanted to do some sit-ups to work off that pizza."

"Sure."

"Do you think it's worth sending a team from the lab over?"

"Naw. There's nothing missing. She's probably already scrubbed the toilet with Lysol; and I'll bet that dime, she's getting the vacuum cleaner out right now to take care of the places where he matted down her rug."

Johanna set the three most recent letters side by side on the desk blotter and read them.

They were all directed at her and Kirsten personally, and they all incorporated some of the same phrases. But things started getting more confusing with the middle one.

Rick was talking about a blond little girl. That must be Kirsten. But who were "the children" and what were the "things I need to do?" And—oh God—what did he mean by a "river of blood."

The third was even more incoherent. The tone swung wildly from persuasion to threats. There were more oblique references to "the children."

What could that mean? For a moment, a crazy thought crossed her mind. Could Rick be the murderer stalking the neighborhood children? He'd always had violent tendencies. Could he be *that* far gone? Could he be striking out at little girls who resembled his daughter?

She shuddered at the thought. There was

probably no connection, she told herself as she focused on another aspect of the letter. Apparently Rick was furious that she'd been seeing someone else. The thought that he had been out there in the dark watching her house made her feel like a tethered goat in a pagan ceremony waiting for the priest to slit its throat.

What was she supposed to do, hire a bodyguard?

She didn't realize she'd mumbled the words out loud until Betty answered her question.

"I could call Norton. Remember he offered to help."

Johanna thought about it for a moment. Jennings still considered himself combat ready. But if she were going to have a bodyguard, it would be somebody a little younger.

That made her think of Dan. *He* was with the police, and he cared about what happened to her. If the rest of the department didn't want to get involved, maybe he'd have some ideas.

She dialed the number of the Rockville District Police Station and asked for Dan Whitmore.

Her call was transferred to his office. But he was out on assignment.

"Do you want to leave a message?"

Johanna's other line rang, and she looked up as Betty answered it. From the expression on her assistant's face, it looked like something she ought to take care of herself. "Just tell him Johanna Hamilton called," she told the policewoman hastily.

"She's free now," Betty was saying to the

other caller. "I'll transfer you." After pressing the "hold" button, she rolled her eyes at Johanna. "It's Carrie Lyons from WRC. The press kit she was supposed to get on Jim Ellingsworth never arrived." Johanna reached for her log. Jim Ellingsworth, a tax accountant with a book on how to survive under the new system, was scheduled for a call-in show tomorrow. According to their records, Betty had sent the packet on him out two weeks ago.

"Carrie, what can I do for you?" she asked.

The producer was upset. "We never got that stuff you promised us on Ellingsworth. And Tom Plymouth is having a fit. You know he likes to sound like he's read every word of his guest's books."

"I know we sent the packet," Johanna said. "But that doesn't help you. I'll send another one down by messenger right away."

"Oh would you? That would be great!"

"Anything I can do to make your life a little easier," Johanna told her.

As soon as she got off the phone, she gave Betty the instructions for sending the replacement informatin.

"It's going to cost us twenty-five dollars to get it down there that fast," Betty pointed out.

"I know." Johanna got up and started pacing around the room. Despite her cheerful reassurances to Carrie, she was still upset by the latest letter from Rick. What was most frustrating was that there wasn't anything she could do about it. But the lost publicity packet was another matter.

"Is it my imagination or is the U.S. Post Office Department falling apart?" she asked Betty.

"I've been having the same thoughts." The older woman shook her head. "Hardly anybody cares anymore."

"Cliff does. He ran back to help me when the wind took the mail out of my hand."

"Lucky it wasn't Perry Windsor—that old buzzard who had the route before Cliff. Remember? If he'd run over you with his mail truck, he wouldn't have stopped."

Johanna laughed. But the situation with the post office wasn't funny.

Homeowners might have to cope with an occasional missing bill or dividend check. But when you had the volume of mail that went in and out of an office like this, you really noticed when service deteriorated. The five thousand dollar check that didn't arrive. The contract that vanished and had to be re-signed by all parties. The letter from D.C. that came three weeks late and looked as if it had been carried by a gorilla through the African jungle.

Over the past year, Johanna had noticed that the incidents were on the increase. Several times she'd received partially destroyed letters sealed in plastic envelopes with a pre-printed apology. The postmaster even had a stamp to identify mail that had been slit open by mistake.

Johanna had complained before. Now she picked up the phone and called the Potomac post office once again. Usually she kept her emotions under control. Today it felt good to vent her anger. But by the time she hung up, she was feeling guilty. She had a legitimate complaint, but it wasn't fair to work out all her frustrations on some poor clerk.

She looked across at Betty. "I guess I went a little too far."

"Oh, it was probably just a computer masquerading as a person anyway."

Johanna laughed. "I hope I didn't just move myself to the top of the post office hit list."

Chapter 10

Tuesday, October 25

Johanna heard the rumor at eleven in the morning at the Gourmet Giant on Rockville Pike. She had meant to go shopping Sunday. But after learning about Jeanie, she hadn't really wanted to go out of the house except to take her casserole to the Waterfords. Monday dinner had used up the last of the fresh vegetables in the refrigerator. Tuesday morning she'd had to open the emergency carton of irradiated milk she kept on the shelf in the pantry. Kirsten hated the flavor and complained bitterly that it ruined her cereal.

"Did you hear that the murderer turned himself in?" the middle-aged woman in front of her asked as she set a Styrofoam tray of boneless chicken breasts on the conveyer belt. It was dripping.

"The one who killed the little girls?"

"Yes."

"Thank God. How do you know?"

"It was on the news a few minutes ago. He was released from St. Elizabeth's about six months ago. They caught him hanging around the woods near Orchard Brook School. Apparently he's confessed to everything."

Johanna sagged against the handle of her shopping cart. She'd known she was uptight. She hadn't realized just how frightened she was.

The woman looked at her sympathetically. "I'll bet you have a kid that age."

"Um hum."

"My son's in college." The woman set a carton of soda on the belt and passed the red order divider to Johanna so she could start unloading her groceries.

"Thanks."

"My daughter's married. Going to have a baby." Her face took on a faraway look. "Things are so different today. You know, I used to leave my kids in the toy department at Woodies and go look at dresses." She shuddered. "Can't do that anymore, the way kids get snatched. Even babies out of the hospital."

"I know." She was only half listening as she began to set cans of soup on the belt. Chicken NoodleO's. Kirsten's favorite.

The woman was going on about all the horrible things that could happen to children these days.

Johanna nodded and made responses. But she was thinking about Rick. Those letters. They'd sounded so crazy. They'd even made her wonder if *he* could be the killer. Now she could admit she'd been worried about that. But the police had the killer in custody. She should be thankful for small favors.

*   *   *

Tommy Beckett heard the news from a customer at the Treasure Chest. Mrs. Sinclair. She was one of those nuts on educational toys. Number games. Spelling games. Birds of North America Lotto. And now she was going to buy a preschool computer and fifteen cartridges. He liked Mrs. Sinclair.

"I'm so relieved they caught that maniac who killed the little girls," she told him as he was ringing up her purchase.

"They did?"

She launched into an account of what she'd heard on the twelve o'clock news.

Tommy was so excited that he hit the twenty-percent discount key and didn't even notice. Thank God they'd caught somebody. Somebody. Anybody. That meant they wouldn't be out looking for him.

Ever since the police had shown up at his house that morning, he'd had diarrhea. He'd been trying to tell himself that they weren't after him. That it was just a coincidence. But when they'd found that second little girl, he'd started expecting some beefy police officer to come up behind him, put a granite-hard hand on his shoulder, and haul him in for questioning about his secret life. Now they wouldn't be looking anymore. He was home free.

He smiled warmly at Mrs. Sinclair. "Let me know how little Gary likes the computer."

"Oh I will."

He stared into the distance as the woman exited the store. But his eyes were unfocused. His body felt hot and tingly. Tonight he'd get Mom to sleep early with some of that antidepression medication. It wasn't supposed to be a sedative. But it sure knocked her out when he gave her a double dose. Then he'd go out and celebrate. He certainly deserved a little fun—after a week like this.

Juanita heard the news from one of the *niños*. Billy. He had come pounding home from school, his face flushed with excitement.

"What is it? You win a prize or something?"

"Naw. I gotta tell you about the weird guy hanging around the playground."

Juanita tensed. "What *hombre*?"

"It's okay. They took him away. My friend Steve was the one who told Mrs. Phillips about him, and she told the principal." Billy kicked his sneakers against the kitchen cabinet and reached into the cookie jar. "Hey. Oatmeal raisin."

"Tell me about the *hombre*."

"I need some milk."

Juanita poured him a glass while he stuffed one cookie into his mouth and brought another over to the table.

"When the police car came, old Phillips was yelling at us because we wouldn't come away from the window. But I saw them take him away. Real handcuffs."

"What did he look like?" Juanita asked. Maybe it was all over. Maybe the bad dreams would stop.

Billy took a swallow of milk. He didn't see the tense expression on Juanita's face as she waited for his answer. "Dark hair with gray streaks in it. Long and scraggly. He was a greaseball, and he was wearin' a dirty sweat shirt and jeans."

"How old was he?"

"Old. I don't know. Older than Dad."

Billy finished his cookies and milk and pushed back his chair. "Gotta go to soccer practice. Bake some more of those cookies for tomorrow. See ya later."

"Don't be late for dinner."

As Juanita automatically wiped up the crumbs and put Billy's glass in the dishwasher, she thought about the *hombre* he'd described. The face in her dreams had been confusing. First it had been one man. Then the features had melted into someone else's. She didn't understand that. But she knew one thing. The man who had killed the little girls and left that strange mark on their wrists wasn't old. Either the dreams were wrong, or the police had locked up the wrong man.

By the time Dan heard the news, the hot scoop had cooled down to a lump of slag.

It was after four. He and Nico had put in a long day. An auto theft. Arson. Four burglaries. A rape. Before they could sign out, Lieutenant Fogel came into the squad room.

"Jesus I wish these reporters hadn't gotten ahold of this so fast," Fogel lamented. "It's like walking on a tightrope in a circus. Half the crowd is hoping you'll make it across. But the other half is secretly waiting for you to fall off and splat all over the sawdust."

"What do you expect?" Nico asked.

Dan tipped his chair back and stretched out his long legs. So Fogel was griping about being on the hot spot this afternoon. He would have felt sorry for somebody else, but not the lieutenant.

Six foot two, two hundred and fifty pounds, Willard Fogel had been a tackle for the Chicago Bears. Now it would be a lot better if he could work his aggression out on the other team. Instead he liked to jump on his own troops.

Fogel was the kind of guy who spent more time looking for reasons to chew you out than pat you on the back. If you did something right, you were just doing your job. If you made a little mistake, you were dog meat. His major redeeming feature was that he knew police work. If you survived under his command, you came out a damn good cop.

Today Will Fogel was on the defensive, and he didn't like it one damn bit. Never mind that it wasn't his fault. Never mind that he had an eight-man task force working on the case. They hadn't come up with anything. But the public was demanding an arrest. So the media had jumped the gun in reporting a break in the case.

Dan could see how it had happened. At first glance, the guy who'd been picked up around Orchard Brook Elementary School had fit the profile. His name was Ed Lynch. A few years ago he'd been found not guilty by reason of insanity on five counts of child molesting and sent to St. Elizabeth's for treatment. A month after they'd released him, the first murder victim had been discovered in Potomac Manor—by that lady with the dog.

When the interrogation team had started questioning Lynch, he'd broken down and confessed to everything. For a few hours there'd been wild excitement around the station house. Too bad the details of Lynch's story didn't check out. He hadn't known the facts that had been withheld from the papers. And he didn't even have the dates right.

"That fucker would have confessed to the Lindbergh kidnapping if anyone had asked him about it," Fogel muttered. "Damn. We need a real break in this case, or in *something*, to get those smart-ass reporters off our backs." He fixed Dan and Nico with one of those stares that made them wish they'd gone into selling used cars. "Got anything on—" He snapped his fingers. "What do you call him—Jack Daniels?"

Dan thought about the coin Nico had found. "Something. Not much."

"I want that case solved. That guy Larry Gardner, the President's speech writer, keeps calling up and asking about it. Remember, he was one of the first houses?"

Dan and Nico nodded. They both remembered the interview with Gardner very well. So he was still bugging Fogel. Too bad. And too bad they were up to their ears in fifteen other investigations.

"You've been on it for nine months, for God's sake," the lieutenant bellowed. "Jesus. What do you guys get paid for, anyway?"

Chapter 11

"Hello," Johanna answered her personal line.

"Hello, yourself."

"Dan!"

"I'm sorry I'm just returning your call, but it's been a real hectic couple of days," Dan apologized.

"But at least there's some good news."

"What?"

"The murderer. They caught him. That guy who was hanging around the school."

There was silence on the other end of the line while he debated with himself. The information was confidential, but it was going to be all over the place by tomorrow anyway. Nevertheless, he looked over his shoulder to make sure Fogel wasn't in the squad room.

"Dan? Are you there?"

"Sorry." He lowered his voice. "It looks like the arrest was a false alarm."

He could hear her sharp intake of breath.

"Oh, Dan. What happened?"

"We're going to have to let him go. He just doesn't have enough of the details of the crimes right. And there's nothing else to link him to either one of those girls."

"I'm really—sorry to hear that. I was just so relieved when I thought you had someone."

"Yeah. I understand. It's put the lieutenant in a bitch of a mood."

Yesterday she'd waited for him to phone. This afternoon she'd been glad he hadn't called back. She'd decided not to tell him about her crazy suspicions. With the murderer in custody, it had looked like things were back to just her problem with Rick. Suddenly everything had changed again. But when it came right down to it, she didn't want to implicate Rick if she was just jumping to wild conclusions. Suppose they pulled him in, and he found out she'd pointed the finger at him. He'd really blow his top. She hated to think what he might do.

Before she could change her mind, she started to speak.

"Dan, there's something I need to talk to you about—business."

"Sure."

"It's something I'd need to keep confidential."

He rubbed his finger across his lower lip. "Johanna—"

"Please don't ask me any more about it now. Could you maybe come over for a late dinner? After Kirsten's in bed. We could talk about it then."

"You know you're getting me hooked on your dinners. But it's my turn to treat. Why don't you let me bring Chinese? There's a pretty good restaurant in the shopping center down the road from here."

"You don't have to—"

"You're making me feel like a freeloader."

"Well—actually—I do like Chinese."

"Do you like it hot? How about kung pao chicken and Szechwan beef?"

"That sounds good."

"What time?"

"Is eight-thirty too late?"

"No, that would be fine. I can finish up some paper work before I come over."

Not far away, someone else was getting ready for the evening.

It was so wonderful that they were making queen-size pantyhose in colors now. Slate blue was going to look fan-tas-tic with the soft navy jersey dress spread out on the coverlet.

Getting ready was half the fun: gray eye shadow accented with a slash of navy, a generous dash of that new mascara that built up your lashes, Very Berry red lipstick, and a generous spray of Obsession at the pulse points.

The shoes were lined up on the rug beside the bed. They were new: two-inch heels and little rhinestone clips on the buckle. Perfect with the rhinestone necklace and earrings.

Which wig would it be tonight? The platinum blond or the curly chestnut. The blond. Blonds have more fun.

Better get into the dress first so as not to muss the hair.

Half an hour later the blond smiled at the reflection in the full-length mirror and then twirled somewhat heavily to catch the full effect of the graceful jersey dress. It was slenderizing. Perfect!

The finishing touches were a dainty leather shoulder purse and a fox jacket that had cost too much. But it had been worth it.

A few moments later the two-inch heels clattered down the steps.

The screeching of Kirsten's violin had grated on Johanna's nerves like chalk squeaking on a blackboard. Then she'd reminded herself how glad she was that her daughter was safe at home. She'd tried to calm herself down by reading Kirsten a story before putting her to bed. It was *Madeline,* a book they both loved and both knew by heart. They laughed together at the end when all the little girls wished they had had appendicitis. Still, the relaxed mood evaporated and Johanna's heart started to pound when the doorbell rang. After she'd hung up the phone, she'd thought of something else. Dan didn't miss much. When she started talking about Rick again, he was going to ask questions. And then she was going to have to tell him the really bad stuff. Maybe she could leave out the worst part. Maybe she could keep that to herself. Before she opened the door, she sucked in a deep breath.

Dan was holding a large white paper bag.

"Come on in."

He looked tired and a bit rumpled, like the first time she'd seen him.

"I guess you've had another long day. I shouldn't—"

"I wanted to come." He started down the

hall toward the kitchen. "Besides the beef and chicken, I got some moo shi pork. I hope you like that, too."

"Yes." Johanna had already put out plates and cutlery and set the kettle on to simmer. "I thought we could have tea. I don't have any green—just black."

"I don't like green tea anyway." Dan sat down and started opening the cartons. "I'm starving. Hope you don't mind if I eat."

"No, go ahead. I'll be right there." She had been wondering if she'd be able to eat anything herself. But the aroma wafting over from the open cartons was surprisingly inviting.

Dan was pushing red peppers into a pile at the side of his plate. "You know not to eat these little devils, don't you?"

"Um hum."

"I found out the hard way. Nico, my partner, took me out for Szechwan food and didn't warn me. I thought my mouth would never stop burning."

Johanna paused in the middle of spooning beef and vegetables onto her plate. "That wasn't very nice of him."

"Somebody had done it to him. I guess he wanted to even the score."

"But with you?"

"I understood."

"Do you need to even the score like that?" Johanna couldn't stop herself from asking.

"Not anymore." His face took on a grim look. "It comes from a rough upbringing. And Nico was a lot younger then. He wouldn't do it now."

She looked at the scar on his chin. She'd assumed he'd acquired it in the line of duty. "Rough upbringing. You don't just mean Nico's."

"Maybe I'll tell you about it sometime."

She wanted to pursue the topic. She knew he wanted to change the subject. "You've worked with him a long time?"

"Yeah. Six years."

She watched as he turned back to his food and began to eat—slowly at first, and then with more enthusiasm.

"You're not getting your share," he pointed out as he began to heap the pork mixture onto his second pancake.

"That's okay."

"So what did you want to talk to me about?"

She looked down at her plate. "Rick."

"Um."

"It's not what you think."

He waited for her to go on.

"Let's finish dinner and go sit in the den. I want to show you some of the letters I've gotten from him recently."

"All right."

They ate in silence for a few minutes longer. Or, rather, Dan ate and Johanna pushed her food around her plate. "Can I get you a cup of coffee?"

"Are you stalling?"

"Yes."

He laughed. "At least you're honest."

Am I? she wondered.

"Let's clear the table while the water's boiling," he suggested.

It was fifteen minutes later before Johanna had settled Dan in the den with a cup of coffee and gone off to her office to get the letters. In addition to the three recent ones, she included a few that Rick had sent several months ago. When she came back, she saw that he had kicked off his loafers and stretched his feet out on the coffee table.

"You said you didn't mind."

"Of course not." She jiggled the letters, partly to cover the fact that her hand was trembling. "Remember, I told you over the phone—I—want to keep this confidential."

"Why do you want to tell *me?*"

"I just need—I have to talk to somebody."

"Okay."

She sat down on the couch and handed him the correspondence. "They're in order by the dates I received them. The first three are old. The last three are very recent."

He thumbed through the sheets of paper and inspected the envelopes. "These are all from your ex-husband?"

A ball of ice had settled in Johanna's stomach. She could feel it expanding and wished she hadn't started this whole thing. But it was the right thing to do; she knew that. "I—yes—I think so."

Dan read the first three letters: threats, directed at Johanna . . . at Kirsten. When he got to the next to the last, he looked up at Johanna. "This one starts off the same. It's got some of the same phrases. But—"

She wanted to jump in and tell him what

she thought. Instead she knit her fingers together in her lap and waited for his evaluation.

"It's not just the fact that it's typed. The tone changes. So does the subject matter. It's not just focused on you."

"Yes."

"*She was a little girl with blond hair and blue eyes,*" Dan read.

"I thought he meant Kirsten. I thought maybe he made a mistake in the verb tense. But the part about the other children . . ." She shrugged.

Dan began to scan the third letter. She could tell when he got to the warning about her seeing someone else; he looked up. "Sounds like—"

"He was out there watching that night—the night he scared Kirsten. Then he saw me come home with you." She couldn't stop herself from blurting it out.

"And maybe he came back again when I came for dinner on Saturday."

Her eyes darted to the drapes that she'd remembered to draw across the windows.

"I guess he's telling you to stay away from me," he finished.

"I guess so."

He held out his arm to her, and she slid across the sofa and turned so that her back was against his chest. She needed his strength —and the warmth of his body.

When he felt her shiver, he drew his arm across her waist and covered her fingers with his.

"It's hard for you to talk about it," he muttered.

"Um hum." She leaned back against him and stared across the room at the bookshelves. Her eyes focused on a framed picture of Kirsten.

"I guess I know what you're thinking. It would be better if you put it into your own words."

"I know. Give me a minute." She closed her eyes and wedged her fingers more tightly between his. "I keep thinking about blond little girls. Those little girls who were killed were both blond. Would he—would he—" She couldn't finish the sentence. "And what does he mean about changing his image? And the rest of it? The crazy part. And the way he didn't sign the last letters—just put that infinity mark."

"I don't know. Do you have any reason to think he's unbalanced? I mean besides his hitting you?"

"Yes." Her voice was very low. "I didn't tell you everything about why our marriage—our life—went to pieces."

He didn't say anything, but he slid his other arm across her middle so that he was holding her against his chest more tightly.

"It—was—cocaine." She'd finally said the words. Now it was a little easier to go on. "We were doing all right—materially anyway. He was good at construction. His business was really taking off. And then he started meeting a bunch of new people. Some of them were into coke. Rick tried it. He said it made him feel good. More competent. Energetic. Alert. I couldn't get him to see what it was doing to him. He started screwing things up with the business. Making mistakes with jobs. Then I found he was taking money he should have used to pay contractors and buying coke with it. We were living in Bethesda, and I was renting out this house. He got angry when I wouldn't sell it so he could take the cash and blow it up his nose."

"Johanna—"

She was too wound up to stop. "It got to where his whole life was centered around getting the stuff. If he wasn't high, he was depressed. He was paranoid. He thought I was going behind his back and ruining his business. He couldn't see that he didn't need any help with that. Sometimes he saw things that weren't there. Heard things. You asked me if he was unbalanced. He was *crazy*."

Still in the circle of his arms, she twisted around toward Dan. "I tried to help him. I tried to understand. I even tried to get him to go in for treatment."

He'd seen it before . . . knew more about it than most people. She didn't have to spell it out. "God—it sounds like hell."

Maybe she would have told him the rest of it, except that his eyes were fixed on her mouth. When he lowered his head toward hers, she lifted her face. His lips met hers in a soft brush that might have been meant to offer comfort. The impulse quickly changed to something even more elemental: attraction ... proximity ... need ... the almost uncontrollable pull that a man and woman can feel toward each other.

So much had been locked inside of her for so long. Now that she had let her guard slip, there was nothing to hang on to except the muscular ledge of his shoulders.

It started off as a kiss. That was safe enough if you kept it under control. She told herself she could.

But she wasn't prepared for the warmth, the pleasure, the strength of his arms around her, drawing her close. Her nerve endings came alive with long-forgotten sensations. The sensations built into long-denied desires. Or had they ever been this sharp, this compelling?

His lips moved over hers. He didn't have to urge her to open to him. She wanted to taste him—to feel his tongue, his teeth. The kiss was long and deep and hungry. It was followed by another and another. Johanna felt restraint slipping away. It was so good, but it was all happening faster than she could think about it.

And faster than he could think about it. He'd wanted to kiss her since that first night he'd brought her home. Until now, he'd held the impulse in check. He'd told himself she wasn't his type ... but, God, she sure felt like it now. His fingers sifted urgently through her hair. His tongue sampled her sweetness even as his senses registered the depth of her response.

Johanna could no longer reason, only react. She wasn't sure how it had happened, but she found herself lying on the sofa, his hard body pressing her down into the cushions.

He wanted more. His lips left hers to explore her face, her jaw, the pounding pulse point at the base of her throat.

"Dan," she gasped, her hands clenching and unclenching on his shoulders.

He raised himself on one elbow and looked down at her. When his weight was lifted slightly away from Johanna, her eyes fluttered open. Passion had deepened the blue to indigo pools. His hands had turned her carefully combed hair into a wreath of dark curls against the cushions. He could feel her skirt bunched up against her thighs. She moved her leg, and the silky knit of her pantyhose slid against the twill of his slacks. That friction, as much as anything else, was driving him crazy.

He couldn't stop himself from sliding down her body so that his erection was cradled in the cleft at the top of her thighs. She thrust up against him and circled his body with her arms. Winding one leg around his, she pulled him more tightly against herself.

Damn it felt good.

He knew then it wouldn't be hard to take her past the point of no return. The realization brought a surge of male satisfaction. She wanted him. Maybe as much as he wanted her.

But what about tomorrow morning? He was

pretty sure she couldn't handle a casual affair. He had told himself he could. He'd done it before. Now he wasn't so certain.

He gently brushed his lips against her cheek, and then pulled back to give them both some breathing space. Yet, he wasn't thinking very clearly, and he'd forgotten they were lying on a narrow couch. When he rolled away from her, he found himself falling off the edge. He hit the carpet with a grunt of surprise.

Johanna blinked and sat up. Her face was flushed and her hand went to her disheveled hair as she stared down at him. "Dan—I'm sorry. Are you all right?"

"More or less."

He started to push himself up. She offered her hand to help him back up on the couch, but when he was sitting beside her again, she pulled it away. She didn't know what to say. Self-consciously, she tugged her skirt down below her knees.

What did he think of her now? "I—thanks for stopping," she said in a low voice.

"I wasn't planning to be quite so dramatic."

"If you hadn't—I guess I'm out of practice with this kind of relationship."

"I didn't mean to push things that far."

"It wasn't just you." She couldn't quite look him in the eye. "Why did you stop?"

"Believe me, it wasn't easy. But I didn't want to rush you into something you weren't ready for."

So it wasn't that she'd turned him off.

He caught the little sigh that escaped her lips. "What?"

"Nothing."

"Tell me."

"I was afraid you would think I was coming on too strong," she whispered.

"I liked it a lot. Not just physically. Why did you think I wouldn't?"

She didn't want to talk about it. But she took the risk—to make him understand. "Rick. He—he was having problems—responding to me. I thought it would all be okay if I showed him how much I wanted him. He said that turned him off."

Dan swore. "Johanna, coke is supposed to be a turn-on. At least that's what the guys say on the street. But I've read about the effects. A lot of men who use the stuff heavily lose their sex drive."

She stared at him. "I didn't know that. I thought it was me."

He pulled her back into his arms and held her against his chest. "That's not true. It made me feel terrific to know you wanted me."

She snuggled her cheek into the warm place where his neck met his shoulder. "Dan, you're a good man."

He laughed.

"I mean that. And I like you. A lot. I didn't think I would that first time I saw you in Susan's living room."

"I was attracted to you, but I didn't think I was going to *like* you. I was wrong."

She reached up and framed his face in her hands. "We could very well have made love tonight. But it would have been too soon."

"Yeah. Not for me. But for you. You should know me better first."

"We *are* going to get to know each other better, aren't we?"

"I'd like that."

"So would I."

Chapter 12

Plato's Republic was tucked between a dry cleaners and an office supply store on a back street in Bethesda. Outside the bar and lounge were sedate Doric columns and white brick. Inside the entrance was a sea-shell fountain adorned with a urinating satyr. A spotlight in the ceiling aimed a pool of light at his penis. Beyond the foyer the decor carried out a somewhat bastardized Greek theme. Among the bowls of wax grapes and the marble urns were red plush banquettes. And down the hall were TV video rooms that couples could rent for a few hours of private entertainment.

Even on Tuesday night, there were several dozen patrons enjoying the ambience when the blond in the navy dress arrived.

"Tammy!" Pete, one of the regulars, called from the bar. "Haven't seen you around in a while."

"I've been otherwise engaged, sweetheart."

Pete gave the blond wig, makeup, and navy dress the once-over. "You look terrific tonight."

"Thank you."

"Join me for a drink?"

"Love to."

Tammy looked around the familiar setting. It had been lovingly decorated by a friend of the owner: garish, but it had a certain appeal. And right now it felt good to be back. To be able to relax for a few hours and stop worrying about life's problems.

Pete slipped his arm around Tammy and the blond sighed. "Coming to the big Halloween party?"

"Maybe."

"You could come as a man."

"Not my style," Tammy answered in a sultry contralto.

"I know that, honey." Pete slid his hand down the navy knit and let his fingers rest on a plump knee. They were old friends. Occasional lovers. Not the excitement of a new conquest. But, in a way, old friends were the best. You knew you could trust them.

"What'll you have?" the bartender asked.

"Don't you remember my usual?"

"Bourbon on the rocks. Right?"

"Right."

The singles scene had changed a lot over the past few years. Once this place had been jammed full of people scrambling to connect. A lot of them had died of AIDS. Those who hadn't were a lot more cautious. And tastes had changed. Not so long ago, lithe and svelte was in. Now the guys were looking for partners with a little meat on their bones and a card that said they weren't carrying the HIV virus.

A group of out-of-towners at the end of the bar was getting noisy. Pete and his companion exchanged glances, picked up their drinks, and moved to one of the back booths.

"This is better."

"Yeah."

"So how's it going?" Pete asked.

"I've been under a lot of stress lately."

"Maybe I can help you relax." His fingers began to massage the tense muscles of Tammy's shoulders.

"That's nice."

"I remember what you like."

Pete leaned over to nuzzle his lips against his companion's neck.

"Want to watch a video in the back room?"

"Um hum." Tammy snuggled closer to him. "Mmm. You smell good."

Why the hell had they gone in the back? Tammy wondered later. That had been their big mistake. If they had just stayed out front, they would have known what was going on and could have slipped out the back door.

As it was, the loud rock music on the video they had turned on, and their own sighs of satisfaction, had drowned out the sound of gunshots and liquor bottles shattering.

Plato's had an agreement with the cops. They kept things quiet on the outside, and the police left them alone. But the bartender wasn't willing to get himself shot for the sake of discretion.

The patrolmen who arrived took the guy with the gun into custody. While they were on the premises, they also checked the rooms in the back. When they opened the door to number three, they found a couple of guys indecently entwined on the couch. The one in back had his pants down. The other had his dress pulled up to his waist and his pantyhose around his knees. His blond wig had slipped to one side.

Tommy Beckett looked up into the police officer's eyes and knew he was in a hell of a fix. He was about to be arrested for engaging in an unnatural sexual act.

Dan heard about the commotion at Plato's Republic on his police radio as he was driving home to his garden apartment in Rockville. He was glad it wasn't his gig. He had a lot to think about.

Things had gotten pretty heavy at Johanna's. He'd certainly been primed for action. And he couldn't remember the last time he'd called a halt when a date was giving him that much encouragement. But he hadn't wanted to take advantage of her. Or maybe he'd been afraid of getting too deep into the relationship.

He stopped for a red light at the turn-off to White Flint Mall. A stream of cars flowed past. Bloomingdale's was closed: must be one of the movies letting out.

The light changed and he turned down Parklawn, his mind still on Johanna. He liked her. He wanted her. But he'd come to understand that the cool professional image she projected in public was a cover for her insecurities. She had a lot of problems. He wasn't sure he really wanted to take them on.

Or was that really what was bothering him? Maybe he was still wallowing in *his* own insecurities. When he'd married Erin, he thought the relationship would make up for what he'd missed as a kid. Maybe Erin had been too self-centered. Maybe he hadn't known how to nurture the marriage. Or maybe he'd been asking too much. Whatever the reason for the failure, it had hurt when she'd wanted out.

Erin had let him down. Or, they'd let each other down. He didn't want to do that to Johanna. She'd asked for his help—confidentially. Now he wished he could talk to someone else about those letters, like one of the staff psychologists, maybe. Rick Hamilton was pretty messed up. The question was; how messed up? He was violent. Was he capable of murder? And where was he? If he thought Rick Hamilton was the guy who'd killed those little girls, he'd have to report it.

But there was another thought that kept nagging at Dan. Were the letters really from Rick, or was someone trying to make Johanna think they were? Who in the hell would want to do that? And why? Something didn't quite make sense. It was like trying to put together a puzzle when all the pieces didn't really fit together properly. Like the Jack Daniels business.

Dan's apartment was in an aging gray brick garden complex called Cambridge Circle. Once, it might have been fashionable. Now it wasn't exactly like living on First Street, but it wasn't in the Montgomery County high rent district either. There were no spaces in front of his building. He had to drive up the hill and around the corner before he found a place to leave his car. As he climbed out, he shook his head, wondering why Jack Daniels had popped into his mind.

Back to the present problem. The place to start was with Rick Hamilton. He'd do some checking. And if he found any scrap of evidence that connected Johanna's ex-husband to the murders, he'd tell her he had to turn it over to the task force.

Chapter 13

Wednesday, October 26

For the first time in six years, Tommy Beckett wasn't at the Treasure Chest when it opened. Wednesday morning he called his assistant manager and said he had the flu. Then he collapsed into bed, pulling the covers up over his head as though that could shut out the world. He felt terrible—worse than he had all week.

Before, he'd just been nervous. Now, he was hurt, humiliated, and scared shitless. Last night had been the worst night of his entire life . . . a lot worse than when Carol had told him she couldn't stand living with a closet drag queen. He'd pleaded with her to stay, told her he loved the kids—and her. But he hadn't really been sure it was true. And he'd known he couldn't give up the men who brought him a lot more sexual gratification than she ever could.

He didn't want to give up the Treasure Chest, either. His hard work had built up the business into something special. But he'd realized right from the start that his customers wouldn't understand any better than Carol had—their children buying toys from a pervert.

After coming home from the police station, he'd climbed into the shower and stood under the hot water, scrubbing his skin until it was raw. Finally he'd realized he couldn't wash the indignity away. He'd seen the looks of disgust on the faces of the officers who had arrested him. It was the same look they would have given a sideshow freak.

He stood naked in front of the bathroom mirror and inspected his potbelly and pudgy legs. It looked like a pretty ordinary body, except for the bruises on his right side. Maybe the problem was that it was a man's body. Maybe if he'd just been born a woman . . . but that wasn't really what he wanted either.

Mentally changing the subject, he focused on the bruises. They weren't from the police. A drunk in the police van had shoved him onto the hard floor.

He shuddered when he thought about everything that had happened last night. They'd snickered over the way he looked, booked him, photographed him, fingerprinted him, and thrown him into a closet-sized cell with a stranger. Pete was locked up in the next cell. But when the jeering had started, his "friend" hadn't said a word to help him.

He'd thought Pete cared about him, a little bit, at least. Well, he'd just been a convenient fuck for good old Pete. That had hurt. So had the verbal abuse from other guys in the lockup who'd taken out their own bitterness on a defenseless target.

He poured himself a swig of Listerine and swished it around in his mouth, welcoming the nasty taste. It couldn't wash away the sick feeling, but it helped a little.

At four A. M. he'd seen a magistrate. Since he had no prior arrest record, he'd been released on his own recognizance. When he came home, his mother was still snoring away. She didn't even know he'd been out of the house. One consolation was that even if she knew, she wouldn't understand what had happened.

He'd like to think the whole horrible experience was behind him, but he knew it wasn't. There was going to be a trial.

Worse than that, the police had let their suspect in the child murder case go, so they were at it hot and heavy again. They'd taken down his name and where he worked. They hadn't made a connection yet between the dolls and the Treasure Chest. But when they did, they'd be back with questions that he didn't want to answer.

Johanna hung up the phone and sat staring into space for a moment.

"Another problem with the embassy reception?" Betty asked.

"Not really. Maurizia says everything's going fine."

"Then what's bothering you?"

"I'm wondering if I should still go."

"But you've been working for over a month on this. And you need to be there, so everyone will know who gets the credit. You know it could be good for business."

"I know, but—"

Betty's brow wrinkled. "You don't want to leave Kirsten with a sitter. Is that it?"

The room was warm, but Johanna shivered and hugged her arms across her chest. "Not after the other night when I went to the meeting—and then Jeanie Waterford. It's hard to concentrate on my clients when I've got so much else on my mind."

"I understand. But I have a suggestion—at least about the embassy reception. How about letting Kirsten come spend the night with Aunt Betty?"

"Oh, I couldn't ask you to give up your Saturday evening. You probably have a date with Norton."

"Don't you remember? He's doing that talk you arranged for him down in Norfolk."

Johanna shook her head. "I must be losing it. I forgot all about that."

"You've just got a lot on your mind. About Saturday night, you know I enjoy Kirsten."

"And she likes you. Okay, you've got a deal."

"Bring her down early Saturday, and I'll take her to a matinee at the Avalon. They let kids and seniors in for two dollars."

"You're a jewel, Betty."

Her assistant flushed. "Tell me that again and I'll ask for a raise."

"They pushed that staff meeting back to one-thirty. We've got time to go out for lunch," Nico Jackson observed. "Want to try that new deli in the shopping mall?"

"Not today," Dan begged off.

"How come?"

"Got some research I want to do."

"Some lead on Jack Daniels?"

"Naw. Something else. See you at the meeting."

"Okay."

Dan grabbed a limp ham and cheese sandwich from the vending machine and made sure there wasn't any mold on the bread before taking a bite. The company that supplied the machines was supposed to color-date and pull the old stuff. But he suspected some of the sandwiches sat around in their little glass slots for more than a week.

While he ate at one of the molded plastic tables, he made a mental list of things he wanted to check. Had Rick Hamilton been stopped for any traffic violations in Maryland recently? Had he renewed his drivers license? What about in other states? Had he been picked up for anything more serious than a traffic violation? Was he in the FBI data base? He'd owned a business. Who were his old associates? Probably some of them would want to talk about the man.

And then there were the records of Johanna's complaints against him. Maybe Dan should start with those.

Of course, he was going to have to stay out of Fogel's way while he did all that. He could just imagine what would happen if old iron-butt found out he was conducting a freelance investigation.

Chapter 14

He eased down into the velvet wing-chair, propped his feet up on the matching foot-stool, and leaned back into the cushion. The soft fabric felt good as he settled his shoulders more comfortably, and he sighed.

Next to him on the cherry end table sat a bottle of Jack Daniels he'd gotten out of the liquor cabinet and a glass of ice. Not the everyday tumblers from over the sink, but one of the good glasses from the china cabinet in the dining room.

He uncapped the bottle and poured himself a generous drink, watching the amber liquid swirl over the ice cubes.

After taking a sip, he looked around the family room with its comfortable furnishings and floor-to-ceiling brick fireplace. The stereo was in the shelves to the right, the T.V. to the left. Maybe in a while he'd check out the refrigerator—and the videotapes. There might be something he wanted to watch.

The good life: Even if it wasn't his, he could borrow it for a while.

The house belonged to Sharon and Bart
Wexler and their two children, Lisa and Lance.
Lisa was seven. Lance was five. The Wexlers
had taken them out of school for a week so
they could visit their grandma and grandpa
in Ohio. Grandpa was recovering from heart
bypass surgery. Seeing the kids was going to
do gramps a world of good.

He reached over and set down the glass of
bourbon, wishing that he didn't have to wear
the damn surgical gloves. He supposed it was
a lot like wearing a condom when you fucked:
a thin membrane of rubber between your
flesh and reality. He wouldn't like that with
sex, but he wasn't going to let it lessen his
enjoyment of this particular experience. He
had to wear the gloves, otherwise he'd leave
fingerprints. His were on file, somewhere
down in Washington. But not his lip prints.
They couldn't catch him that way and spoil
the fun. And what was the harm, after all, of
borrowing someone's nice house every once
in a while?

He slid his shoulders against the chair cushion. Sometimes he needed to relax in nice
pleasant surroundings, all by himself. It made
him feel good. And not just because of the
luxury. It was more than that. He was pulling
something over on all the smug bastards who
thought they had him pegged.

The liquor went down his throat smooth
and easy. Just like sucking on a lemon drop.
Jack Daniels. His favorite. He'd read about
himself in the newspapers. They didn't know
who he was, so they called him Jack Daniels.
That suited him fine.

Jack Daniels. It had a nice ring. He liked it better than his own name. Momma had given him a real wimpy name.

Damn! Now why did he have to think about *her* and spoil everything. His mother. What a filthy-minded, vile old bitch. It was all her fault. Everything that had happened to him was her fault. Damn her to hell! He knew just which part. He'd read about it. The third circle—in the stinking garbage snow and freezing shit rain. Let it bury her, the fat old cow.

He set the glass down on the table with a resounding crack, kicked the footstool out of the way, and stood up. The mellow mood had evaporated. He was feeling restless—and angry. At Momma. At himself. At Johanna! She had betrayed him. No—maybe it was all right. He'd find out about it. There was no use getting angry at her until he knew for sure. He redirected his wrath at Sharon and Bart Wexler. They had a nice house full of expensive furniture. Two sweet little kids. All the good things. And what did *he* have—really?

The chest near the entrance to the kitchen was covered with pictures of the Wexler family, all in matching silver frames. Sharon. Bart. Lisa. Lance. Even Grandma and Grandpa. One big happy family. All smiling. Taking their good luck for granted. But it could all just come apart at the seams so quickly, and you couldn't put it back together again.

As he walked past, he dashed the pictures onto the floor with a wide sweep of his arm. The breaking glass gave him a feeling of satisfaction. But it wasn't enough. Not tonight.

He kicked at the mess, sending shards of glass across the tile floor.

He hadn't been going to go up to the bedrooms. Now he headed for the stairs. To Lisa's room. That was probably where she kept her doll collection. He could imagine them up there—all those unblinking eyes staring out at him. Blue eyes. They were almost always blue.

For a moment he shuddered. He didn't want the Goddamn dolls to see him. But it was going to be all right. If he smashed them to pulp, ground their heads under his feet, it would be all right.

"Mommy, I forgot to tell you something important!"

It was almost eleven. Johanna had been on her way to bed. Now she pushed open Kirsten's door and stepped into the room. In the light from the hall, she could see her daughter under the covers, surrounded by her usual coterie of dolls.

"What are you doing up at this time of night, young lady?"

"I couldn't sleep, so I was playing school, and I was the teacher. Then I remembered this notice I should have given you."

Johanna moved aside a Cabbage Patch doll, Princess Leia, and Strawberry Shortcake and sat down on the edge of the bed. Kirsten smiled up at her, and she smoothed a hand across her daughter's brow. "You're going to fall asleep during math if you don't watch out."

Kirsten giggled. "It's so oogy, I could fall asleep anyway."

Oogy was a word Kirsten had made up to describe anything she found distasteful—from broccoli to math. It made Johanna smile.

"Oogy or not—you have to learn your math."

Kirsten reached up and wrapped her arms around her mother's neck, pulling her down into the warmth of the bedding. "Did you like arithmetic when you were a little girl?"

Johanna snuggled against her daughter, hugging her tight for a moment. "No, I didn't like arithmetic. But I think you're looking for an excuse to keep this conversation going way past your bedtime," she murmured against the little girl's silky hair.

"No. I really did need to tell you something important. About the notice. Miss Pinder gets mad if we don't give them to our parents. I was going to show you this afternoon, but you were busy. And then I forgot. It's in my knapsack, downstairs."

"Um."

"There's going to be a talk in the auditorium tomorrow. The principal says it's important. Parents can come if they want."

"A talk?"

"Yeah. You know—like what you and Officer Whitmore told me—on Sunday."

Johanna's hold tightened on Kirsten again. "Oh. Well, that's a good idea."

"He's going to talk to the *whole school*."

Johanna looked down at the upturned face. "He? Do you mean—Officer Whitmore?"

"Yup. I told some of my friends we know him. And about his having dinner at our house and all. Is that okay?"

"Of course that's okay."

"Will you come to the talk?"

"I'll try."

The bar was a low cinder-block building on U.S. 1 in Beltsville. A neon sign announced the name: the Yellow Rose. There were two dozen cars and pickup trucks in the gravel parking lot. More trucks than cars, actually. That told Dan something about the kind of crowd he'd find inside. He shouldn't have any trouble fitting in.

Behind the heavy wooden door, the air was thick with smoke and the rhythm of a country and western number blaring from the jukebox.

It was easy to spot Joe McClure. He'd described himself well. A big man with curly reddish hair and a big brush of a mustache, he was wearing a plaid shirt, jeans, and cowboy boots.

The barstool next to him was vacant.

"Joe McClure?"

"You Whitmore?"

"Um hum. Appreciate your meeting me."

"Like I said over the phone, got a business to run during the day. But I don't mind talking to you on my own time—'specially since you're willin' to come out here."

"Buy you another beer?"

"Sure. Miller Lite."

Dan ordered one for McClure and one for

himself. When they came, he took a swallow. "You're a plumbing contractor?"

"Right. Action Plumbing. We do commercial and residential. Most of my jobs are with new construction. Steady work."

"You did some contracting for Rick Hamilton about three years ago?"

"Wish I'd never met the bastard."

"How come?"

"Never saw a penny past the first advance on those last eight houses I did for him. He skipped town without payin' me. And a lot of other people, too, the way I heard it."

"Would have made me mad. Working on eight houses and not getting my money out of it."

"Yeah." McClure took a swallow of his beer and looked inquiringly at Dan. "Guess I shoulda asked to see your badge or something. Why'd you say you were looking for him?"

Dan got out his police identification and passed it to the red-haired man, who gave it a quick inspection and handed it back. "It started off as a domestic violence case. There could be more to it, but I wouldn't want to say anything else right now."

"Sure, I understand."

"Did you know Hamilton very well?"

"Not really. Only did a few jobs for him. Got the first one on a referral. Didn't like the guy much."

Dan nursed his beer and waited for McClure to elaborate.

"When I first met Hamilton, he came across

as sure of himself. A go-getter. Full of energy. I thought he was going places. That's why I let him talk me into waiting for my money that last time. But just before he skipped town, I saw these highs and lows. Like he was *on* something. Then I heard some things about him. Does dope figure in this?"

Dan shrugged. "What did you hear?"

"About the crowd he was hangin' out with. Marty Barnette. Ed Carnero. They were good buddies of his. I think they used to party together. Them and their wives."

"Where could I find them?"

"Marty bought the farm. Coke—the way I heard it. Ed used to own a nice little lumberyard down by the railroad tracks. Used to come in here every once in a while and shoot the breeze with the guys. Then he got a big fancy office in Greenbelt." He laughed. "Let me know if you find out what he does there."

Dan murmured something noncommittal.

"And if you find that son of a bitch Hamilton, tell him he owes me ten thousand dollars."

Dan set down his half-empty glass. "Thanks for your help."

"Don't mention it."

Chapter 15

Thursday, October 27

Johanna had planned to be at school for Dan's presentation by two o'clock, but Betty had already left for a dentist appointment. She was probably going to need a tooth capped. Johanna had made the mistake of answering her phone on the way out of the office. It was the printer, calling about the invitations to a book-signing. They wanted to go to press, and she had to stop over to proofread the copy before heading for Kirsten's school.

By the time she stepped into the back of the auditorium, Dan was well into his talk. All the chairs were taken, so she stood against the wall. When Dan saw her, he looked up and nodded. She smiled back. Automatically, she glanced around to see how many parents had come. Susan was there, and Ted had taken off work to attend. There were maybe fifty others—mostly mothers. It was a pretty good crowd.

She leaned back against the cool cement-block wall and listened to Dan. Once again she was struck by how well he was handling a difficult situation. A child in the neighborhood had been abducted and killed. But, just as with Kirsten, he knew how to mix precaution with reassurance.

When the principal dismissed the students to go back to their classrooms, there was a sudden burst of noisy activity from kids who had been on their best behavior for an hour. After the youngsters had cleared the room, the parents looked around at each other. A group of mothers got up to ask Dan questions. Several of the voices were shrill enough to vibrate across the almost-empty room. He was probably getting the kind of questions Ted had prevented at the meeting the other night. But Dan calmed the group down and then stood, talking quietly.

Johanna gravitated toward Ted and Susan.

"You should have asked *him* to give that T.V. interview the other day," Susan said.

"You were good too. Sometimes it's better to have a mother, rather than a policeman."

"We got a lot of feedback from that T.V. program," Ted added. "Thanks for arranging it."

"Glad they called me. The hard part was persuading Susan to do it."

Susan nodded. "She dragged me down there kicking and screaming."

Ted gestured toward Dan. "We really were lucky to get him involved."

"Yes."

After the mothers had finished asking questions, Ted and Susan both thanked Dan. She had the feeling that the committee chairman would have continued the conversation, but Susan took him by the arm and led him out of the room.

Johanna was left alone with Dan. She stuck her hands in her pockets. "Looks like you were a big hit with the kids."

"How could you tell?"

"If you'd been boring, they would have been wiggling and talking to each other instead of listening."

"Thanks for coming."

"I'm sorry I was late. Business."

They hadn't talked since Tuesday night. After that session on the couch, she couldn't help feeling self-conscious.

He shuffled through his note cards before gathering them up. "How have you been?"

"Fine."

"Good." He slipped the cards into his pocket. "I was wondering—would you want to go to a movie Saturday night?"

"I'd really like that—"

"But?"

"But I have this embassy party." She saw the look of disappointment in his eyes. "I didn't want to leave Kirsten alone with a sitter—because—you know . . . but then Betty volunteered to take her for the night. And really I should be at the reception." She laughed. "I arranged it. It's for one of my clients, Gino Dinelli. To kick off his U.S. opera tour."

"Maybe some other time, then."

"Yes. Or you could come with me. It's at

the Italian Embassy, and it's going to be a real bash."

He was about to say no. Then he thought about her driving down to D. C. by herself and coming back late at night to an empty house. What if Rick—or whoever it was—was still watching the place.

"Are you sure I wouldn't be out of place?"

"Of course not."

"Then you're on."

Her pleasure showed in her face. "Good."

"What do I—uh—wear to a fancy embassy party."

"Black tie."

"Oh."

"Is that a problem?"

"No. I'll rent one. A tuxedo." He shifted from one foot to the other.

The door flew open and Kirsten burst into the room, an indignant look on her face. "*Where* have you been? I've been waiting for you."

Johanna turned to her daughter. "Sorry. I'll be right there." She looked back at Dan. "Then I'll see you Saturday. Could you pick me up at seven?"

"Sure."

He watched mother and daughter link arms as they disappeared around the bend in the hall. A reception at the Italian Embassy. Black tie. An opera singer. What had he gotten himself into? He didn't even like opera.

Kirsten was going to play with her friend

Mandy and asked to be dropped at the Donovan house.

"You call me when you're ready to come home, and I'll come over and get you," Johanna said as they pulled up in front of the Donovans' Cape Cod.

Kirsten looked as if she was about to protest.

"Remember what Officer Whitmore just said."

"Yeah," she agreed reluctantly.

The wind had started to blow again, and clouds were gathering. It looked as if it might rain. "Button up your coat," Johanna said.

"Aw, Mom. I'm just going to take it off in a minute."

Before they could get into an argument, Kirsten opened the door and scrambled out.

Johanna shrugged as her daughter dashed up the Donovans' walk, open coat flapping out behind her. A minute in the wind wasn't going to give her a cold, she told herself. After waiting until the front door had closed behind Kirsten, she headed up the hill.

She'd told Betty not to bother coming back for the rest of the afternoon if she wasn't up to it. Still, she didn't like the empty feeling of the house when she stepped through the side door that led directly to her office.

There was a crumpled maple leaf on the wide wooden floorboards, and she automatically stooped to pick it up. She stared at it a minute before dropping it in the trash can. Funny, she hadn't seen it blow in behind her.

The room was cold and gloomy with the weak light of an overcast afternoon. After hanging up her coat, Johanna shivered and rubbed her arms. Then she switched on a couple of lights and pushed up the thermostat a few notches.

She was tired, but she needed to take care of some things in the office before starting supper. On her desk were several client folders. Phil Hanover from WUSA had called about using Mitch Johnson for a Veteran's Day program. She needed to make some suggestions for possible topics. But Mitch's folder wasn't where she expected to find it. She would have sworn she'd set it to the left of the blotter. Now it was closer to the middle of the desk, and when she opened it, the papers inside were out of order.

Her brow wrinkled as she looked at the jumbled collection of material. Had Betty dropped the folder before leaving and just swept everything together because she was in a rush to get to her appointment? That didn't sound like her tidy assistant.

Automatically, she put the papers back in order. Nothing seemed to be missing. But as she sorted letters, press releases, and clippings by date, she couldn't shake off a nagging feeling of disquiet.

She glanced around, swiveling her chair so that she could see over her shoulder. The door to the file room was ajar. Had she left it that way?

The crazy thought crossed her mind that someone had searched her office and dropped the folder. But that didn't make any sense. Who would do something like that? And what were they looking for? An image of another folder, the one with Rick's letters in it, leaped into her mind. Maybe she should get up and see if it was still there.

Johanna pressed her fingers to her suddenly throbbing temple. God, was she coming unraveled? She'd ask Betty about the Johnson folder tomorrow. There was no sense getting worked up about it now, or about anything else. Of course Rick's letters were still there.

When the doorbell rang, she gave a startled little jump.

Had Kirsten come home without calling after all?

But when she answered the door, it wasn't her daughter. It was Clifford Fuller. His sandy hair was windblown. His boyish face was tight with distress.

The mail had long since been delivered. Johanna gave him a puzzled look. She wondered if he might be feeling ill. Had he come to her for an aspirin or something? "What are you doing here at this time of day?"

He rubbed his heavy black shoe against the welcome mat. "I wanted to talk to you. I stopped by a couple times and you weren't here. So I made a special trip back."

"Oh?" The wind was making a draft in the hall. "Come in."

"No." He braced his legs. "You complained to my supervisor about some mail that got lost." He looked hurt.

She pulled her sweater closed and wrapped her arms across her chest. "Cliff, I was upset.

An important press kit I sent out didn't arrive. But I didn't mean to get you in trouble."

His fingers were clenched at his sides. "I got called in and chewed out about your stuff anyway. I tried to tell Barringer that I'm doing the best job I can, but he wouldn't listen."

Johanna looked into his earnest blue eyes. "I'm sorry if I got you into trouble." He'd always been so friendly. She hoped her rash behavior in complaining about the press kit the other day hadn't alienated him too much. She didn't need that, too.

He shifted his weight from one foot to the other. "I try to look out for you."

"I know you do. Really. I guess I wasn't thinking when I flew off the handle." She desperately wanted to make amends. "I was going to sit down and have some cookies and coffee," she improvised. "Want to join me?"

He looked torn. "No. I'm sorry; I can't right now. But maybe I'll take a raincheck."

"So what happened while I was gone?" Dan asked.

Nico shrugged. "Just your typical afternoon. The task force brought in another guy for questioning on the Morrison/Waterford case. Some crazy woman called up to tell me about her dreams—in Spanish. And Jack Daniels went berserk again. Take your pick."

"I think I'm going to need some fortification for this one."

"Sure."

As they walked down the hall, Dan looked

over at his partner. "Give it to me in that order."

"Remember hearing about that drag queen they picked up on a morals charge down in Bethesda a couple of days ago?"

"Vaguely."

"Turns out he's the owner of the toy store at White Flint."

Dan put fifty cents in the machine and pressed one of the buttons. "Not so good for him."

"Right, and it turns out he sells the kind of dolls both the Morrison and Waterford kids were found with."

"Oh shit." Dan lunged at the soft-drink machine. Instead of coming out straight, the paper cup was tilted at a forty-five degree angle. Most of his soda was going down the drain. He managed to rescue a couple of ounces and a handful of ice.

To make it worse, Nico threw back his head and laughed. "Good save, man."

Dan flicked ice off his wrist. "Thanks."

"Think I'll get coffee," Nico observed.

Back in the squad room, Dan sat down in his swivel chair, and Nico perched on the edge of the desk.

"I'll bet it's not going to pan out," Dan mused. "These guys don't usually mix their perversions."

"Yeah. But the lab made the killer's blood type—from his semen, so they can check it."

"I'll be interested to hear what happens." Dan leaned back in his chair. "So give me the comic relief. What about the Spanish lady?"

"Man, that was really strange. The front desk got me on the line because I speak Spanish. She wouldn't tell me her last name. Juanita something was all I could get out of her, and she didn't even want to give me that. Said she was calling to make sure we caught the *hombre muy malo.* The killer."

"Think she knows something?"

"I was hoping at first she might. But from what I could get out of her, it was all some kind of crazy dreams. She kept talking about *las niñas muertas.*"

"The dead children—little girls?" Dan translated slowly.

"Yeah. And the *hermosa,* dark-haired woman who's in danger. Not just her, but her little blond daughter, too."

Dan unwrapped his hand from around the cup. The ice-filled drink had given him a sudden chill. A pretty dark-haired woman with a blond daughter. "What woman?"

Nico shrugged. "She didn't know who the woman was. When I pressed her about the killer, she said something about his face melting. Then she hung up."

"Maybe she was just a nut," Dan said slowly. "A case like this brings them out."

"Sure."

Dan was still trying to shrug off his uneasy feeling. "Was she young or old, do you think?"

"Young. Why?"

"Don't know. You think of old ladies—you know, like that woman we talked to the other day. What was her name—Beckett?"

Nico gave him a strange look. "Beckett.

She's the mother of the toy-store guy. Jesus. It's weird how these things get connected."

"Yeah. They live next door to one of the houses Jack trashed."

Nico nodded.

"So tell me what our buddy Jack's been up to."

"Took apart another house. I was out there while you were being Officer Friendly."

"And?"

"Looks like Jack's losing it. This time he smashed a bunch of pictures in the family room and then went upstairs to tear the bedrooms apart. Everything that could have been broken up there was broken—" Nico stopped suddenly.

"What?"

"Dolls. In the little girl's room. Jack sure as hell doesn't like dolls. Other things were just broken, but the dolls were torn limb from limb, and the faces were all smashed. It looked like he ground the eyes under his heel. Gruesome."

Dan took a sip of soda. "Dolls again. I wonder—is it just a coincidence?"

"Better mention it to someone downstairs with the task force."

"Yeah."

Chapter 16

Friday, October 28

"Why don't you sit down, dear, and let me make you a nice cup of tea?"

"No!" Muriel Beckett glared at Mrs. Wilson. "Tommy's upset." She scratched her brittle hair and a few flakes of dandruff fell onto her shoulder. "I don't know why. But I want to make him something special."

"Oh, I'm sure it's nothing important," the woman who'd been looking after Muriel for the past year soothed. There were some days when all you had to do was sit her down in front of the game shows. There were others when you had to watch her every second or she'd get into some kind of trouble.

She shook her head. You never knew. But it was really nice of Mr. Beckett to want to keep his mother home. So many people just put parents with Alzheimer's disease in a nursing home and forgot about them.

Muriel ignored Mrs. Wilson and opened the refrigerator door. Tommy always liked her cornbread sticks. She remembered when he was a little boy, he'd sneak downstairs in the middle of the night and snitch some, when she'd told him she was saving them for breakfast. But he was grown up. He was married to Carol. Or was that right?

Things got so mixed up. But it didn't matter. She'd make him . . . what was it? Cornbread. She'd make him that. She knew the recipe by heart. Cornmeal. Flour. Baking . . . was it baking powder or baking soda? She'd figure that out later. She needed eggs, and oil. Or was it margarine? Maybe she'd use both just to be sure.

Tommy had been in a good mood this morning, until he had gotten that phone call. Then he'd started using that bad language. How many times had she told him not to use those words? His teachers would think he was such a bad boy.

She stopped and shook her head. "He's not a boy any more."

"Who?" Mrs. Wilson asked. She was a tall, sturdy woman with dyed red hair styled into a tight finger wave. When she'd first taken this job, it hadn't been so hard. Now things were deteriorating.

"Tommy."

"Of course not, dear. Don't you remember? He's a grown man. He owns the Treasure Chest. You've been down there. They have such pretty toys. Train sets. And dolls."

"Dolls. Pretty dolls. He was talking about the dolls this morning. He thinks the police want to—want to—" She turned her head and looked at Mrs. Wilson. "You know. He likes to get dressed up like the dolls. That's why Carol left him." There was a sudden look of panic on her face. "Tommy's a good boy. The police have to understand that. But what'll happen to me if the police take him away?"

Mrs. Wilson clicked her tongue. She didn't know what Muriel was talking about, but that was often the case. Half the things that came out of her mouth were garbled. Her husband had been dead for over thirty years. A lot of the time she thought he was upstairs sleeping or getting ready for work. And then she'd surprise you and come out with the question to one of the answers on *Jeopardy*. On the other hand, Mr. Beckett *had* seemed upset this morning. Was he in trouble with the police? She hoped not. He was such a nice man.

Muriel set eggs and buttermilk out on the counter.

What was the harm in letting her make the cornbread? It probably wouldn't be any bigger mess than letting her grandchildren bake cookies. "I'm sure there's nothing to worry about," Mrs. Wilson murmured. "Tommy is going to be so surprised with your cornbread."

"Yes. I need cornmeal. And flour. Where did you hide the flour?"

Mrs. Wilson pointed to the canister on the counter right in front of her. "Right here where we always keep it. Why don't I measure it for you?"

"All right." Muriel stopped and rubbed the bony bridge of her nose. "I don't know how much. I can't seem to remember the recipe."

"Then I'll look it up in one of your cook-books."

"They're in the family room."

Mrs. Wilson was out of the kitchen for less than two minutes. When she came back, the refrigerator door was open, two cracked eggs were dripping down the counter to puddle on the floor, and the room was empty. "Muriel? Muriel? Where are you?"

No answer. When she ran into the hall, she saw that the front door was open. Muriel was standing on the walk in her robe and slippers. The mailman had her by the arm.

"Oh, I'm so glad you caught her."

"We were having a nice chat," Cliff said.

"I like men in uniform." Muriel cocked her head to one side, her brow wrinkled. "My husband wears a uniform. But it's a different color. And you—"

"Come on back inside, dear," Mrs. Wilson interrupted. "You'll catch your death of cold."

"No! Mr. Fuller and I are having a nice chat. Aren't we?"

"Sure." Cliff looked a bit uncomfortable. Then he handed her a stack of mail. "Don't you think you ought to put this inside?"

"Why didn't I think of that? You're right. Put it inside."

Mrs. Wilson sighed with relief. And maybe by the time Muriel put the mail down she would have forgotten about the cornbread.

The part of the week Dan hated most was Friday, when the Weekly Activity Reports had to be turned in. Around the office everybody

called them "WAR items." Nico did them half
the time, but this week it was his turn.

They had a heavy case load. With most of
the investigations there was damn little of
significance to report. The trick was making
it sound like something had happened when
nothing really had.

The office had cleared out by five-thirty
when he tossed the reports on Fogel's desk.
Finally he was free to get out the file he was
keeping on Rick Hamilton.

As far as he could tell, the guy was lying
low. He hadn't shown up on the FBI computer or any other national or international
data base. Maybe his fingerprints weren't on
record. Maybe he was operating under a new
identity. So Dan's only option was the route
he'd been pursuing—talking to Rick's former
associates to see if he'd made contact with any
of them recently.

He'd gotten a lead on Ed Carnero, the former lumberyard owner, from Joe McClure.
Carnero had opened an import/export business. Dan had asked a friend of his in P. G.
County to check it out. On the surface it
looked legit, but he got the feeling Carnero
didn't want anybody poking into his books.

It was a good bet Carnero wasn't going to
return his call. He knew the man was in the
office Saturday mornings. The thing to do
was to drive over there after he picked up his
rental tuxedo and have a friendly little chat
with Ed.

It was funny how a particular smell could

trigger a memory. He'd stopped at the market on the way home from work to buy some milk and there had been a Halloween display outside. Pumpkins and apples and a grinning scarecrow sitting on a bale of hay. The dry, dusty smell of the hay had reminded him of the loft in the barn where he and Emily used to play. Beautiful, blond-haired Emily. The sister he'd loved.

Momma had yelled at them and told them to stay out of the barn. It was dangerous. But they couldn't play in the back room anymore where she kept the out-of-season clothes. She'd caught them in there once, and she'd spanked his bottom, and Emily's, too, until it had hurt to walk.

"I'll teach you two to play dirty games," she yelled. "Dirty, dirty games."

They hadn't thought it was dirty. They hadn't started out with the idea of taking their pants off and touching each other. It had just happened. Maybe it was because they were alone together a lot. Emily was eight and he was nine—old enough to watch her while his mother did the chores around the farm. His mother was angry because he'd fallen down and hurt his leg and couldn't help with the work, just when they'd lost their foreman and she was at her wit's end. But at least he was good for something. And he liked taking care of Emily a lot better than feeding the chickens.

They'd been playing hospital. Emily's dolls were sick with chicken pox. Momma had said dolls were for babies, but he didn't care.

They'd arranged them on beds that they'd made out of old blankets and towels. Emily had a doctor kit, but he made her let him be the doctor. The girl had to be the nurse. At first she said she wasn't going to play, but then she let him be in charge. She always ended up letting him be in charge.

They'd taken the stethoscope and listened to the walking doll's heart. Then Emily had giggled and pulled down the doll's pants and tried to take her temperature the way Momma did. But of course she couldn't, because there was no hole in her bottom, just smooth molded plastic.

"I'm not like that," Emily had said and looked at him.

He remembered trying to sneak into the bathroom when Momma was giving Emily a bath. He wanted to see what she looked like. She was different from him. He'd seen that much. But Momma had said that was dirty.

"Can I see what you're like?"

She threw a quick glance over her shoulder. He'd closed the door. She pulled up her dress and pulled down her pink cotton underpants.

"Lie down."

She did. He didn't have to ask her to spread her legs apart so he could see.

Seeing her made him feel all warm inside. He rubbed his hand against his pants. Then he reached out to touch her.

"Don't." But she didn't sound like she meant it. She was different from him, all right. Soft and moist and musky smelling. When he stroked her, she closed her eyes and wiggled her bottom against his fingers.

"That feels funny."

It made him feel funny too—and kind of good. He didn't understand why, but it made his penis get hard, like at night when he lay in bed and touched himself. "Do you want to see me?" His voice was a little hoarse.

Emily nodded.

"You can touch me, too."

He had just pulled down his underpants when Momma came in. Both of them tried to get their clothes back on, but she saw. She started screaming at them.

"God almighty, is this the way you take care of your sister?"

They were filthy. *Disgusting!* And they were going to go to hell. Then Momma spanked them with a coat hanger until they were both sobbing and begging her to stop. He hated her. He wanted to hit her back, but he just clenched his fists instead.

After that, they didn't play in the back room anymore. His leg was better, so he had to work, but he'd learned how to get the chores done fast. Then he and Emily would sneak into the barn.

There was a place up in the loft that was all soft with old hay, warm and snug. They brought the dolls up there and the lemon drops they both liked. Sometimes they played with the dolls. And sometimes they played a rhyming game they'd made up.

She'd say "Eat grass."

And he'd say "Not on your ass."

And they'd both giggle.

But the rhyming games and the dolls weren't as much fun as touching each other. There was nobody to tattle on them, so they had a lot of time to try different things. He discovered it felt really good to slide his penis up and down against that warm, moist crack between her legs. Then, after a while, they found a hole down there where he could put it inside. It hurt Emily at first, but she let him.

His breath came in unsteady puffs. It made him hard now when he thought about it—how she'd take off her pants and pull up her dress and lie down in the straw. By the time she'd open her legs, he'd already be hard. And then he'd lie down on top of her and put it inside and bounce his hips up and down. He knew it was wrong. But he hadn't wanted to stop, and neither had Emily.

They were doing that one afternoon when Momma came into the barn. Maybe that was why they didn't hear her come up the ladder.

But Emily saw her. She shrieked and pushed him off and tried to get away.

He remembered the hideous look on Momma's face. And he remembered Emily's terror. She hadn't been thinking about anything but escaping from Momma.

"Watch out," he had screamed. But it had been too late. She'd run right off the edge of the loft. Her foot had caught one of the dolls, and it had tumbled off with her.

He squeezed his eyes shut and pressed his

hands against his mouth to hold back the sobs.

God, he'd never forget that scream as long as he lived. Maybe if she'd only fallen onto the straw, she'd just have hurt herself a little bit. But there'd been a machine down there, a machine with long sharp spokes. Emily had fallen on them. They'd gone right through her body like long knives. He remembered crawling to the edge and looking down. The image of what he'd seen was burned into his brain: Emily's body with her dress pulled up around her chest and the sharp spokes sticking right through her. She was lying all curled up on her side. The doll had landed right beside her. It was in the crook of her arm like she was holding it.

"Look what you've done. Look what you've done," Momma screamed at him. "You killed your sister. Killed her with your filth."

Later she said there was no way for him to atone for it. He didn't know exactly what "atone" meant, but he knew that he was going to hell. It was right after that he'd started reading about hell so he'd know what it was like when he got there. He didn't understand all the words at first. But he learned. Momma had made sure he learned.

She'd always been there to make sure he never forgot what he'd done, and to make sure he never did anything filthy like that again. Then last year she'd died. He'd been free for the first time. Really free. And he'd needed to explain to Emily that he hadn't meant it. Only, she was dead. So he had to explain it to someone as much like her as he could find.

He cradled his throbbing head in his hands. Nobody understood him. Nobody understood what he was going through. Why he did what he did. And he wanted them to know.

Johanna was the one to help him with that. There were so many secrets he'd kept from her. But she *had* to help him. Until lately, he'd thought she was his friend. Now, he wasn't so sure. Sometimes it seemed like she was looking for excuses to betray him. Like with the letters she was saving in that file. Maybe he should have taken them when he had the chance. Johanna. His Johanna. Seeing another man.

The thought made the throbbing in his temples flare white-hot. Maybe he could kill that other guy. Maybe that was the thing to do.

Or maybe he'd give Johanna one more chance. Test her, the way he'd done before. And if she didn't cooperate, there was a way to force her to do what he wanted.

Chapter 17

Saturday, October 29

Johanna had to be at the embassy in the morning to make sure everything was set for the party. On the way down, she dropped Kirsten at Betty's.

"Now, I don't expect to hear you gave Aunt Betty any problems," she told her daughter firmly.

"Aw, Mom. Aunt Betty and I always have a good time."

"That's right," the older woman confirmed. "So don't worry about anything. I'll bring Kirsten home Sunday afternoon."

"You don't have to bring her."

"You go ahead and sleep in. And have a good time tonight."

After hugging Kirsten good-bye, Johanna tore herself away. For the next few hours she was busy at the embassy with Maurizia and the Ambassador's wife, going over the last minute details.

When she got back, she checked her office answering machine. There were two calls. The first time, no one left a message—just twenty

seconds of ragged breathing on the other end
of the line. The sound made the blood drain
from her face. It was like the other anony-
mous call.

But the next message was worse.

Johanna heard the breathing again and then
an explosive curse. "Why the hell aren't you
home taking care of our daughter?" His voice
was hoarse and rough, but it was Rick.

Johanna slumped into the chair. Her hand
reached out to slam the "off" button. Instead,
she sat there rubbing her wrist and listening
to him scream that he wasn't going to let any
fucking police keep his daughter away from
him.

It wasn't a long message, but she couldn't
stop shaking. Instead of erasing the tape, she
pulled it out of the machine. She would save
it as evidence. It was hard to think straight.
She should call Dan. He'd know what to do.
But he wasn't at the station. And when she
tried his home number, he wasn't there either.

My God. She'd thought someone had been
in her office Thursday. Could it have been
Rick? His last letter had been postmarked
right here in the county. Where was he now?
Did he still have the key from when they'd
rented the place out? She should have changed
the locks. Why hadn't she taken care of that?

She leaned her head against the chair-back
and took several deep, steadying breaths. She
had to calm down. She had to think.

The party was important. She'd put so much
time and effort into it, and she was looking

forward to going. Could she still drive down to D. C. tonight?

Yes. Kirsten was safe at Betty's. She'd get a locksmith in this afternoon so no one could get into the house while she was away. Dan was taking her to the embassy. He was a policeman. She trusted him, and he cared about her. How much safer could she be?

Tommy Beckett sighed as he rang up a five-dollar Halloween mask and put it in a paper bag.

In a way, he should be happy. A simple lab test had proven that he wasn't lying when he said he hadn't raped and murdered those little girls. He hadn't known you could do a blood type from semen. Maybe the killer didn't either. But thank God he was an O positive and the guy who'd snatched those kids was Ab. And, as an added bonus, he'd tested negative for the HIV virus.

But he hadn't been able to keep any food down since he'd opened the *Gazette* on Friday. Under other circumstances, he would have killed for an article in the local paper. But the couple of paragraphs in the county weekly had made him run into the bathroom and throw up.

"Toy Store Owner Arrested" the headline read. The short article described his humiliation.

Apparently a lot of his customers had read it, too. Saturday was usually his best day. From the amount of business this morning, you might think there was a snowstorm outside, except that the rest of the mall was plenty busy.

Usually by this time his Halloween costumes were cleaned out. Today he probably had the best selection left in town.

The shoppers who'd come in were giving him some pretty strange looks, and there hadn't been many unaccompanied children. What the hell was he going to do if this kept up through the Christmas season?

Then there was the problem about the dolls. He sold the kind that had been found with the little girls. They could have come from his store—or twenty other places in the D. C. area.

Shit! How was he supposed to remember who he'd sold every doll to? He had five employees who manned the registers. The police were asking for the impossible. After what he'd been through with them, he wasn't in any mood to be accommodating.

Dan finished struggling with the last shirt-stud and picked up the black tie. Why couldn't this damn outfit just have buttons like everything else? But that would take away the fun of figuring out how to get into it. At least the bow tie was already tied. But where did the points of the collar go? Over or under the bow?

What about his gun? He was going to feel naked without it. But he could imagine it would make the diplomatic crowd edgy, and he didn't want to end up explaining it to the security guards. Better leave it at home.

But why fool himself? It wasn't really the tux or the embassy party that was making him so uptight. It was what he'd learned about Johanna from Carnero. After he'd gotten back from the meeting, he'd thought about calling her and canceling out tonight. Then he'd decided he really ought to hear her side of the story. Maybe it was different. Or maybe it just didn't matter anymore.

He just wasn't the kind of guy who went back on his word. He'd said he'd take her down to D. C. tonight, and he was going to do it.

He wasn't prepared for how lovely she looked when she answered the door. She was wearing a long, pale blue silk dress that brought out her slender elegance. Her dark hair was swept up from her neck and piled on top of her head with just a few artful wisps curled tantalizingly over her ears. A simple pearl choker circled her throat.

He hadn't planned what he was going to say when he saw her. Somehow, the eager look in her blue eyes decided for him. This evening meant a lot to her. Why spoil it?

She gave him a quick inspection and grinned.

"What's so funny?"

"Your tie." Reaching up, she pulled the points of the collar over the black bow. "There. That's better."

"I haven't worn one of these things since my wedding. Glad to provide you with a little amusement."

"Dan, I'm sorry. I didn't mean—"

"Forget it."

The stiff way he was standing and the look in his eyes made her stomach contract. She shouldn't have teased him about his rented tuxedo. Or was something else bothering him? Maybe the whole idea of the party made him uncomfortable. Maybe she shouldn't have jumped at the idea of having him take her.

Johanna got her lynx jacket out of the closet and picked up her blue leather evening bag from the sideboard. "We'd better go."

"Yeah."

"Why don't I drive?" she offered.

"Okay with me."

She hadn't felt so uncomfortable with him since that first night at Susan's house. He didn't seem to want to keep a conversation going, so she finally turned on the radio and pretended to be absorbed in the Brandenburg Concerto WGMS was broadcasting.

The party wasn't actually at the embassy downtown but at the far more elegant Villa Forenza, the Ambassador's residence near Chevy Chase Circle.

Johanna had always thought the massive stone and timber building with its wide lawns sweeping down toward Rock Creek Park was the perfect setting for gracious entertaining.

Tonight the Ambassador, his wife, and the tall, handsome Gino Dinelli were greeting their guests in the foyer. Gino touched his lips to her hand and kept them there for a moment.

"Johanna, *cara,* this is magnificent. I couldn't have asked for a better way to launch my tour."

"We're certainly indebted to the Ambassador." She turned to him and thanked him once again for offering the house.

"Think nothing of it. It's my pleasure. Gino is one of our most precious Italian exports."

Other guests had come in behind Johanna and Dan. They moved down the stairs into the grand reception hall with its lead glass windows and high balconies.

"You and that guy are pretty friendly, huh?" Dan observed.

Johanna shot him a startled look. What was that supposed to mean? "I'm just his publicity agent. But you know how Italian men are."

Dan didn't pursue the subject.

In the grand reception hall, she was drawn into half a dozen conversations with Washington personalities and media people. Even though she was careful to introduce Dan, he seemed restless.

"Why don't I go get a drink," he finally said. "Want me to bring you one?"

"I'll get something later."

"Then I'll see you in a while."

"Dan—I—" She wasn't sure what was really wrong between them this evening, or what to say. But this was no place for a private conversation, and she was determined not to let anything spoil the evening. "I'll see you in a while. Make sure you try the fresh Parmesan cheese. It practically took an edict from the Godfather to get it."

He didn't laugh.

Johanna felt a pang of regret as he disappeared in the crowd. Then she forced a light expression onto her face and took a glass of champagne from one of the waiters circulating through the crowd. This was a big night for her. She was going to enjoy it.

Senator Carlson waved from across the room, and she went over to say hello. "I understand you're responsible for all this," he said.

"I had quite a bit of help."

"Don't be modest."

"It's true."

They talked for a few more minutes before Johanna excused herself to circulate. The mansion was quickly filling up with elegantly dressed party-goers. Lucky they'd gotten those heaters for the terrace, Johanna thought as she stepped through the French doors.

Dan was already outside. He was talking to the Italian Air Force attaché. They were both tough-looking men who seemed just a bit out of place in this gathering. Yet even though she knew Dan was uncomfortable in evening clothes, she liked what the black tuxedo did for his athletic body. She smiled at him, and he nodded. But before she could cross the flagstones, the conductor of the National Symphony touched her arm.

"Misha. I'm so glad you could make it."

"Always glad to support a colleague."

They chatted for a few moments about the PR for the fund-raiser she was handling for the symphony. By the time she looked up, Dan had gone back inside, and their paths didn't cross for another hour and a half.

Old friends and business associates came up to her throughout the evening. Everyone was lavish in their praise of the party. She accepted the compliments graciously. Inside she was glowing. This was one of those perfect evenings that would be remembered for a long time.

Dinner was served buffet-style. Over the fettucini and veal Marsala, Carol Corsini asked if she'd be interested in arranging a tour to promote her book on the new Italian cuisine. Johanna got her card and said she'd call early the following week to talk about details.

Then it was time for Gino Dinelli to perform. He charmed them all with a selection of arias from his most famous roles. Don Giovanni, Figaro, Boris Godunov. He was superb.

Before Gino began to sing, Johanna made a point of finding Dan in the crowd. He was drinking bourbon on the rocks. He'd had a glass in his hand most of the evening. "Having a good time?"

"You were right. It's quite a bash," he answered noncommittally.

"Did you get enough to eat?"

"Sure."

"I can't leave for at least another forty-five minutes."

"Whenever you're ready."

Johanna would have liked to stay and chat with the small crowd gathering in the sitting room. Instead, she made their excuses.

In the car, she couldn't help noting that Dan smelled rather strongly of bourbon. And she couldn't shake the speculation that he'd deliberately drunk more than his usual limit.

"I get the feeling you didn't have a very good time. I'm sorry."

"I'm fine."

Again the conversation died before it even started. It was a relief to finally pull into the driveway.

Dan walked her to the door.

"Well, thank you for taking me down to the reception." Tonight she wasn't sure how to say good-bye, with a kiss or a handshake.

"I'd like to come in and talk to you."

"It's pretty late."

"Johanna, we need to talk."

The tone of his voice didn't allow for arguments. Suddenly she thought she knew how he might behave with a suspect.

Inside, she hung up her jacket. "Let me make you a cup of coffee."

"I could probably use one." He turned back toward the front door. "You had the lock changed."

"Yes." She'd wanted to tell him about the phone call. Now she decided to find out what he wanted to talk about first.

He didn't follow her into the kitchen. When she brought two mugs of coffee into the den, he was sitting in the easy chair facing the couch. He'd taken off his bow tie and opened his shirt collar, but he still didn't look very comfortable.

She set a steaming mug on the square wooden table beside him and brought hers to the sofa. It was impossible not to remember the last time they'd been in this room together.

He didn't reach for the coffee. She took a small sip of hers.

"Dan, something's been wrong all evening. What is it?"

"Tell me about the party at Marty Barnette's," he demanded in a flat voice.

Her fingers tightened on the hot mug. "What party?"

"*The* party. You know. The one where you were snorting cocaine like a pro, and then you and Rick and Marty went back to one of the bedrooms."

The blood drained from her face. "It wasn't —I didn't—"

She swallowed.

"*Tell* me about it, dammit. What did you think was going to happen when I started digging into Rick's past?"

"Rick wanted me to go to bed with Marty— because he couldn't make love to me. As soon as I went into the bedroom, I knew I was making a terrible mistake. The whole idea made me sick and I left. I took a cab home. You can ask him."

"Sorry, sweetheart. Marty's dead. Or didn't you know?"

Johanna set down the mug on the coffee table with a clank. "No. I didn't know."

"Convenient for you."

She drew her knees up under her long skirt and wrapped her arms around them. "Do you think I'd lie to you?"

He shrugged. "I don't know anymore. I

guess I think I was a chump for not taking what you were offering me the other night."

"So that's the issue. Your macho pride. Well that's still safe. I haven't—I haven't—been with anyone since Rick. Or anyone else *but* Rick for that matter."

His dark gaze bored into her. Johanna wondered why she'd been compelled to tell him that. Now she felt like a fool. She wanted to look away; somehow she couldn't.

"Are you going to tell me you weren't snorting cocaine either?"

"I— No, I won't lie about that."

"Now we're getting somewhere. Are you still on the stuff?"

"My God, Dan. How could you think that? You've been with me a lot recently."

"Some people hide it pretty well—for awhile."

"For awhile? That party was four years ago. I didn't want to go. And I didn't enjoy the cocaine. I only tried it a couple of times. For Rick. I didn't like being—out of control."

"What the hell do you mean—for Rick?"

"I mean, it was so important to him. I was trying to understand why. I was trying to hold my marriage together."

He didn't say anything.

"I don't expect you to understand. *I* don't even understand now. But at the time—"

"You said you weren't going to lie."

She nodded.

"Then why didn't you come clean with me when we were talking about Rick?"

"The truth? Well, I was trying to get up the nerve. Then you kissed me, and I didn't want to talk about the past anymore. You were so—I just wanted to—" She couldn't finish the sentence. Her voice broke. Instead of trying to continue, she stood up. When she realized she was rubbing her wrist, she let it go abruptly. She couldn't look directly at Dan anymore. She didn't want him to see her go to pieces. "I can't handle this," she managed. "So I hope you won't mind letting yourself out." She turned quickly before he could see the first tear slide down her cheek. Then she walked stiffly out of the room and up the stairs.

Chapter 18

Sunday, October 30

It had been a long time since Johanna had lain in bed sobbing. That night she couldn't help it. Finally, at four in the morning when she was all cried out, she got up and splashed cold water on her face.

The confrontation with Dan was bad enough in itself, but she knew there was more to it than that. The past week and a half had been hell—except for two really memorable occasions. The first had been on the couch with Dan when she'd lost herself in the joy of discovering him. The second had been tonight at the reception.

With a few harsh words, he'd taken the pleasure of both away from her.

Johanna leaned over the sink, peering at her puffy face and swollen eyes. It would be easy to let herself wallow in misery, but she wasn't going to do that. And she wasn't going to let Dan spoil the triumph of this evening by grilling her about things that had happened four years ago.

Tonight had been a wonderful party. A

rousing success for her and Gino Dinelli. No one could take that away from her.

She'd been too dispirited to do more than throw her dress over a chair and climb into bed in her long slip. Now she took that off and changed into a flannel nightgown.

For the first time in years, she'd let her guard down with a man. She hadn't tried to deny her attraction for Dan, and she'd been incautious enough to hope there was a future in their relationship. Well, she'd been wrong. A mistake in judgment. Wishful thinking. Maybe that was why she hadn't wanted to tell him about her naive encounter with cocaine. It was something she wished she could forget, something that never should have happened.

Sometimes you couldn't tell what kind of weird thing you were going to do when you were in the middle of a crazy situation. She'd read about it in psychology books. It was like being in combat. You couldn't predict how you'd act. Thank God she hadn't been able to do anything quite so stupid as sleep with one of Rick's friends. Some ingrained morality must have taken over to prevent that.

But when she thought back about her marriage, she couldn't believe how off-balance she'd been. Living with Rick had done that to her. At least she'd had enough sense to get away.

She hadn't known how to explain any of that to Dan. If you hadn't been there, you weren't likely to understand. And perhaps, knowing the kind of man he was, she'd been afraid he couldn't have accepted something like that in her past, even if she *had* been able to somehow explain her motivation.

The thought made her squeeze her eyes shut for a moment. It hurt. There was no way to pretend it didn't. But she'd been through a lot worse with Rick and survived. Just the way she would now.

Rick. Oh my God. She'd pushed that phone call out of her mind. She'd been going to talk to Dan. It had been a mistake to lean on him so much. When it came to the crunch, the only person you could rely on was yourself.

She'd wait until Monday and call the Rockville station. This time, she had the tape. She'd pack that up and send it to them—along with the letters.

Betty didn't bring Kirsten back until almost dinnertime. When Johanna heard a car in the drive and looked out, she was surprised to see a beige Mercedes instead of Betty's old Ford.

The luxury car belonged to Norton Jennings. Apparently, he'd gotten back from his speaking engagement and called Betty. When she'd told him that Kirsten had stayed overnight, he'd proposed taking them both to the National Zoo.

Kirsten came in the door smiling from ear to ear and hugging a stuffed panda. "We had a real neat time."

Johanna hugged her daughter. "I missed you."

"I would have missed you if I had time."

"You stinker."

"Can I get you something?" Johanna turned

to Betty and Jennings. There was a subtle intimacy about the way they were acting with each other. They were standing with their shoulders touching—and all at once Johanna realized that they'd become lovers. Well, good for Betty, she thought, biting back a small twinge of envy.

"Coffee?"

Jennings accepted her offer.

Kirsten turned to the colonel. "Come upstairs so I can show you my dolls."

"Kirsten, I don't think Colonel Jennings really wants to—"

"Nonsense. Of course I would. I collect toy soldiers myself. I'd enjoy seeing Kirsten's dolls," he interjected.

"Then I'll get your coffee."

"I'll help you." Betty followed Johanna into the kitchen.

"You and Norton seem pretty happy," she observed.

"I guess it shows."

"I'm really glad for you both."

Betty twisted the gold bangle on her wrist. "Do you think I'm acting too giddy?"

"Of course not."

"Getting into a new relationship at my age can be scary."

"At any age."

"There's a lot I don't really know about Norton. And he does like to take charge."

"I've noticed that."

"When he gets to talking about guns and stuff—sometimes it frightens me. He wants to take me to the range at Ft. Belvoir and teach me how to shoot."

Johanna's laugh had a hollow sound. "Well, maybe that's not a bad idea for self-defense."

"You could ask Dan to teach you."

"No."

Betty looked at her consideringly. "Is there something wrong?"

Johanna turned away to get the coffee from the refrigerator. "Do you think Norton wants Kona or something fancy like Seville Orange?"

"Oh, let's go for the orange." Betty stroked her chin. "You didn't answer me."

"No. There's nothing wrong."

"Come on. I know you too well. Something happened last night. I thought that after the reception you might—"

"We didn't."

"Did you and Dan have a fight?"

"I don't think it's going to work out with us . . . but I don't want to talk about it."

"And here I am telling you about me and Norton."

"Betty, I *am* happy for you. And thanks for taking Kirsten." She poured boiling water into the coffee grounds.

Betty changed the subject. "I haven't asked you about the reception. How did it go?"

"It was terrific." Johanna filled her assistant in on some of the details.

"I'm glad. You worked so hard."

Johanna nodded. "By the way, I've got a couple of new keys for you. And I have to remember to give a set to Susan."

"New keys?"

"I had the locks changed."

"What made you do that all of the sudden?" Betty inquired.

"Rick left a message on the answering machine."

"Oh no."

"I don't want to talk about that either. I'm trying to pretend, this afternoon, that I don't have any problems."

Betty patted her on the shoulder. "You're too nice a person for things not to work out all right."

Maybe she should have used Betty as a character reference with Dan, Johanna thought wryly as she began to pour the coffee into the cups.

Billy liked to sit and read the comics with Juanita. He said he was trying to help her improve her English, but usually he ended up laughing till his sides split at her fractured pronunciations.

But Juanita didn't mind. Señora Hempsted had an important job over at NIH. She didn't have a lot of time to spend with *los niños*. That was a shame—at least for Billy. So Juanita tried to spend some extra time with him.

Her favorite comic was *Henry*, because it didn't have any words. But Billy made her read him *Peanuts*.

Today in the strip, Snoopy was dreaming about the Great Pumpkin. That made her think about her dreams.

"Hey, you're not paying attention," Billy complained.

"*Perdon.*" She made an effort to concentrate, but even the short words were coming out mangled.

"You're not even trying. I'm going over to Alan's house," Billy finally said.

"Maybe we try again later."

"Maybe."

"You call me if you go anywhere else."

"Okay."

He didn't always remember. Juanita watched out the window as he headed down the block on his bike. *Gracias a Dios* the bad man wasn't stealing little boys. Then she pressed her fingers to her mouth. What a terrible thing to be grateful for. What was wrong with her? Maybe it was because she wasn't going to church. Maybe if she could just talk to a priest. But what would she say? A priest in her own country might understand. Up here he'd probably just think her dreams were crazy.

It would just be another dead end, like that policeman. He hadn't made fun of her, but halfway through the conversation she'd known he didn't believe about the dreams. He thought she'd seen something in real life. When he kept asking who she was, she'd gotten scared and hung up.

Opening the pantry, she began to straighten up the cans and boxes. Tomatoes down on the right. Cereal up on the left. How did it get so messed up?

The dreams hadn't bothered her for a few days. She'd thought they had gone away, but last night they'd come back. Something *muy mal* was going to happen ... to the dark-haired lady and her daughter. Now she really believed it. And she didn't know what to do.

His hands were shaking as he got out the newspaper articles he'd photocopied at the library. He spread them out, all across the dining room table.

It made his heart start to beat faster as he looked at them. Millions of people had read about him. Some of the stories were from the *Gazette*. That was chicken shit.

Covered with spit. Totally unfit.

Eat grass. Not on your ass.

Bloody hell. Not that. He pounded his forehead with his fist, trying to beat the rhymes out of his brain.

He never knew when they were going to come back.

Sometimes they seemed to expand in his mind until he could think of nothing else.

They wouldn't go away, and he stumbled into the kitchen for the bottle of bourbon. Without even bothering with a glass, he tipped up the bottle and gulped down some of the fiery liquid. In a few minutes he stopped shaking and he could think straight again, even if everything was a little fuzzy.

He was losing it. What if he couldn't keep up that nice-as-pie front that had everybody fooled? The thought made him close his eyes and press his palms to his throbbing temples. He had to think of the good things . . . like the *Washington Post* article about him. That was really the big time. And he'd even been mentioned in a piece in *Newsweek* on serial killers. That made him smile.

Then he remembered how angry he'd been at the library. He couldn't bring bourbon to the library, only lemon drops. He sucked them while he tried to make the fucking machine work right. The damn thing had made the copies too dark. He'd screamed at the woman behind the counter before he remembered to be nice. She'd given him his money back and showed him how to change the setting, but he could tell she was afraid of him. He couldn't afford to let that happen. People had to think he was nice, kind, and helpful. And well groomed.

You had to make a good appearance if you wanted to have them respect you. Johanna had taught him that. And he'd learned from her how to put together a press kit. He could even send it out himself. He'd stolen some of her stationery. But he couldn't write as well as she could. That was her job. And what she said would have more impact than anything he could put together. The press didn't pay attention to ordinary people. You had to know who to call and who to flatter. He wanted to make sure everybody understood about him . . . and Emily . . . and Momma.

He wanted to ask Johanna about it, but he was afraid to let her know exactly who he was until he was sure she understood.

He leaned down and pressed his throbbing face against the cool surface of the table. Then he lifted his head and banged it down against the hard wood. The physical pain helped drown out the hammering inside.

This was so tricky. He hadn't thought it would all be this complicated. Careful. He had to be careful.

It was so hard to think. Johanna. Kirsten. She was like Emily. Like the others. Emily was dead. So were the others. And Johanna would get angry at him if Kirsten were dead.

He couldn't afford to make Johanna angry. Not yet. He needed her. And she needed him . . . wasn't that right? Or was he confused again?

Johanna was going to help him make everybody understand. That was important, because if people didn't understand, then he was going to be in a lot of trouble. They'd probably lock him away in a mental hospital. He sure as hell didn't think he could survive being locked up like that. He needed to be out in the fresh air every day.

Just right. Everything had to be just right. Soon he'd find the right time to leave the clippings at Johanna's. Not in the mailbox. He giggled. That wasn't safe; it was right down there on the street. Somebody could take an envelope out. He'd leave it in the door. That way he could use the special postmark he'd made up.

Chapter 19

Monday, October 31

If it hadn't been for Kirsten, Johanna would have thrown Dan's pumpkin in the trash. But Kirsten would want to know why, and she wasn't up to any explanations.

"Officer Whitmore said he liked to carve pumpkins when he was a little boy," Kirsten said as she scooped seeds onto sheets of newspaper.

"Um hum."

"I wish he were here to help us now. You're not very good at it."

"Sorry."

"Where is he?"

"Busy."

Luckily Kirsten hadn't pressed the point.

After finishing the pumpkin, they went out trick-or-treating.

Johanna didn't like leaving the house unattended on Halloween, but going out with Kirsten was more important than worrying about toilet paper on the trees and soap on the mailbox, and tonight she wasn't going to think about anything worse.

The weather was too cold for the princess outfit Kirsten had worn to the school party. They'd had a fight about covering it with a coat, so they'd compromised. Johanna had agreed to let her daughter wear her expensive rhinestone-studded evening sweater from I. Magnin if she put on a tee shirt and a turtleneck under it. The sweater was like a dress on Kirsten, so they'd added a silver stretch-belt and rolled up the sleeves.

Kirsten had grinned as she'd twirled in front of the mirror. Then she'd dragged her mother out the door.

There were a lot of parents out tonight, Johanna noticed as she looked up and down the street. They must feel the way she did about keeping an eye on their children. The difference was, most people could leave a spouse at home while they made the rounds.

"Kirsten," Johanna called.

"What?"

"Slow down. I need to keep up with you." She'd known there was no way she could talk her daughter into staying home this evening. But being out in the dark gave her a spooky feeling. Sort of like the night of the meeting, when she'd walked down to Susan's and felt as if someone were following her.

"But I won't get a lot of candy if I go slow."

"You won't get any candy at all if you don't, because we're going to go right back home."

"Mommy!" But the little girl waited at the driveway to the next house before skipping up to the front door.

The dark shape of a compact car went past

on the street, and Johanna tried to catch a glimpse of the driver's face. Hadn't that car passed them before? Maybe it was someone looking for a house number.

It was too dark to see who was behind the wheel. Maybe it was some parent who didn't like walking.

Rick hunched over and pulled his cap lower on his forehead as he cruised by Johanna the second time. If he'd rolled down the window and put his arm out, he could have touched her. But it wasn't Johanna he wanted to touch. He wanted Kirsten. And he'd figured this would be a perfect night to grab her. In a couple of days he was going to get some more stuff to deliver. Three hundred thousand dollars—street value. He and Kirsten could go pretty far on that.

Damn Johanna! Damn that bitch. She was always interfering with his plans. Why couldn't she stay home giving out candy where she belonged tonight?

Johanna heard the big dog bark as soon as Kirsten set foot on the walk.

The girl turned to her mother. "Don't worry. That's just Baron. He's nice."

Baron. He and Marian Lewis had been at the Waterford's the day Jeanie had turned up missing. She'd remembered then that Marian and Baron had found— She stopped herself from finishing the thought.

From the sidewalk, Johanna could see Marian open the door and smile down at Kirsten before bringing out a basket of candy.

Kirsten came back waving a Mounds bar. "Not just the little kind. She's giving out big ones."

"That's nice." And just maybe I'll snitch it for myself, Johanna thought, as a reward for plodding around the neighborhood on a cold dark night like this.

He drove around the block and came up behind Johanna and Kirsten again. Which way were they going? His hands tightened on the wheel. Maybe they'd turn onto Orchard Hill Run. There was a place with a lot of scraggly bushes where the path crossed the road. If they went up that way, maybe he could get Kirsten anyway. He could pull up beside her and open the door. It would only take a moment to get her into the car. Then he could zip right out of there. He could be out of the state in twenty minutes if he headed toward D.C. Then he'd cut across the Four-teenth Street Bridge to Virginia.

He looked over his shoulder. Was some-body out there stalking him? The police?

He was starting to feel shaky. He needed a little pick-me-up. From the glove compart-ment he pulled out a tin that had once held throat lozenges. Inside was a plastic bag of coke and a cut-off straw. He laid out a line and snorted. In a moment he was feeling a lot better.

Johanna and Kirsten reached the corner,

and he held his breath. *Turn. Go ahead, turn,* he chanted. Kirsten hesitated and then darted down Orchard Hill Run. It was a sign. A sign that she wanted to go with him.

His heart was pounding in his ears. He was going to put something over on that bitch Johanna. It was hard to make himself wait, but he counted to three hundred, picturing them moving down the block. Then, slowly, he put the car into gear and drifted around the corner.

A kid dressed like a hobo darted in front of him, and he slammed on the brakes. Damn fool. Lucky he was going so slow. He might have hit the kid and spoiled everything.

Easy. Easy, he told himself. You've gotten this far. Don't blow it now.

Kirsten was almost to the bushes. Good. Just a little bit more, he thought, getting ready to pull into position.

Then Kirsten stopped. What the hell was she doing?

A bunch of other little kids came running up to her. One was dressed up as a witch. One was a devil. There was a football player. A clown. They were opening their bags, seeing who had the most candy.

Get away from her! Had he screamed that out loud?

Two women came up behind Johanna. They all went to join the kids.

He waited, heart pounding, but it was no good. They were all going to stay together. He'd lost his chance. He'd have to come back another time. Soon. Maybe he'd pick up the stuff first. Or if he didn't show up for the delivery, they wouldn't miss him till maybe Thursday. He and Kirsten could be in West Virginia by then. Who would look for them in some little burg in the mountains?

Chapter 20

Tuesday, November 1

The bite had been too high on Betty's crown every since she'd gotten it. When she called the dentist, he said she could come in at three-thirty and have it adjusted. But she'd taken the Metro instead of her car that morning because Norton Jennings was supposed to come over and pick her up after work. Now she couldn't get in touch with him, and she hadn't any transportation.

"What should I do?" she asked Johanna.

"If your jaw's sore and it hurts every time you bite down, you'd better get it taken care of. You can use my car."

"Are you sure you don't mind?"

"Of course not."

"Then tell Norton to wait for me."

"Will do."

Kirsten called after school to say she was playing at Amy's. Johanna had just hung up the phone when Jennings knocked at the door. It was overcast and dismal outside, the kind of day where it gets dark early, but Jennings hadn't bothered with an overcoat. He was wearing a muted Harris tweed jacket with leather patches at the elbows. His blue Oxford cloth shirt was crisp. His tie was a burgundy and navy silk stripe. Obviously he'd dressed for Betty.

He followed Johanna into the office and looked around. "Where's your assistant?"

"She had to make a quick trip to the dentist, and she gave me strict instructions to make sure you waited."

He grinned.

"Can I get you a cup of tea?"

"Do you have Earl Grey?"

"I think I can scare some up."

Jennings sat down on one of the couches near the fireplace and looked out the window.

After she had brought a mug of tea for each of them, the phone rang. Johanna excused herself to take a call from one of her authors who was worried because his books hadn't arrived for the National Press Club Book Fair. After calling the publisher and being assured that the books had been shipped, she turned back to Jennings.

"I didn't realize how many little details you have to take care of," he observed.

"That's what you pay us for. I've got your new press kit almost finished. The picture really looks good. Want to take a look at it?"

"Why not?"

Johanna crossed to the walk-in closet where they kept the filing cabinets. She had just opened the drawer and started to pull out Jennings's folder when she heard a sharp rap at the closet door.

"Johanna—don't panic, but there's some guy sneaking around out by your garage."

Johanna gasped. "I'll call the police."

"Nothing I can't take care of. You wait there."

She tried to reassure herself that the colonel would find it was something innocent—like a teenager cutting across her property. But her heart had started a wild drumming in her chest.

"Be careful," she called after Jennings. He didn't answer. Then the outside door opened and closed softly behind him.

Johanna reached for the doorknob. He had said to stay in the closet, but she couldn't just cower there waiting for something to happen. She peered out the window into the gathering gloom.

At least she didn't see an intruder. But she didn't see Jennings either. If nobody was there, why didn't he come back? God, she wished she knew what to do. Maybe she should call the police after all. But she'd bothered them so much recently that she suspected they'd just think she was crying wolf.

Her hand hovered above the phone. Then she froze.

"Give that to me, you son of a bitch." It was Jennings, bellowing.

The order was followed by a curse in another voice. That voice. She should recognize it. But there was no time to try and think about it now.

Johanna looked wildly around for a weapon. After snatching up the poker from the fireplace, she rushed to the door and opened it. It might have been her imagination, but she thought she heard scuffling feet and grunts of effort from the other side of the garage.

Then there was a low groan and the sound of something heavy hitting the ground. Without any thought of her own safety, Johanna dashed out into the dusk. As she rounded the corner of the garage, she could just make out a figure disappearing into the darker shadows beneath the pine trees, fifty feet away.

Was that Jennings, chasing someone she couldn't see? No. Not Jennings. It looked as if this man's jacket and trousers matched. That was all she could tell in the dim light.

As she ran forward, she almost tripped over a limp form sprawled on the ground. She gasped. Then, afraid of what she might find, Johanna knelt. Her hands brushed against soft tweed. It was wet and sticky. Blood. She hadn't heard a shot. What had happened out here?

Jennings was lying on his side. She was afraid to roll him over until she knew where he was injured.

"Colonel Jennings. Norton. Can you hear me?"

He didn't move, didn't answer.

She was trembling from cold and shock as her hand reached frantically for the pulse in his neck. There was a slow beat under her fingertips. Thank God he was still alive.

Then she saw the deep gash across his forehead. It was gushing a river of blood, which was soaking onto her skirt. She bit back another gasp. She had to stay calm. She had to get help. She didn't want to leave him bleeding like that, but there wasn't anything else she could do.

As she stumbled back across the driveway, headlights blinded her, and she threw up her hands to shield her eyes.

The car screeched to a halt, and Betty jumped out. "My God, there's blood all over you. What's happened?"

There wasn't time to tell her gently. "It's Norton. He's been hit on the head."

"No!" Betty's face was an anguished mask.

Johanna grabbed her arm, leaving five bloody fingerprints. "You stay with him. I'm going to call an ambulance and the police."

She made the calls and then scooped up a stack of clean towels and a blanket from the laundry room before hurrying back out.

Jennings was lying just as she'd left him. Betty was kneeling beside him pressing her wool scarf to the gash on his head. Her face was white as paste as she replaced the scarf with the clean towel Johanna handed her and continued to apply pressure. "So much blood. Oh God, please don't let him die."

Johanna unfolded the blanket and spread it over the still form.

Betty crouched over Jennings, clutching his hand.

"He's going to be all right," Johanna whispered.

Betty nodded numbly.

The wail of a siren sounded in the distance.

"Thank God," Johanna breathed. "I'm going down to the end of the drive in case they can't find us."

A few minutes later, Johanna was back, leading a stretcher crew. Betty moved away as the paramedic squatted down beside the victim and checked for vital signs.

"Dilated pupils. Elevated blood pressure. Possible skull fracture." The quiet words of the rescue worker made Johanna reach out and clutch Betty's arm. They watched silently as a rigid collar was fitted around Norton's neck to prevent further injury. Then he was moved to the stretcher.

Johanna suddenly noticed that two uniformed police officers had also arrived.

Betty went with Jennings to Suburban Hospital. Johanna went back into the house with the policemen. Not until she'd stepped into her office did she realize that her skirt and blouse were stiff with blood. Both of them were sticking to her skin.

She gestured toward her ruined clothes. "Could I—clean up?"

"Sure. Go ahead."

"I mean—I want to take a shower."

"No problem."

"I'll be back down in a few minutes."

Upstairs, she stripped off her clothes and stuffed them into a plastic bag. Then she turned on the shower and stepped under the steaming water. She wanted to stand there for a long time. Instead, she scrubbed the blood off as quickly as possible, washed her hair, and blew it dry as quickly as she could.

Without makeup she looked pale and drawn, but she didn't want to take any more time. Twenty minutes after she'd stripped off her blood-stained clothes, Johanna was back down-stairs clad in jeans and a navy sweatshirt.

"I'm sorry to keep you waiting," she apologized. The words were automatic. She still felt numb.

"We understand," the younger of the two officers assured her. He was tall and blond, named Stevenson. His partner was short, dark, and compact, named Marotti.

"Can you tell us what happened?" Marotti asked.

Johanna sank onto the sofa opposite them. Up until now, adrenalin had kept her going. All at once she felt like a rag doll that had lost its stuffing. In a voice that she couldn't quite hold steady, she related the incident.

"So you didn't see the assailant?"

"I only caught a glimpse of him."

"Are you sure it was a man?"

She shook her head. "Not really. I think he was wearing trousers and possibly a jacket of the same color. Denim, maybe. He wasn't a large man, I don't think. The voice—"

"What about the voice?" the dark-haired officer asked.

"I think it was a man's. Someone I should know."

"Your ex-husband?" Stevenson asked.

Johanna's head jerked up.

"We called in to the station while you were upstairs and got the scoop on your complaints about him," Marotti explained.

"You mean the tape on Saturday?"

"What tape?"

"On my answering machine," Johanna clarified.

"There wasn't anything in the complaints about that."

"I didn't want to come down there, so I mailed it in. And some letters. I guess it's too soon for them to have gotten there yet."

"These letters and the tape—they were threats?" Marotti asked.

"Yes. Against me—and Kirsten, my daughter." Without thinking about what she was doing, she rubbed her wrist.

The questioning lasted half an hour. Johanna wished she could give a better description of the person who had hit Jennings, but she simply hadn't been able to see much in the dim light.

When Stevenson and Marotti finally closed their notebooks, Johanna leaned back against the sofa cushions. "Do you think it was Rick?"

Marotti shrugged. "No way to tell yet."

"But who else—?"

"We'll put out a bulletin on Hamilton, and we'll get back to you as soon as we have something. Or maybe Jennings will know—if he's in any shape to talk."

"Thank you."

After Johanna showed them out, she called the hospital. Jennings was still unconscious, but she was able to reach Betty.

"Do you want me to come down there?"

"There's no use two of us sitting around here."

"Let me know as soon as you find out anything."

"I will."

Her next call was to Susan, who was horrified to hear what had happened.

"Do you want to come over here?" her friend asked.

"I don't feel like going out."

"Well, why don't I keep Kirsten overnight?"

"I'd appreciate that. But are you sure that's not too much trouble?"

"Of course not. She and Amy will love it."

"Susan—thanks."

"Glad to do it."

Well, at least she didn't have to worry about Kirsten tonight, Johanna thought as she put down the phone. Methodically, she walked around the first floor checking the locks. Then she went into the den and got out a bottle of sherry. Maybe a drink was what she needed.

She was just pouring the amber liquid into a small glass when the doorbell rang.

Her whole body tensed. Was that the man who'd attacked Jennings coming back? No, that was ridiculous. He'd hardly ring the bell.

The chimes sounded again.

"Just a minute."

When she peered through the sidelight, her heart gave a painful lurch. Dan Whitmore was standing on the front porch.

Chapter 21

Johanna opened the door a crack, shivering in the unexpected blast of cold air. The temperature had dropped considerably in the last hour. "What are you doing here?" she asked Dan.

"I heard about what happened with Jennings. I came over as soon as I could get off."

"I don't— We don't—"

He pushed against the door, and she gave way. Before she could protest any further, he had stepped into the hall and closed the door behind him.

"Johanna."

The way he said her name made something inside her chest contract painfully, and she looked up to search his eyes.

Instead of saying anything else, he closed the space between them in one long stride and pulled her hard against him. His muscular arms wrapped tightly around her. For a moment she stood rigid. Then her self-control snapped, and she started to shake. God, how she'd tried to be strong. But she'd needed someone to hold her. She hadn't dared admit how much she'd wanted it to be Dan Whitmore.

She didn't protest when he swung her up into his arms and carried her into the den. In fact, she braced her arms around his neck. Lowering himself to the sofa, he cradled her in his lap, stroking and rocking her. When the trembling finally stopped, she felt calmer than she had in days.

"Thank you," she whispered.

"Marotti told me how you looked with blood all over you. You didn't cry or anything. He said he thought you were in shock. I knew you needed—someone."

"And you thought you'd offer your services." She couldn't keep the sudden sharpness out of her voice as she tried to push away from him.

He held her fast. "Maybe that didn't come out the way I meant it. You've been through a hell of a lot, and I wanted to be with you. Even though I knew I wasn't very—helpful— the other night."

She nodded, relaxing fractionally. "What you said— No, the way you said it—hurt."

"I know." It wasn't easy to apologize. Maybe he could slip into it gradually. Test out the right words. "I was upset, and I'd had a lot to drink. I was overreacting."

"I knew you were upset—and drinking a lot. Every time I saw you, you had a glass in your hand. All evening I wanted to ask you what was wrong. I thought maybe you were uncomfortable in that crowd."

"I was. But that was nothing compared to

the way I felt after talking to Carnero." He shook his head. "I didn't have any right to go after you about the cocaine like that. Or anything else."

"There wasn't anything else!"

With his thumb and forefinger under her chin, he tipped her face up toward his. "I didn't mean— When I cooled down, I knew you were telling me the truth."

She nodded.

"Maybe I should tell you where I'm coming from," he said in a low voice.

"If you want."

"Believe me, I'd rather not. I don't talk about this much."

"You don't have to tell me."

"Yes I do." He swallowed. "I mean literally— where I come from. I grew up in a run-down housing project in Riverdale. I don't know who my father was. My mother dumped me on my grandmother and skipped town. We found out when I was nine that she'd died of a heroin overdose. But I'd only seen her a few times. It wasn't like she meant something to me."

"Oh, Dan. I'm sorry." So that was why he'd reacted so strongly to the fact that she'd tried drugs.

"I don't want you to feel sorry for me."

"That isn't what I meant. I remember what you said about your childhood being rough. It must have been hell."

"You remember my saying that?"

"I wanted you to talk about it, but I didn't want to press you. I guess I realized it was like my marriage. Something—you'd rather forget."

"Yeah, like your marriage. It wasn't any picnic. Grandma was pretty pissed about having to raise a kid on her pension. But she did her duty. And she was determined I wasn't going to turn out like my mom. God, was that old lady strict."

She reached out to trace the scar on his chin. "Are you going to tell me more about it?"

"Later. If you still want to hear." He cleared his throat. "Johanna, I told myself that first night you were too good for me. Too polished. You went to college. I went to Prince Georges Junior College for a year before the Police Academy, and then got my degree at night."

"None of that has to matter."

"Yeah. I kept telling myself that. Then when Carnero had those things to say about you—I felt like you'd slipped one over on me—me, the street-smart cop. So I wasn't just hurt, I was angry."

"And now?"

"Now I want you to forgive me for hurting you. And forgive me for not being here when you needed me."

"I'm glad you're here now."

She lifted her head. He lowered his, and their lips met. It was like the last time. Urgent. Powerful. Hungry. Only now it meant more, because the fear hovering in the background had come a little closer, and because of the way they had parted last time. He wanted her to know how he really felt. She wanted him to know she understood.

His lips ravaged hers, tender and savage by turns. His hands slipped under the back of her sweatshirt to knead her back. When he discovered she wasn't wearing a bra, he couldn't stop himself from reaching around to the front of her so that he could cup her breasts.

As he took their soft weight in his palms, he watched her face intently. The way she sucked in a sharp little breath of air told him what he wanted to know.

"Jesus, you feel wonderful," he muttered as his fingers played across her tense nipples. Then he pulled the sweatshirt up. For a moment he was captivated by the sight. Then he bent to suck one taut nipple into his mouth.

Johanna gasped and clasped her hands around his head, her fingers stroking mindlessly across the bristle at the back of his neck.

He drew back slowly, and she looked up to meet his eyes, answering his unspoken question. This time they weren't going to stop.

"I think we should go up to my bedroom— before somebody falls off the couch again."

He laughed. "Um hum."

They had both stood up, and he reached out and stroked his finger across her cheek. "Where's Kirsten?"

"Spending the night at Susan's."

"Good planning."

"I didn't know how good. Susan just thought I needed some time to myself."

They walked up the stairs hand in hand.

She switched on one of the bedside lamps and folded back the covers before turning to face him again.

He knew she was nervous, stalling for time. Now that they were up here, he wasn't quite so sure of himself, either. It had been a long time for her. What if he hurt her? Or what if it wasn't any good for her?

He looked around the room, liking it. She'd furnished it in antique walnut: dresser, night tables, an armoire, and a beautifully carved headboard. The walls were papered in a delicate diamond pattern in rose, or some muted color. He couldn't quite tell in the dim light.

She watched gravely as he took the 357 Magnum from the holster in his belt and put it on the dresser.

"Betty said I should get you to give me shooting lessons."

"That's not a bad idea. Do you want me to?"

"I don't know about a gun in the house with Kirsten."

"I'd make damn sure she knew how dangerous it was."

She didn't want to keep talking about guns or danger or intruders bashing clients over the head. Instead, she crossed the room and began to unbutton his Oxford cloth shirt.

Underneath, he had on a white tee shirt. Her hands slid it upward, inch by inch, revealing the broad expanse of his chest. She pressed her face against him, drinking in his masculine scent, rubbing her cheek in a circle against the crisp hair.

"God you're sexy," he growled.

"Am I?"

"Yes."

She tipped her face up to his. "So are you."

They began to undress each other then—she, still a little shy; he going slowly to make sure she was comfortable with him.

She was the one who led him to the bed. When he pulled up the covers around them and took her in his arms, she gasped.

"Okay?"

"It's just so—nice—feeling your body against me like this."

He pressed his cheek to hers and turned to kiss the side of her face just along her hairline. "I need you to tell me what you like. What turns you on."

"Just being with you."

"I mean it. Tell me if I'm being too rough. Or too soft."

She laughed and surprised herself by slipping her hand down to clasp his erection. "You're not too soft."

He closed his eyes for a moment. "That feels real good. But if you keep it up, you're going to make things happen too fast."

He rolled her onto her back and began to caress her. After awhile she forgot to tell him what felt best. But he knew by the little sighs and catches in her breath—and by the hot, damp readiness of her.

Almost as soon as he entered her, she cried out and came. And then she did again, a few minutes later, with him. Then he was hugging her against him and rocking her, and they were kissing each other on the cheeks and eyebrows and chin.

He could see where his beard had made her face red, and he reached up to smooth a finger across her cheek the way he had downstairs. Only now the gesture had a new intimacy.

"I should have shaved before I came over."

"I'm glad you came right from work. I needed you. And I didn't want—couldn't—call you."

"I know." He hugged her tighter.

"I needed you," she repeated. "Not just for sex. Oh damn, that didn't come out the way I meant it. The sex was wonderful. But I was feeling like—it was all too much."

"I understand."

"I don't want to be anything with you except honest—ever again."

"That's how I feel, too."

"Even if it hurts?"

"Yeah." His serious expression turned to a grin. "So when you said the sex was wonderful—"

"Hum. Maybe spectacular is more descriptive."

The phone rang. Dan glanced over at the clock radio. It was ten-thirty. He watched the way Johanna picked up the reciever, as though it were her enemy. He saw her expression change, and he gathered from the conversation that it was Betty.

"How's Jennings?" he asked when she got off the phone.

"He's got a skull fracture and internal

bleeding—something called a subdural hematoma."

"Too bad."

"They can't tell what kind of recovery he'll make, but they're going to have to operate to relieve the pressure."

He reached out, and Johanna sat down beside him. He held her, stroking her back. "I saw the way you looked before you answered the phone."

"That bad?"

"Marotti said you told him you sent in a tape from your answering machine."

"Of Rick." Briefly she told him about it.

"I don't like your being here alone."

She tried to make a joke of it. "Does that mean you want to spend the night?"

"It means I can't help worrying about you. And yes, I'd like to spend the night."

"Susan will call me to come get Kirsten. I wouldn't want her to walk in and find you in my bed."

"Yeah."

"You didn't have dinner, did you?" Johanna asked.

He shook his head.

"I wasn't hungry," she said. "Now I think I could eat a sandwich."

"Sounds good. Anything'll do."

"Liverwurst and onion?"

"I hope you're kidding."

"Yes. How about ham and cheese? Or chicken?"

"Could I have one of each?"

"Sure."

He knew she was self-conscious about getting out of bed naked, but he watched appreciatively as she crossed the room and took her robe out of the closet.

"I don't really know what Miss Manners would advise, but would you like me to—uh—throw your underwear and your shirt in the washer and dryer while I'm downstairs?"

"I'd appreciate clean underwear tomorrow. The shirt's got at least another good day."

She raised her eyebrow.

"Honesty, remember."

"I'll bring the food up."

Johanna was smiling as she left the room and went down to the kitchen.

Her forgotten glass of sherry was still on the counter. Well, she'd found a much more enjoyable way to relax. Humming, she began to get out makings for sandwiches. One for her and two for Dan. She hadn't asked him what he wanted to drink. Hoping he liked cranberry juice, she poured two large glasses and set them on a tray with the sandwiches.

She was getting ready to go back upstairs when she heard the storm door open. Tensing, she waited for a knock, but there was only the whoosh of the door closing again.

"Kirsten?" she called as she peered through the sidelight.

There was no answer, and nobody to be seen. Slowly she opened the door, and a fat manila envelope fell inside. Picking it up, she looked at the address. Her name was printed across the front. Instead of a stamp in the upper right hand corner, there was a block of

four old Christmas seals. Across them someone had drawn wavy cancel lines. But it was
the postmark that made the hair on the back
of her neck stand up. It wasn't the usual
circle with the name of the post office around
the inside edge. It was an infinity mark, just
like the signature at the bottom of the last
few letters.

Chapter 22

Dan was sitting up in bed, his bare back propped up against the pillows. "Clever move, taking my underwear," he quipped. Then he saw Johanna's face. "What's the matter?"

She set the tray on the bureau and held up the envelope. "Special delivery. I heard someone leave it in the storm door."

He swore under his breath.

"I'm afraid to open it."

He held out his hand. The first thing he did was heft the envelope. Then he carefully inspected the outside—with particular attention to the sealed end.

"What are you doing?"

"Making sure it's not a bomb."

She drew in her breath.

"It's not." He picked up a pencil, inserted it under the flap, and slit the envelope. Before he pulled out the contents, he looked up at Johanna with a wry expression on his face. "Mind passing me my sandwich."

"How can you eat now?"

"I'm starving."

She set one drink on each night table, brought the tray over, and climbed back into bed with him. Johanna watched Dan take a hearty bite of ham sandwich. "This is good. You eat some too."

"I don't know if I can."

"Small bites, then. You need the nourishment."

She followed his directions, but her nerves were so taut that the ham sandwich had about as much taste as wallpaper paste.

After polishing off one of the sandwiches and starting on the other, Dan drank some of the juice, and then he pulled a simulated leather folder out of the envelope. She could see he was being careful not to touch anything but the edges. It was a two-pocket folder like the ones she used for press kits, only the outside was fancier. The two interior compartments were stuffed with photocopies of newspaper articles and typed sheets of paper. The top one was on *her* letterhead.

"My God," she gasped. "I knew it. Somebody was in my office last week when I went to school to hear you talk. But I didn't know what was missing."

Dan slipped an arm around her shoulder. "Why didn't you tell me about it?"

"I wasn't sure—until I saw this. I was going to mention it Saturday, but—"

"Yeah. I didn't exactly make things easy for you Saturday. Did you change the locks because of the break-in?"

"No. I half-convinced myself I was imagining someone had been there. But I couldn't make the phone call from Rick go away. It was on tape."

He riffled through the material. "Any significance in the way this is put together?"

"It's just the way Betty and I do a press kit."

Typed on her letterhead was a short paragraph directing the reader's attention to the clippings.

"Of course, I would have written a longer letter, pointing out some of the important facts," Johanna added.

"I guess the sender wants you to draw your own conclusions." Dan pulled out the photocopies and began to thumb through them. They were all accounts of the two local murders —except for the *Newsweek* article, which was a feature on serial murders.

Dan spread them out. In all of the articles, certain sentences had been underlined with a red pen. Words and phrases leaped up at Johanna:

No clue to the murderer's identity
They had both been sexually assaulted
What drives a serial killer is the perception of some hurt he has experienced in the past. . . . He picks his victims with discrimination.

Johanna clutched Dan's forearm so tightly that her fingernails dug into his skin. He didn't flinch away.

Ritualistic patterns
Many of these people, when they were quite young,

were themselves victims of sexual, physical, or emo-
tional abuse. That abuse leaves a scar.

Rampage of revenge

"Oh, God," Johanna moaned. "It's him. The only thing this can mean is that he's the murderer."

"Who?"

"Rick. Don't you see? I was right. It's got to be Rick."

"Maybe."

"His voice was hoarse, coughing, but I'm pretty sure it was Rick on that tape the other night."

"A rough voice—from coke maybe," Dan mused. "Was he talking about the murders then?"

Johanna shook her head.

"What was he saying?"

"That he was going to come and snatch Kirsten. My God, Dan, we both know she looks like the little girls who were murdered. Blond hair. Blue eyes. Eight years old."

"He wasn't saying he was going to murder her, was he?" he persisted.

"No. But the letters. You remember some of the letters talked about murder."

"Has a psychiatrist seen them?"

"No."

He gave her a direct look. "You remember when we first talked about this, you asked me to keep it confidential?"

Her head bobbed fractionally. She knew what he was going to say.

"We can't. You know that now?"

"Yes," she whispered.

He set the tray on the floor and pulled her against his chest.

She buried her face in his neck and he stroked her shoulders. He'd promised he was going to be honest with her. He couldn't be honest now and tell her just how frightened he was. For her. This material sure as hell looked like it had come from the killer. Even if it wasn't Rick, it was from someone close enough to Johanna to have been at her house four times in the last week. One of those times he'd been inside—going through her papers, and the last time he'd done his best to kill Norton Jennings.

She needed protection. If he could move in with her, he'd be here at night. But how could you ask a woman if you could move in when you'd just taken her to bed? You couldn't.

"I don't like this setup one damn bit," he muttered.

"You're worried."

He didn't want to give her any false reassurances. That was dangerous for her. "I've got to be. You do too. I'd feel a lot happier if you and Kirsten could just get out of town until we caught this guy."

He felt her body tense. "I'd leave too many people in the lurch. I can't do that. Besides, Rick would find me, and I'd rather face him on my own turf."

"Then we'll make sure Rick can't get to you."

"When you have to depend on other people, they might not be there," she said in a low voice.

"I'm going to be here—for you."

Before she could voice any more doubts, he stopped her with his lips. She didn't want to resist the heat that leaped up inside her as his mouth moved over hers and his hands began to part the front closing of her robe.

Both of them knew they were holding fear at bay, but soon there wasn't room in the bed for anything but their passion.

The last time he'd played a tape of a phone call to Johanna, she'd been doing all the talking.

But this tape was different. It was from the answering machine, so he couldn't hear her saying anything at all. He would have liked to listen to her reaction. But he could imagine it. The message had frightened her. Maybe she'd drawn in her breath. Maybe she'd started to shake. Maybe she'd rubbed her wrist the way she did.

Then she'd bundled the tape up with some of the letters and sent the whole thing to the police department.

Bloody hell! He didn't like that. Only he was smarter than Johanna and smarter than the police. He'd taken the package out of the mailbox.

He pressed the "rewind" button and started the tape again. He'd listened to it a dozen times. He didn't want to listen to it anymore, but somehow he couldn't stop his hand from hitting the "play" button again.

The tape made him angry. Sweat stood out on his forehead, and his head was already pounding. He needed a drink. More and more often now he needed a drink to stop the pain in his head.

Head. Led. Seeing red.

"Stop it!" he screamed out loud. For a moment he thought he was going to start smashing things. But he got ahold of himself—just barely.

There were a lot of things that made him angry lately. Like when he'd stopped over at Johanna's this evening to leave the press kit. There had been a car in the driveway. It belonged to that guy who'd been hanging around her. He was going to fix that guy. Just the way he'd fixed that old fart Jennings.

He laughed. The old fool thought he was so tough just 'cause he'd been in the army. He'd seen him out by the garage and come charging out of the house like he was John Wayne or something. But he'd dropped the old guy like a steer in a slaughterhouse. Probably, he was dead. He'd better be dead!

He'd gone back again tonight with the press kit, thinking he was in the clear. He'd worked hard on that press kit. He wanted Johanna to see it. But he almost hadn't left it when he'd seen that Chevy in the drive and the low light up in her bedroom. Bloody hell! He could just imagine what they were doing up there, and his hands had started to shake.

Then he'd made himself calm down. He'd put a lemon drop in his mouth and sucked it until it was just a little sliver. He needed to know if Johanna was going to help him.

His hands clenched. He was getting angry at her. Just like he'd gotten angry at Momma.

Johanna had disappointed him so many times lately. She better not this time! She'd better help him! Otherwise she was going to be sorry.

Chapter 23

Wednesday, November 3

Dan slammed on his brakes and came to a halt a foot behind the Buick that had stopped abruptly in front of him.

As he waited for the rush-hour traffic to start up again, he rubbed his fingers across the bridge of his nose. He hadn't gotten much sleep, maybe an hour or so. After he and Johanna had made love again, they'd talked in low voices—about the letters, and the press kit . . . and then about other things. She'd asked more about his childhood, and he'd told her. Not just the bad parts. She'd talked about her childhood, too. And he'd told her about his partner Nico and how they hadn't liked each other at first but found they had a lot in common.

"Like us."

He'd laughed. "Yeah." Then he'd smoothed his hand along the inside of her thigh. "But Nico and I aren't quite *this* close."

When he thought about Johanna now, he got a tight feeling in his chest. He hadn't wanted this kind of complication in his life, but she was starting to mean a lot to him. It was surprisingly easy to get close to her, once they'd started opening up with each other. He liked that. It wasn't like with Erin where neither one of them had really been able to be honest.

Johanna had even been able to talk about her husband. "I suppose you wonder why I stayed married to him for so long. He changed so gradually that I didn't realize what was happening at first. He was always moody. But he had a lot of aspirations. And he wanted to be part of the 'in' crowd. That's how he got mixed up with cocaine."

Dan nodded. "I knew a lawyer who had to eat off paper plates. He had everything in the house in storage so his wife couldn't sell the stuff to buy coke."

"But the thing I keep asking myself is—how could Rick have gotten so crazy?"

"There's something called cocaine psychosis. I know paranoia is one of the symptoms." He shrugged. "A lot of addicts are pretty messed up." He went on to tell her about a drug deal that went sour down on First Street. "The customer was paying for crack with a stolen VCR. The dealer had been told it was VHS. When he found out it was a Betamax, he started shooting. I guess there's better movies on VHS."

"You're kidding!"

"Scout's honor. Coke makes a lot of people wig out."

Now he glanced down at the manila envelope on the seat beside him. The one with the press kit.

Just how fucked up was Johanna's ex-husband, and what *exactly* did he want from her?

He remembered when Kirsten had come home in the morning, Johanna had knelt in the front hall and wrapped her arms around her daughter.

Kirsten had been embarrassed, maybe because he'd been there.

"Why are you hugging me so tight?" she'd protested.

"Because I missed you."

"But I was just spending the night at Amy's."

Johanna hadn't tried to explain, but Dan had understood.

He'd wanted to hold her tightly like that after she'd fallen asleep, but he hadn't because he'd been afraid he'd wake her up. So he'd just lain there in the dark, thinking. Somehow the letters and the press kit and the phone calls didn't quite make sense. They didn't all add up. Maybe because he just didn't have enough information. As soon as he got to the station, he'd pull the files on the murders of the little girls. Maybe they'd give him something else to go on.

As he turned into the parking lot, he started thinking about Kirsten again. Johanna had told him some of the problems the child had had because of Rick: wetting her bed, crying fits, being afraid to let her mother out of her sight. For a while it had been bad, but she seemed pretty normal now.

She'd wanted to know what he was doing there so early in the morning.

He'd explained that he and Johanna were having breakfast together so they could talk about some things. That had satisfied Kirsten. It hadn't been a lie, either. It just wasn't the whole truth. He knew that made Johanna uneasy. Not just the explanation, the idea of having an affair—with a kid in the house. Probably Johanna wasn't going to let him spend the night when Kirsten was home.

He'd wanted to take her in his arms and kiss her good-bye. Really kiss her. Taste her. But Kirsten had been watching them, so he'd settled for a quick squeeze of Johanna's hand. At least she'd squeezed back.

He pulled into a parking space and cut the engine. For a moment he leaned back against the headrest and closed his eyes. He'd been awake most of the night. He was dead tired. Yet when he began thinking about the length of Johanna's body pressed to his and how her breasts had felt in his hands, he started getting hard again.

Damn!

Johanna had a lot of work to catch up on, but it was going to have to wait until after she'd been over to Suburban Hospital to see how Jennings—and Betty—were doing.

She'd talked to her assistant on the phone again this morning. Betty hadn't been home at all, so Johanna had volunteered to stop at her apartment in Chevy Chase and pick up a change of clothing for her.

As she sped out of the development, a man in a yellow compact car caught the corner of her eye. For a moment there was a flash of familiarity. Rick? The Cougar lurched as her foot left the gas pedal and reached for the brake. Then she shook her head. The man in the car looked too old to be Rick. She'd better get a grip on herself.

Dan tucked the manila envelope under his arm and stopped in front of the blue door marked "Police Only." After pressing the combination on the cipher lock, he let himself in.

The squad room was upstairs. Instead of going up to his desk, he headed down the hall past the chief's office to the large room that had been taken over by the task force.

Desks, chairs, and file cabinets had been moved in. On the bulletin board along the far wall were photographs of the two crime scenes.

Dan had intended to read the files. Now something drew him to the pictures. Several showed Jeanie Waterford's body nestled in a pile of pine needles. Others were of Heather Morrison, the first victim. Each child was lying on her side, clutching a doll in her right arm, but the left arm was stretched out so that the wrist was visible. On each, a serpentine figure had been drawn in dark ballpoint ink. It appeared to be a figure eight when you looked at it across the wrist. But was that the intent?

Dan held up the envelope he was carrying and inspected the homemade postmark: an infinity sign drawn in black ballpoint ink, like a figure eight on its side.

He could feel the hair on the back of his neck bristle. The same damn mark. He'd seen it on the letters, too, which meant the mail Johanna had been receiving was from the killer. Rick? Or someone else?

Whoever he was, he'd singled her out. He wanted something from her. And that meant she was in danger, and she needed protection. But did he have enough evidence to get police security for her?

He needed the rest of those letters. Johanna had sent them in, so his next stop was the mail room. But nothing had been logged in. Where the hell had they gone? he wondered.

Back in the task force room, he got out the files and read the reports. There was no mention of any letters sent to the victims or their parents. Maybe that detail had been overlooked. Or maybe the letters didn't tie in the way he thought they did.

Dan pounded up the stairs to the squad room. He found Nico at his desk.

"Man, you look terrible," his partner observed dryly. "Late night?"

"Tell you about it later. I want to check something out."

Briefly, he told Nico about the letters and showed him the envelope.

"You're sure it's the same mark?"

"Come on downstairs and look at the pictures of the little girls."

"I believe you."

"What we need to find out is whether the parents of the two other victims got any mail like this."

"What do you mean—we? Turn it over to the task force."

"Nobody's down there now . . . and it can't wait."

Nico glanced toward the small office at the end of the room. The lieutenant was bent over his desk. "What about Fogel?" he mouthed.

"Screw him."

Nico stood up. "All right, you've got it."

Before he left, Dan tried to call Johanna to tell her about the postmark. All he got was her answering machine. He asked her to call him the minute she got back.

Nico had said he'd take the Morrison house. Dan drove over to the Waterfords'.

Johanna made it to the hospital by ten o'clock. Betty was in the waiting room outside the intensive-care unit. Except for the deep circles under her eyes, her face was colorless. She looked as if she'd aged ten years over the past twenty-four hours.

Johanna wrapped her arms around her friend, and they stood in the middle of the waiting room clasping each other for a few moments.

"I should have been here with you," Johanna murmured.

"You had to stay home with Kirsten."

A stab of guilt shot through Johanna. But what good would it do to explain how she'd spent the night?

"How is Norton?" she murmured.

"Still in the recovery room."

"Oh, Betty."

"It was worse than that. He doesn't have any next of kin, so I said I was his fiancée and authorized the surgery. What if he dies?" Betty started to cry.

Johanna led her to one of the plastic sofas and rocked her back and forth until the outburst subsided. "You did what you had to do."

"I keep telling myself that."

After a while, Johanna persuaded Betty to change her clothes and wash her face. When she came back from the restroom, she looked a little better.

"Did you get to see Norton last night?" Johanna asked.

"Just for a few minutes."

"Did he say anything about who attacked him?"

"No. He was unconscious."

"He's going to be all right," Johanna repeated, praying it was true.

"Oh God, Johanna, I hope so."

"Do you want me to stay down here with you for a while?"

"A little while."

"Long enough to make sure you get something to eat, anyway."

"I suppose it's no use saying I'm not hungry."

"Right."

Betty tried to smile. "But if you don't go back to the office, I'll have twice as much to do when I finally get back there."

"Then I'll try to get as much done as I can."

Dan remembered how Mrs. Waterford had looked at the meeting. Pale and sick. Now the pale color seemed to have sunk into her skin, as though the pallor radiated from within her.

"Mrs. Waterford, I'm Detective Whitmore. I'm sorry to bother you, but I'd like to ask you a few more questions about Jeanie."

"I've already told the other detectives everything I know."

"Please. There are a few details I need to check on."

She sighed and gestured toward the living room. "I guess you might as well come on in."

The room was dusty and cluttered. Apparently Mrs. Waterford wasn't taking much interest in housework anymore. Or maybe she just didn't have the energy.

"I want to know if you received any unusual mail during the weeks before Jeanie was—abducted."

Mrs. Waterford looked blank. "Unusual mail? No, I don't think so."

"No letters that might have come from the man who abducted her?"

"Nothing like that. Why are you asking me this?"

"I'm trying to find a tie-in to—the next possible victim."

"Oh."

Knowing he'd hit a dead end, Dan looked around the cluttered room. There was a stack of mail on the table next to the sofa. He had to restrain the urge to thumb through it. On top was a brochure from the U. S. Mint, advertising a new issue of silver dollars.

Mrs. Waterford followed his gaze. "I should clean that up."

Silver dollars. Silver coins. Dan wasn't sure what made him hold his breath after he'd asked the next question. "Does someone in your house collect coins?"

"Tony. My middle chi—my younger son. Mostly he collects dimes."

"Dimes?"

"Yes. Silver dimes." Her face took on a melancholy look. "He was so angry with Jeanie for getting into his collection. She liked to play with them. The day she disappeared— But that's not important now."

Dan leaned forward. "What about the day she disappeared?"

"She didn't mean any harm." Mrs. Waterford glanced up at him.

"Of course she didn't."

"She'd taken some of his dimes to school to show her friends. Tony is so particular about his collection. He knew exactly what was missing. All of them were in her desk. Except one."

Dan's mouth was dry. "Was it minted in 1961?"

"Why, yes. How do you know? Did you find it?"

"Yes. I think we did." He stood up. "Thank you Mrs. Waterford. Thank you very much. You've been a big help."

He'd been looking for a link to the letters. That wasn't what he'd found. It wasn't the letters; it was the dime. It had been dropped in one of the houses Jack Daniels had used. He and Nico hadn't known why Jack had moved the furniture. Now he guessed it was to spread a tarpaulin on the rug. That must be where he had kept Jeanie before he took her to the woods. And the other little girl, Heather, had he kept her in a house where the owners were away? Right in the neighborhood. Dan had a sick feeling that that was what had happened.

Johanna kept Betty company while she ate some chicken soup and a muffin. When they went back upstairs, Norton still wasn't out of the recovery room. Johanna waited until the doctor came by to say that he was doing as well as could be expected, but that the next twenty-four hours would be critical.

"You go on back to the office now. I'll call you as soon as I know anything more," Betty insisted.

"All right," Johanna agreed reluctantly. She wanted to go straight home. But as she turned the dial on the car radio, she caught a weather report.

Winter storm watch, the first of the season. Oh damn, she thought. Just her luck. She hadn't picked up much at the grocery store last time, and she was out of bread, milk, and meat again. If she didn't lay in some food now, and it snowed, they'd be reduced to eating macaroni and cheese all week. But the store was going to be packed if she didn't get there right away.

The dime was in the storage room next to the sergeant's office. The key was supposed to be secured. Dan knew it was in one of the desk drawers.

He put the envelope containing the coin into his pocket and went back downstairs to Captain Lindsey's wood-paneled office.

He didn't have much contact with Lindsey, and he wasn't happy about going over Fogel's head to see him. But he knew the commander of the station was the only one who could authorize a stakeout at Johanna's, and he didn't want to waste time explaining to Fogel what he'd been doing all morning.

Lindsey eyed the manila envelope he'd brought along with the pictures from the task force bulletin board.

"Sit down, detective," he invited.

"Thank you, sir."

"What can I do for you?"

He hadn't been sure what to expect from the captain. The man didn't interrupt while Dan showed him the three infinity marks and explained where the envelope had come from.

"It looks as if Mrs. Hamilton has been receiving mail from the killer," he agreed.

Dan gave him a rundown of the recent incidents at Johanna's house.

"But the additional letters and the tape from her husband have disappeared?"

"Yes. Mrs. Hamilton says she sent them in to us, but they were never received."

"Any theories about that?"

Dan shook his head.

"I take it you think the killer's getting ready to do something to her or to the child," Lindsey summed up.

"Yes, sir. I'd like to ask for a stakeout of her house."

"You've got it." But when Lindsey called to talk to Johanna about it, she still wasn't home. All he could do was leave another message.

"I'll send a man over there to wait for her," the captain said.

Dan nodded but didn't get up to leave.

Lindsey raised inquiring eyebrows. "Is there something else?"

"Yes. I want to work with the task force."

"Your other investigations—"

Dan pulled out the envelope with the dime and set it in the middle of Lindsey's immaculate desk blotter. "This coin was found in a house that was broken into by a suspect Nicolas Jackson and I have been tracking for months. I think it's the same man who killed the little girls."

Lindsey eyed the dime. "Want to tell me how this fits in?"

"Yes, sir."

Johanna knew as soon as she pulled into the parking lot of the Giant Food Store on Rockville Pike that she hadn't been fast enough to avoid the first wave of panicked shoppers. Briefly, she considered going right home. Then she glanced at her watch. if she hurried, she could still beat the school bus.

Fifteen items. She'd just get fifteen items. Then she could go through the quick-check line.

The aisles were crowded. Johanna was concentrating on fighting her way up and down them, so she didn't notice the startled expression on a young dark-skinned woman's face as she maneuvered her cart past.

*   *   *

Juanita dropped the can of stewed tomatoes she was holding, and it clattered into the metal cart. *Madre de Dios.*

She stared in shock at the slender figure a few feet away. The dark-haired woman had just gone right past her. Close enough to reach out and touch. *The* dark-haired woman.

She'd dreamed about her again last night. This time it was more frightening than ever, because the danger was closer, about to swallow her—and the little girl—up. The woman had seen the bad man, and she'd been frightened. Not for herself. For her daughter. Then she was getting in a car—no, a little truck—to chase the bad man. Juanita had known that was the wrong thing to do.

Don't get in, don't get in, her mind had screamed. But the woman hadn't heard. She'd gotten in and driven away, and Juanita had woken up with sweat covering her body.

Now she stood paralyzed beside her grocery cart, with the same words frozen in her mouth.

Somehow she found her voice. "Wait!"

The store was crowded and noisy. The woman was already at the end of the aisle and didn't hear.

A cart blocked the way. Juanita tried to push past. The owner gave her a dirty look.

Suddenly Juanita was uncertain. What was she doing?

Señora Hempsted had taken off work to drop her at the food store. She was going to be angry if she came back and found her maid wasn't waiting outside with the groceries. How would she explain her lateness?

Then she shook her head. So she made Señora Hempsted angry. She wasn't going to get fired for that. And the danger was real. It was going to happen like in the dream. She had to warn the dark-haired woman, to make her understand.

The woman she was chasing had long since disappeared around the corner. Feeling panic rise in her throat, Juanita left her cart and threaded her way to the end of the aisle, looking both ways. The woman was nowhere in sight. Had she gone right or left?

Muttering under her breath, Juanita picked the aisle to the right. The woman wasn't there . . . and not in the next aisle, or the next.

Sweat had broken out on Juanita's forehead. When a hand came down on her shoulder, she jumped.

"There you are. Where's your cart?" Señora Hempsted asked.

"I—"

"Come on, I'll help you finish in here. It's already starting to sleet. We have to get home."

"But I—"

"What's wrong with you? We have to go."

Chapter 24

Johanna had been in the food store only forty minutes, but when she came out, the car was covered with a sheet of ice. After stowing the grocery bag in the back, she started the engine and turned on the rear defrost. She groped under the seat for the scraper and offered a silent thanks when her fingers closed around the handle.

She hadn't worn gloves. By the time she'd cleared her windshield, her hands were cold and raw, and her left wrist was aching. She was tempted to leave the side windows. But that wasn't really safe, so she gave them a going-over as well.

Shivering, Johanna joined the line of cars creeping out of the lot. Snow was bad enough. Ice storms were even worse.

She might have gone straight to the school, except that the buses were probably already loading. What she ought to do was park by the bus stop and wait for Kirsten to get off.

It was a slippery fifteen-minute ride. Sleet was still coming down, and her windshield wipers were only smearing the mess. Along the route there were half a dozen cars that had slipped off onto the shoulder, and she just missed being part of a four-car collision.

By the time she arrived at the bus stop, her fingers ached from gripping the steering wheel.

Just as she stopped at the curb and cut the engine, the mail truck pulled up alongside her. Cliff Fuller leaned out and rapped on her window. Johanna rolled it down and looked at him inquiringly.

"I don't want to worry you, but there was a guy in a yellow Mazda hanging around your house."

A yellow car. She'd seen a man in a yellow car this morning and thought for a moment it might be Rick.

"When I asked if I could help him, he wanted to know what time school let out."

"Did he have blond hair?"

"Yeah. With a lot of gray in it. I think it was your ex-husband."

Panic rose in her chest and she didn't think to wonder why Cliff would know Rick. "How long ago?" She gasped out the question.

"About twenty minutes."

"Oh, my God. He's gone to get Kirsten. I've got to get to the school." With shaky fingers she reached for the ignition key.

"Wait. Let me take you. The mail truck's got four-wheel drive."

As Johanna scrambled out of her car, Cliff made room for her in the front of his truck and folded down the jump seat.

He revved up the engine and pulled out into the street. "I know which route the bus takes. We'll go that way."

"Oh, Cliff. I don't know what I'd do without you. But what about your route?"

"It can wait."

Johanna gave him a grateful look. The ride was bumpy. Johanna sat on the edge of the jump seat bracing herself against the door with one hand and twisting the strap of her purse with the other. Cliff was right; he could make better time on the slick roads. They arrived at the school to confront the worst traffic jam Johanna had ever seen there. The buses, loaded with children, were still in the driveway, hemmed in by cars. Cliff didn't try to pull in. He let her off on the street. Johanna jumped out before the mail truck came to a complete stop.

Kirsten's bus was number 107. Johanna ran up to the driver. "I need to get Kirsten Hamilton."

"Her father already picked her up," one of the kids shouted. "She was crying."

Johanna's heart stopped. Don't panic; think, she commanded herself. Icy water pelted her head as her gaze probed the curtain of rain, trying to find the car she'd seen earlier. Yellow was not a common color. She spotted one up near the front of the driveway. It was a compact, like the one this morning.

Her feet were soaked. Her hair was plastered to her head. Ignoring the cold and wet, she wove frantically through the tangle of vehicles. Three cars ahead of the yellow one, the traffic jam started to break up, and a blue Buick pulled away.

Johanna ran faster. If she didn't get there in the next few seconds, the yellow car would get out of the driveway, too.

She had just reached her goal when the driver turned his head and saw her. Rick! His hair was dirty gray instead of blond, and his face was pale and lined. He'd aged twenty years in the last two, but the hatred in his eyes was bright.

"Mommy!" Kirsten and Johanna reached for the door handle at the same time. It was locked.

Rick slapped at Kirsten's hand as he pressed on the accelerator.

Johanna screamed, but her cry for help was lost in the squeal of Rick's tires as he pulled out of the drive. He was getting away. She'd never catch him now.

Everyone else was preoccupied with the treacherous weather. Everybody except Cliff, who must have been watching Johanna's frantic chase.

She turned and saw that the mail truck had swung around on the street.

"Over here," Cliff called above the sound of idling engines.

She caught up with him and jumped in.

"He's up there. He's got Kirsten."

"I saw. That bastard's not going to take her away. Not if I can help it."

Ahead of them the yellow Mazda skidded, and Johanna held her breath as it sideswiped a parked car. Rick didn't even slow down.

"That man's crazy," Cliff observed.

At least the sleet was letting up, so they could see. Rick was heading into the country-side. He turned off Falls Road onto South Glen. Cliff kept him in sight. He was hunched over the wheel, his face tense with concentration.

"How dare he! How dare he do this to me," the postman muttered over and over.

Johanna only half heard and mumbled a response. Her attention was focused on the car weaving from side to side ahead of them. He was going much too fast for the icy condi-tions. The only saving grace was that there wasn't much traffic. God, what if Rick crashed into a phone pole or something? She held her breath.

The Mazda turned off onto a narrow lane. The mail truck was half-a-block behind.

"Interfering bastard," Cliff growled between clenched teeth. "First Jennings. Now this."

She'd been afraid that Rick had been the one who'd almost killed Jennings. Now she nodded in agreement.

They were gaining on the yellow car. It took a curve too fast and tipped over on two wheels.

"Kirsten!" Johanna screamed and closed her eyes so she wouldn't have to see the crash. She felt the mail truck screech to a halt. When she opened her eyes, the Mazda had nosed into a dirt bank just beyond the shoulder. Both she and Cliff tore out of the truck. She didn't even notice that she'd kicked her purse under the front seat.

Cliff yanked the driver's door open, pulled

out a dazed Rick, and started to shake him. "How dare you try to interfere like this," he raged.

Johanna screamed a warning as Rick pulled a revolver out of his belt. Cliff knocked the weapon out of his hand.

Diving into the car, Johanna unbuckled Kirsten's seat belt.

"Mommy! Mommy!" Her daughter sobbed, throwing her arms around Johanna's neck. "I didn't want to go with Daddy. But he made me."

"It's all right. It's all right now." Johanna hugged her daughter as if she would never let her go, thanking God that they'd gotten there in time. But it wasn't over yet. Outside in the rain, the two men continued to struggle.

When she saw Cliff lose his footing, she looked wildly around for a weapon, but didn't see anything she could use. Then she heard a groan and saw Rick sink to his knees.

When Cliff turned back toward her, there was a look of triumph in his eyes—and a bloody knife in his hand. Even then, Johanna didn't really understand.

"We've got to get an ambulance."

"No. He's finished. I wasn't going to let him get you."

Johanna shuddered and pressed Kirsten's face against her shoulder. Everything had happened so fast that she still couldn't take it all in. Rick had been terrorizing her, but she hadn't wished him dead. "We've got to get to a phone and call the police," she whispered.

Cliff shook his head as he stooped to pick

up the gun, which lay behind the wheel of the car, where Johanna hadn't been able to see it.

"You don't have anything to worry about. It was self-defense."

The mailman hefted the weapon and smiled. "This is going to come in handy."

"Handy?"

She glanced up and saw the gun pointed at her and Kirsten. But it was no less frightening than the maniacal look in Cliff's eyes.

He giggled, a strange high sound that made her blood as icy as the sleet that soaked her. "I fooled you with the letters." Another mad giggle. "You thought I was Rick. Wrong, wrong, wrong." He waved the gun menacingly. "I've got you now, and you're going to help me make them understand, aren't you, Johanna?"

Chapter 25

The door to the task force room flew open, and Dan looked up. The towering figure of Will Fogel was framed in the doorway. Dan had been expecting him to appear.

"I don't like it when one of my men goes over my head."

Dan shrugged, hoping the tension in his shoulders didn't show. In twelve years on the force, he'd always gone through channels. What was he supposed to say? That he was sleeping with Johanna Hamilton? That he hadn't been able to stand by and wait for something to happen to her or Kirsten? He'd gone out on a limb, but it was worth it because she was going to be all right. There would be plainclothesmen with her in the house, guys outside in the woods, and in unmarked cars on the street. Nobody was going to make a move on her without their knowing about it.

Fogel braced himself on muscular legs and folded his arms across his chest like a coach about to chew out a wide receiver who'd gotten his signals crossed.

From the other side of the room, Greg Greenway, one of the detectives assigned to the task force, glanced up and then back down at the doll catalog he'd been scanning: Hardly his usual reading material. During the past week he'd learned more than he'd ever wanted to know about the subject. At first he'd thought they might be able to trace the killer through a purchase at the Treasure Chest. But the dolls found with the murdered girls were from a popular series available at dozens of locations in the D. C. area. Someone would have to check them all, and it was probably going to be another dead end.

Dan waited for Fogel's next words, wishing the two of them didn't have an audience. He was probably going to find himself back in a uniform, directing traffic on Falls Road.

"Captain Lindsey was impressed with your hotshot detective work. Said this was the first real break we've had in the Goddamn murder case."

"Um."

"Well, you and I know it's no break at all. So you've got a silver dime that connects Jack Daniels to the Waterford girl. So what? You're no closer to knowing who Jack is than you were last week, are you?"

"He could be Rick Hamilton."

"Any evidence that Hamilton has been in the area?"

"The tape that didn't arrive."

"Maybe she's lying about that."

"No!"

Fogel gave him a penetrating look. "Well,

get me something on Hamilton, or a real lead on Jack—PDQ—if you don't want to find your butt in a sling."

When Fogel left, Greenway looked up at Dan again. "I take it you've joined the team."

"Yeah."

Greenway filled him in on the procedures they were following. Dan explained the Jack Daniels and Johanna Hamilton connections.

Greenway sighed. "So now we get to question everybody around those houses that were broken into."

"Sorry."

"At this point we'll take whatever leads we can get."

Johanna tightened her arms around Kirsten and pressed her daughter's face into her shoulder. Automatically her fingers smoothed across the wet blond hair. My God. Rick was dead. Murdered right before her eyes. Desperately, she sucked cold air into her lungs. He'd been her husband. She'd loved him once. But it had all gone wrong, a long time ago. Now she felt as if someone had turned her upside down and shaken her by the ankles, spilling out every thought in her head like loose change from her pockets.

All along, she'd been so sure Rick was stalking her. And he *had* been. But Cliff Fuller—

Her brain simply couldn't accept the evidence in front of her face. Cliff Fuller. Boyishly helpful Cliff. Who always knew when she had a letter from Rick—who made sure Kirsten didn't see them.

"You've been reading my mail."

"I had to."

She watched wide-eyed as he knelt and wiped the bloody hunting knife on Rick's shirt. Then he tossed it carelessly into the mail truck. As it clattered on the metal floor, she winced.

He'd loved her chocolate cake.

He'd given Kirsten lemon drops.

Had he been in her office that afternoon? Taken her stationery? Written that press release? She shuddered. That press release had been from the murderer. And she'd thought it was Rick.

Oh God.

The little girls.

Not Cliff. No. Please, not the kind-hearted mailman who was everybody's friend.

But the man who was holding her at gunpoint was a stranger. She took a step backward and the gun jerked in his hand.

"You don't want to hurt me—or Kirsten."

"No, I don't."

Her sigh of relief was cut short by his next words.

"But I might have to."

"You've always been so nice to us. Let us go." Johanna struggled to keep the quaver out of her voice.

He took a step closer. "Good old Cliff. Everybody thinks I'm nice. Everybody but Momma." His mouth twisted into a hideous parody of a smile.

She could feel every wet hair on her head tingle. That smile. And the giggle a few minutes ago. He was a man on the edge. Pushing him the wrong way could be deadly.

"I like you, Cliff," she managed. "But I need to take Kirsten home now."

"You know I can't let you do that. I've been counting on you to help me make them understand."

The letters. That's what he'd said in the letters. My God, what did he want from her?

"Mommy, I'm cold." Kirsten sneezed against Johanna's coat.

Johanna looked up at Cliff. "I've got to get her out of the sleet."

"It wasn't supposed to be today." He seemed to be musing to himself. "But I knew Rick might come, so I was ready. I'm always ready." He looked at Johanna. "I have to finish delivering the mail, and you're going to be very cooperative or someone is going to get hurt."

"Please. I'll do anything you want. Just let Kirsten go."

"Don't ask me to do that." He reached out and stroked the little girl's blond hair.

Johanna jerked backward, fighting the nausea that rose in her throat.

She could see him fumbling with something in the back of the truck. Before she knew what was happening, he'd pulled out a bottle and pressed a strong-smelling cloth over her nose and mouth. She gagged and tried to struggle.

The last thing she heard as the ground rushed up to meet her was Kirsten's scream.

The phone in the task force room rang, and Greg Greenway picked it up. He looked across at Dan. "For you."

Johanna, he thought with relief. But it was Susan Randolph. "I hate to bother you," she began. "But have you heard from Johanna this afternoon?"

"No. I called her this morning, but she hasn't gotten back to me." Suddenly his mouth felt dry. "Is something wrong?"

"My daughter Amy just told me that Kirsten's father came to get her at school. She said Mrs. Hamilton was looking for her on the bus." Susan gulped. "I just called, and they're not home."

He'd thought everything was taken care of. Now he felt all his muscles tensing up. "What's the number of the bus?"

"107."

"Thanks. I appreciate your calling me right away."

The logical thing to do was to speak to Amy and the bus driver. Instead, he went straight to Johanna's.

Her gray Cougar, covered with a sheet of ice, was angled along the curb at the school-bus stop on her street. She hadn't bothered to lock it, even though a bag of groceries sat on the floor in back.

But she'd been seen at the school. Someone must have given her a ride. Who? And why?

Hoping against hope, he turned back toward Johanna's house. An unmarked car was at the bottom of the drive. Inside it was Larry Innis from surveillance. He was a small man, in his early forties, but his receding hairline and wrinkled face made him look older. Dan knew he was tough, and good at what he did. This afternoon he was understandably irritable. He'd been waiting for Johanna since lunchtime, but she'd never come home.

Dan told him about the new development. "See if you can get hold of the driver of bus 107—or anyone else at the school who might have seen something."

Innis seemed glad to have something to do besides freeze his buns off in the car.

When his colleague had driven away, Dan scuffed his foot against the icy curb. He needed a picture of Rick, and there was probably one inside. Betty, Johanna's assistant, must have a key. But she was at the hospital.

He rang the bell. There was no response, but he didn't expect one, since Innis hadn't seen Johanna. His feet crunched on the ice-crusted grass as he walked around the house. All the doors were locked. He could break in, but Fogel would probably suspend him for that, so he drove to Susan's and asked if she had a key. He explained that he wanted to get a picture of Rick. Luckily, Johanna had given her a new key after changing the locks.

The key fit the side door to the office. Inside, the house was dark and silent. "Johanna?" His voice echoed through the empty rooms. He ought to do a quick search anyway. Upstairs, he stood and looked for a moment at the bed where they'd made love. She'd been in a hurry when she'd left this morning. Instead of making the bed, she'd just pulled up the covers. The tray was still on the floor. He carried it down to the kitchen.

In the den, Dan began to open drawers

and poke through papers. She kept receipts in a wall-unit in the den. Next to them was a handmade Mother's Day card from Kirsten, telling Johanna she was the best Mommy in the world. The picture, done in vivid crayon colors, showed a woman and a girl with their arms around each other. The woman had dark hair. The girl was blond. The house in the background resembled Johanna and Kirsten's. The card made his throat constrict, and he slammed the drawer shut.

He remembered what he and Johanna had said about being honest with each other. He didn't like going through her belongings behind her back. Maybe she'd come in and chew him out. She could have just taken Kirsten and gone shopping.

Christ, he'd be relieved if the two of them suddenly came banging into the house. But that didn't happen.

With a growing sense of urgency, he opened and shut drawers.

In the cabinet below the shelves in the den, he found a picture album. It started with smiling snapshots of a young couple. Johanna looked fresh and innocent. He wished he'd known her then. The guy had Kirsten's coloring. Must be Rick.

Dan removed a couple of snapshots from near the back. They had been taken at an amusement park. Both showed Rick holding Kirsten's hand. In one, they were standing in front of a merry-go-round. In the other, Kirsten was holding a huge pink cotton candy. She looked a couple of years younger. Her father was smiling for the camera, but there were tension lines around his eyes.

After slipping both pictures into the inside pocket of his sports jacket, Dan went back to Johanna's office. No papers or folders on the desk. The answering machine said it had eleven messages. He'd bet she hadn't been there all day.

He listened to the calls. One, at 9:30, was from him. Another was Captain Lindsey. Most were clients. The last was from Betty at the hospital, twenty minutes ago, thanking Johanna for coming down that morning and saying that Norton was out of the recovery room. She asked Johanna to call back.

So she hadn't gotten in touch with Betty either. Where the hell was she?

Before going back to Susan's, he turned and looked back at Johanna's house. Someone had been watching her—the night he'd first brought her home, and later when he'd come to dinner. Then there had been the episode with Colonel Jennings. How many other times had someone been here? There must be a place where you could watch the house without being seen.

Pulling his collar up against the sleet, Dan turned in a complete circle and surveyed the scene around him. Up on the hill was a grove of pines that overhung the road.

His shoes crunched on the frozen grass as he climbed the hill, and he almost lost his footing once or twice. But it was relatively dry under the thick limbs.

Someone had hacked away a few of the

lower branches. Kids making a fort? He'd done that himself enough times. But there was no evidence of the junk kids liked to drag into a hideaway—old blankets or boxes to use as furniture. He looked down at the dry needles on the ground, searching for some clue to confirm that an observer had been here. The smooth blanket of brown needles had been disturbed. Resting on them were a few squares of clear cellophane—the kind that were used to wrap candy. That could still be from kids. As he picked one up and put it in his pocket, he remembered the photographs in the task force room. This was a lot like the stand of pines where Heather Morrison had been found.

On his way back to Susan's, Dan stopped at the houses near the bus stop and asked if anyone had seen Johanna get out of her car and leave with someone else. No one had been driving by or looking out the window at the right time.

It was dark. She was cold and cramped. There was a wad of cloth stuffed into her mouth and taped into place. Her head throbbed. When she tried to move her hands, she found they were fastened behind her back with some kind of heavy tape.

Postal tape. For strapping packages. The sudden realization made her want to gag.

She needed to lift her aching head up off the cold metal surface where it rested. Where was she?

Then she remembered the handkerchief over her mouth and the medicine smell.

Cliff had drugged her. She shuddered in revulsion.

For the first time, she realized she was in a moving vehicle. The mail truck?

Kirsten. Oh God, where was Kirsten?

There was some kind of heavy tarpaulin over her, and on top of that, lumps of weight. Bags of letters? Packages?

The truck lurched to a stop and something limp and heavy banged against her shoulder. Kirsten?

She held her breath and strained her ears. Was it her imagination, or could she hear muffled, even breathing?

Yes. Breathing. She was sure of it. Kirsten was next to her. Cliff must have drugged her, too. At least if she was asleep, she wouldn't be afraid.

Something hit the ground. The weight above her shifted slightly. She heard the crunch of shoes on ice and then a rasping sound of metal. Cliff had picked up a bundle of mail, gotten out of the truck, and opened a mailbox. My God. He was finishing his route just as cool as you please, with the two of them bound and gagged under the mail.

He got back in. Gears shifted. The truck moved forward and stopped again.

"Godawful weather," someone observed. "I guess it got you off schedule."

Johanna didn't recognize the man's voice, but it didn't matter. If only she could get his attention. Her heart started to thump.

"Yes. But I'm almost finished now."

Frantically Johanna tried to kick her legs

against the side of the compartment. She could
barely move.

The truck started up again. Heart in her
throat, she counted as Cliff put mail in six
more boxes. She concentrated on trying to
pry her hands apart. All she accomplished
was making her wrist ache.

Cliff was just opening another box when
the sound of a dog barking next to the truck
made Johanna jump.

"Baron! What's wrong with you? It's just
Mr. Fuller. You know Mr. Fuller."

Baron. Marian Lewis. She was only a few
blocks from home. Making a superhuman effort, Johanna thumped her legs against the
metal floor.

The dog growled and then started to bark
ferociously. Cliff scrambled back into the truck
and gunned the engine.

Tears of frustration welled up in Johanna's
eyes, and she couldn't even wipe them away.
The dog had heard her. But what good had
that done?

The mail truck sped away with no more
stops. She'd missed her chance. How was she
going to save her daughter, and herself, now?

Chapter 26

When Dan returned to Susan's, she was waiting by the door. As soon as she saw his face, her own expression turned grim. "I don't suppose Johanna came home." Her voice was edged with worry.

"No. But I'd like to show Amy the picture of Rick."

"Of course." She gave him a considering look as she ushered him in out of the cold. "You must be frozen. How about some hot coffee?"

"Thanks."

"I've been calling around. Several children saw Johanna get on the bus. And one said she ran over to a yellow car that was stuck in the traffic jam."

Susan led the way to the kitchen, where Amy was doing her homework.

The little girl looked up as Dan came in. "I know you. You gave that talk at school. And you were at Kirsten's house the night me and Brenda were there."

"That's right." He sat down. "And now I'm

looking for Kirsten and her mom. Did you see the man Kirsten left with?"

"Everybody was running around trying not to get wet. I heard Kirsten say 'Daddy,' so I looked at him real hard, because she never talks about her dad."

"Did you see the yellow car?"

Susan set down a mug of coffee in front of him, and he took a quick swallow.

"No."

"Is this the man you saw?" Dan brought the pictures out of his breast pocket and laid them on her notebook.

The child studied the snapshots. "Kirsten was little. Is *that* her dad?"

"Isn't it the same man?"

"I'm not sure. He looked old."

Dan thought for a minute. The guy had aged a lot in the photographs in the album, and he'd been on coke for four years. That could make a difference in his appearance. There was an Identakit in the car. Maybe he could put together a composite that Amy would recognize.

She was fascinated with the box of facial features on plastic sheets. Twelve noses. Fifteen sets of ears.

He picked the basic facial shape and the eyes. Then she helped select plastic overlays to get the rest of the features. By the time Dan left, he had a picture of a man who looked a lot like the one in the photographs— only about twenty years older. Now he was pretty sure Rick had been the guy who'd picked up Kirsten.

"Do you think he has Kirsten and Johanna?" Susan asked in a low voice as they stood by the front door.

"I don't know."

"If Johanna saw him take Kirsten, she'd follow him."

"But in whose car? Hers is down by the bus stop."

Susan shook her head. "Do you think Johanna could have taken Kirsten and left town?" she asked hopefully.

Dan thought about that for a moment. "I asked her to do that last night. She said she wouldn't."

"Is there anything else I can do?"

"Let me know right away if you hear from Johanna. And keep making calls. Maybe somebody else saw something." He put a hand on Susan's shoulder. "Ninety percent of the time when someone's missing, there's a perfectly harmless reason for their absence," he said, as much to reassure himself as for her. "But—"

"But what?"

"If she hasn't come back by tomorrow, we'll file a missing person's report."

Betty had tried to prepare herself. Still, it was hard to hold back a sob when she saw Norton. His head was swathed in bandages. He was attached to more monitors and tubes than she would have thought possible.

Dr. Cohen had said he was doing better, and that he might know that she was there, even if he couldn't respond.

They were only going to give her a few

minutes with him. She wanted to make the most of them. Reaching out, she wrapped her fingers around the limp hand that rested on top of the covers.

"Norton." She squeezed his hand.

Did she imagine that he squeezed back?

"It's Betty. I'm here. I've been here the whole time. You're going to be all right."

His eyelids fluttered and his lips moved. She leaned closer.

"mmmaaa"

Had he forgotten his mother was dead? Was he calling for her? Or just making a random sound?

His fingernail dug into her hand. He seemed to be making a tremendous effort to speak.

"Please, Norton. Don't exert yourself."

"mmmmaaa—annn"

She stroked her hand on his cheek. "It's all right, Norton. You just concentrate on getting better."

At least the sleet had stopped. But the roads were littered with cars that had been abandoned during the worst of the storm.

When Dan arrived back at the office, there was a message from Larry Innis saying that he'd talked to the bus driver. The extra hour and a half it had taken him to complete his route had put him in a foul mood, and he hadn't wanted to answer a bunch of questions. He remembered Mrs. Hamilton coming to the bus, but he claimed he hadn't seen the man Kirsten had left with.

Frustrated, Dan arranged to put out an

APB on Rick Hamilton—last seen driving a yellow compact car of unknown make and model. He might or might not have Kirsten Hamilton with him. And Johanna Hamilton. It would be broadcast that night over the local police channel and to neighboring counties and D.C. as well.

Then he checked the accident reports. At least they didn't include Johanna's name. But where in the hell was she?

She'd said she wasn't going to leave town. She could have changed her mind. But would she do that without telling him? Last night he wouldn't have thought so.

He brought another cup of coffee over to the vacant desk in the task force room. His head ached, and his eyes burned. There were some eye drops upstairs in his own desk, but he was too tired to climb up there and get them.

It was only five o'clock, time to go home, but it seemed as if he'd been working for forty-five hours straight. Still, how could he go off duty not knowing what had happened to Johanna?

She'd been last seen running toward the car of her ex-husband, who presumably had Kirsten. But what then? And why hadn't he heard from her?

He remembered when he was a kid. Sometimes he'd go off with his buddies and come home to find his grandmother furious with worry—when he hadn't even realized there was a problem.

It could be like that with Johanna. Maybe

she was at the home of the friend who'd taken her to school, and just hadn't thought anyone would have missed her. He comforted himself with that, but he really didn't believe it, and he couldn't stop thinking about what might have happened.

Right from the beginning, there were pieces of this damn puzzle that didn't fit . . . like Rick Hamilton. He was selfish. Violent. A cokehead. But was he a killer? Or did he just want his kid back? He was angry at Johanna for taking Kirsten away. Would he kill her to get at his daughter? Dan shuddered. He couldn't dismiss that possibility. But what about the two other little girls who'd been raped and murdered? How did they fit in to the out-of-kilter picture?

He'd read the interviews with the parents. Both of them had talked with their children about being cautious of strangers. Had a stranger shoved them in a car in broad daylight? Or had they been snatched by someone they knew, someone they wouldn't be afraid of?

Someone they knew . . . someone who knew the neighborhood . . . who knew which houses were vacant and broke into them. The killer had held Jeanie Waterford in one. Maybe Heather Morrison in another, back in May. But those weren't the only times. He'd been in a lot of houses, sometimes just to sit and have a drink and a sandwich. And sometimes he went berserk.

Dan went back upstairs to get the Jack Daniels file. Nico was still at his desk.

"You still here too?"

"Yeah. Fogel's making me give him a status report on every fucking open case we've got. Says he wants to reassign the work load if you're hotshotting it downstairs for awhile."

"Jesus. Sorry you got caught in the backlash."

"Yeah. Just remember you owe me one."

"Two."

Nico raised an eyebrow.

"You're the one who picked up the dime."

"Un hum. Wasn't that something? I never could walk past a piece of change on the street without picking it up."

For the first time that day, Dan laughed. Then his expression turned grim again. "God, I wish I knew where Johanna was."

"What's happened?"

"A hell of a lot." Dan began telling him about it—starting with the first night, when Kirsten had seen someone in the yard.

Nico cocked his head to one side. "And this long conversation you had last night with Mrs. Hamilton. I take it that's the reason you didn't get much sleep?"

"Something like that."

Nico tipped back his chair and propped his feet in a desk drawer. "So somebody took her over to the school," he mused. "Then she and the kid just disappeared. And you think she would have called you. But officially—as far as the department's concerned—there's nothing to get excited about yet."

"Yeah."

"It could be that she and Hamilton are off somewhere, reconciling their differences."

"If she's with him, she's doing it to protect Kirsten."

"You don't think she'd cozy up with you one night—and him the next?"

"That's right," Dan said through gritted teeth.

"Just getting the picture straight."

Dan stood up. "I came back to check the Jack Daniels file. Maybe I'll just do that and clear out of your way."

"Don't get your nose out of joint. I'll help you."

Dan sighed. "Sorry. I'm just uptight."

They divided up the file. Twenty minutes later, Nico raised his head. "As far as I can see, the only person who may have seen Jack is Muriel Beckett."

Dan snapped his fingers. "That's right. The old woman. She heard breaking glass, didn't she? But she sounded pretty rattlebrained."

"Her son thought she was confused. I did too."

"Her son. The drag queen." Dan shuffled the reports back into the file. "I wonder—if I talked to her, could I get anything coherent? Maybe if I show her the composite of the aging Rick Hamilton it will jog her memory."

"Want me to come along?"

"No. I'll do it."

Johanna knew where Marian's house was —on Orchard Hill Run. After they pulled away, she tried to count the left and right turns, to figure out where Cliff was taking them. But her head was still fuzzy, and she suspected he might be driving in circles to confuse her.

The truck stopped. A garage door ground open. Cliff pulled inside and closed the door again. As Johanna felt the bundles on top of her being pushed aside, she tried to stay limp. Let him think she was still out.

He swept a piece of heavy canvas aside and pulled her across the bed of the truck so that her legs scraped painfully against the hard surface. Then he hoisted her up like a sack of potatoes and carried her inside. The muscles in her arms and legs screamed as he shifted her position. Her hands and feet were numb from the bonds.

He didn't stagger under her weight. Unfortunately, he was stronger than he looked. And even if he freed her hands and feet, she knew she'd barely be able to move.

Johanna tried to keep her breathing easy, but she was afraid he could feel the pounding of her heart. He dumped her on a heavy pile carpet. When he ripped the tape off her mouth, her eyes flew open and she gasped with pain.

"I knew you were awake. I heard you pounding on the side of the truck."

She stared at him. The murderous anger in his eyes made a cold sweat break out on her forehead. God, how could he have fooled her like this? But it wasn't just her, it was everybody. Betty, Susan. The whole neighborhood. She remembered the day he'd come to the door, after she'd complained about the missing press kit. Now she could see the conversation in a new light. He'd been angry. What had it cost him to keep himself under control? And how should she deal with him now: Lie? Cooperate? Play up to him?

"My legs hurt. I was trying to move them," she whispered.

His expression changed. "I don't want to hurt you." He reached down and massaged her ankles.

It was all she could do to keep from retching when he touched her.

"Where's Kirsten?"

"Still sleeping in the truck. I'm going to bring her in."

"She needs to be with me, so she won't be afraid."

Cliff's gray eyes took on a thoughtful look. "I'll think about that."

When he went out again, she looked frantically around the room. On the mantle was a framed family portrait—a father and mother and two little boys. She recognized them. The Goodwins. Alice Goodwin was a friend of Susan's. My God, he'd taken her to a house right in the development!

Maybe they'd come home and find her . . . end this crazy nightmare. Her heart leaped at the thought. Then she remembered what Susan had told her the night of the meeting. Alice and Bill traveled a lot. They were on a cruise, and the kids were at their aunt's.

The sleet and the abandoned cars all over the streets had turned rush hour into a horror show. Dan thought about stopping at the mini-mall and getting a slice of pizza, but he didn't have any appetite.

The light at Falls Road and Seven Locks was out, and there was a bedraggled uniformed cop in one of those orange day-glow vests directing traffic. Dan nodded sympathetically as he turned onto Falls.

A few downstairs lights were on at the Beckett house, and two cars were in the driveway. As Dan pulled up, a middle-aged woman came out. He studied her in the light of the porch. She was too tall and too well-groomed to be Mrs. Beckett. After she got into a white Ford and drove away, he opened the car door. An icy branch hung in his way, and he pushed it aside.

"Did you forget something, Mrs. Wilson?" a male voice called out when he rang the bell.

"It's not Mrs. Wilson. It's Dan Whitmore from the Montgomery County Police."

An anxious face peered out the sidelight, and then the door opened a crack. "I thought they said down at the station that they were through with me."

"I'm not here about your arrest."

Tommy's expression turned belligerent. "So this is just general harrassment?"

Dan stuck his hands in his pockets. "No. I was here a couple of weeks ago to talk to you and your mother about the break-in next door. I'd like to speak to her again—about what she saw the night of the incident."

"Don't you guys have anything better to do?"

"This is important."

"Too bad. Mom's so out of it, she wouldn't be able to tell you anything anyway."

"I'd still like to talk to her."

"Well, I've had enough of the police department to last me the rest of my life, and I'm not going to let one of you guys in unless you have a warrant."

Beckett started to close the door, but Dan stuck his foot in the opening.

"I have evidence that may link the break-ins to the child murders."

Beckett looked undecided for a minute. "Are you bastards trying to tie me into the case again? You don't care whose reputation you destroy, do you?" he hissed.

"I'm not trying to tie *you* into anything. I know you went through a rough time, but—"

"That's right. So just go away and leave us the hell alone."

"Listen, I wouldn't be bothering you except that we're desperately looking for a rapist-murderer. He may already have picked up another little girl this afternoon." Dan took out his card and scribbled his home phone on the back. "If you change your mind, call me—either at work or at home. It doesn't matter how late."

Beckett slammed the door before he could hand him the card, so he slipped it under the rubber band around the newspaper on the front porch. As he walked slowly back to the car, he hunched his shoulders against the wind. He was so frustrated that he didn't see the icy branch blocking his car door until it slapped him in the face. Uttering an oath, he reached out, snapped it off, and tossed it onto the ground.

There wasn't much else he could do until morning, but he did stop by Johanna's. The house was still dark. Nothing had changed except that someone named Potter had taken over for Innis.

Cliff's hands were shaking with anticipation as he opened the tailgate of the mail truck. He turned on the overhead light and looked down at Kirsten. She was still asleep, sprawled on a bed of scattered letters, her mouth slightly open and her blond hair streaming out in back of her. Her coat was open and her dress had ridden halfway up her thighs. He reached out to stroke a finger across her soft cheek, ending just at the corner of her bow-shaped lips.

What kind of panties was she wearing? He hoped it was pink cotton like Emily's favorites. His hand moved like a snake up her leg, and she murmured something in her sleep. The sound and her warmth made him hot all over.

He remembered Heather and Jeanie. They hadn't liked the things he and Emily had done, so he'd kept them asleep a lot of the time. That way he could do anything he wanted, and they wouldn't kick and scream, or cry.

His trembling hand reached the edge of Kirsten's dress. He wanted to look at her now, the way he had that first time with Emily. Just the thought of that made him hard. And after he looked at her, he was going to do all the other things he and Emily had liked. One last time.

He was glad the Goodwins were out of town. Their two-story house was solidly built, and the neighbors on either side weren't too close. Even if there were screams, nobody would hear. And the police wouldn't find him, either. By now, they might have guessed that he picked vacant houses—ones where the owners notified the post office that they'd be away. Yes, the Goodwins had filled out that form, too. But he'd never turned it in. He was the only one who knew they were away. He giggled at his cleverness.

Outside, the wind moaned around the corner of the house, and he looked up from the sleeping child. It was cold. What if it got too icy to drive? He had a lot of things to do this evening. Kirsten was going to have to wait until later. That was all right. Good things came to those who waited.

Chapter 27

When Cliff came back in carrying Kirsten snuggled against his chest, he saw Johanna's eyes rivet to the possessive way his hand cupped her bottom. He wondered if she was jealous of the attention he was giving her daughter.

He wanted to explain to her that she was just as important to him as the child—only in a different way. But he didn't have time for that now, either. So he just laid Kirsten, still asleep, down on the carpet beside her mother.

He made sure their hands and feet were bound so they couldn't get away, and he taped Johanna's mouth again. For good measure, he secured her hands to the heavy leg of a credenza.

Her eyes followed him around the room as he made sure the drapes were closed and that everything was the way it should be. Then he found the thermostat and turned up the heat so they wouldn't be cold.

Unbearable tension built in Johanna when

Cliff walked out of her line of sight into the next room. Where was he going? What was he doing? She strained her ears, but she couldn't hear anything, so she forced herself to lie still, with her legs curled up against her stomach the way he'd left her.

Her blood pounded in her ears, almost making her dizzy as she waited for him to come back. She could imagine a knife in his hand. Or something worse. An acid taste rose in her throat as she tried not to think about what he might do to her—and Kirsten.

When she heard his footsteps on the kitchen floor again, she swallowed a silent scream. Although his hands were empty, there was a satisfied expression on his face. Her heart started to pound more wildly. But he didn't come near them, just stood there looking down at her and Kirsten on the rug.

What was he thinking? She didn't have a clue. How could she follow the thought processes of a madman?

When he came back into the family room, Johanna hadn't moved. That was good. She understood there was no use trying to interfere with his plans.

He smiled at her reassuringly, conscious again of the need to hurry and get everything done so he could return to the two of them. "I'll be back real soon."

She couldn't answer, of course, because of the tape on her mouth.

After he closed the garage door behind him, he turned and checked the house. From the street, it looked dark and empty.

*   *   *

Johanna strained her ears again, listening for some sound that would convince her he was really gone. Even when the garage door whooshed up, and the motor of the mail truck turned over, she was still afraid to move. This could be just a trick, a test to see what she'd do. . . .

Near her on the rug, Kirsten stirred in her sleep. My God, if *she* was scared, what about poor Kirsten? How would she respond to all this—Rick coming to school and snatching her away, the wild ride ending with the car nosed into a dirt bank, and then Cliff pulling open the door and stabbing Rick?

She wondered how much Kirsten had seen—and what she must think was happening. At least she didn't have an adult's insights. Thank God she didn't know Cliff was the man who had killed the two other little girls.

Johanna began to tremble violently. She wouldn't think about that or she'd go crazy. Under the circumstances, it was a mercy Cliff had put her daughter to sleep.

She longed to put her arms around Kirsten's limp form, to murmur that everything was going to be all right. But the most important thing was to get away—get the two of them out of here before Cliff came back. The thought of him coming through the door again made her panic surge, and she started to shake again. When he returned he was going to— He was going to— She couldn't finish the thought.

She wanted to shut her eyes and curl into a

tight ball. She couldn't give in to that. She had to get herself under control—for Kirsten. At least Kirsten wasn't like the other little girls. She was with her mother. That gave her a better chance.

Cliff had been gone five or ten minutes. He'd have to return the mail truck or the post office would miss it. How long would that take? Trying to keep her mind calm and analytical, Johanna looked around the room. In the dim light, she could see a wall phone in the kitchen. Could she get to it?

She pulled at the tape that bound her hands to the leg of the credenza. It was tight and unyielding. She pulled again and again, but it didn't loosen. The only thing that happened was that the tape cut into her wrists and the left one started to ache terribly.

She glanced over at Kirsten. Her daughter's eyes were open, staring at her. She tried to say something, and coughed. It was a muffled sound through the gag. Her expression went from sleepy to frightened in the space of a heartbeat. She struggled to sit up but couldn't.

The best Johanna could do was stretch out her bound legs and touch Kirsten's foot.

Through her own gag, she tried to murmur soft reassurances. The little girl looked at her beseechingly. Tears filled her eyes as she strained to free her hands.

Johanna nodded her head slowly and made her eyes reassuring.

"Mommy." The plea was muffled.

"I know, sweetheart." The words were so

distorted by the wad of cloth in her own
mouth that she wondered if Kirsten could
hear.

"Help me, Mommy."

"I will. Just as soon as I can. I will. You just
lie still now so you don't hurt yourself."

Kirsten must have heard, because she stopped
struggling.

First he took the mail truck back to the post
office parking lot. With a flashlight, he double-
checked to make sure Johanna and Kirsten
hadn't left anything in the truck. When he
saw Johanna's purse, he swore. A little detail
like that could hang him. It was open. Her
keys and a Cross pen had spilled out . . . and
the knife, my God—he'd almost forgotten the
knife. Resenting the delay, he felt around on
the floor, but he couldn't find anything else.
Satisfied, he locked the mail truck, picked up
his own car, and drove carefully to his own
home.

Lucky he had real good tires on his car, or
he wouldn't have made it. But he was prepared for bad weather. He was prepared for
everything.

Before, he'd been jumpy. Now a calm had
settled over him. It was almost over.

He went in the kitchen and carefully washed
off the knife. Then he wiped it dry until he
could see his reflection in the blade. The image was distorted. His face looked long and
thin and wolfish. For a moment he was afraid
of what he saw. His arm swung in an arc, and
the knife came down into the cutting board

beside the sink. When he pulled it out, it left a raw gash. Food would get in there, but that didn't matter. It was all going to be over soon.

While he'd been planning this, he'd liked to tell himself that he and Johanna and Kirsten could be together for awhile. But he knew that he'd just been fooling himself. It had to be quick, like with the others . . . as soon as Johanna did what he wanted.

He slipped the knife into the sheath that fastened around his calf, then he changed into corduroy slacks and a green cardigan. He would put on his blue nylon jacket just before he went out. Right now he wanted to check again to make sure he had everything he needed.

It was all in the spare bedroom, laid out neatly on the bed: the handcuffs, the pen, his typewriter, and paper. The new doll he'd bought for Kirsten—a Victorian girl, just like Emily's favorite. His fingers smoothed the frilly fabric of the dress.

On the way back he would stop at McDonald's and get them all something to eat. They'd missed dinner. He'd bring hamburgers and fries and milk shakes. He and Johanna liked chocolate. But Kirsten had told him once that she liked strawberry.

He remembered he was in a hurry and began to stuff everything into a duffel bag. Maybe after they ate he'd explain everything to Johanna: How she was going to help him tell his story, and then why he had to kill her and Kirsten. Or it might be better not to tell her that part.

* * *

Juanita had felt nauseous and shaky ever since she'd come back from the food store. She scorched a Ralph Lauren shirt with the iron and let the chicken paprika cook until it fell apart. Señor Hempsted was furious, but the señora looked worried and took her aside.

"Juanita, are you feeling all right? You've been acting funny since the grocery store."

It was on the tip of her tongue to talk about the dark-haired woman and the blond little girl. But once, when she and the señora had seen a T.V. program on psychics, Señora Hempsted had called it rubbish and a bad influence on developing minds. She couldn't let the señora think she was a bad influence.

"My throat hurts," she croaked. It did . . . from tension.

"I hope you're not coming down with strep." Señora Hempsted took her temperature and gave her a glass of Alka Seltzer Plus. It was bitter tasting, but she drank the whole thing and thanked the señora.

"Try and get a good night's sleep."

"*Si.*" Juanita went down to her room in the basement, but her bed was no refuge. She didn't want to go to sleep, because she was terrified of what she might dream tonight.

After stopping by Johanna's, Dan took Montrose to Rockville Pike and turned right. But he was too restless to go home, so he pulled up at the first McDonald's he came to and went in. The restaurant was noisy with kids who'd just come from a soccer game. Dan looked for a table in the corner.

He opened his Quarter Pounder and emptied his French fries into the lid of the Styrofoam carton, but he didn't have much enthusiasm for the meal. He took a small bite, remembering what he'd told Johanna the night before. God, was it only last night that they'd made love?

His stomach lurched, and he had to put the burger down. He'd been trying to pretend that he could handle this like any other case that came in.

It didn't help to keep reminding himself that ninety percent of missing persons turned up perfectly okay. They were just statistics.

He remembered how he'd reacted when Nico suggested Johanna might be reconciling with Rick. The very thought had twisted in his gut like a piece of barbed wire.

Now he closed his eyes for a moment and thought about the way it had been in bed last night. She'd wanted him to know it wasn't just the need for comfort—or just for sex. It wasn't that way for him either. He cared about her a lot, more than he wanted to; he had to admit it.

He made himself drink some of his Coke. He needed the caffeine, because he knew he wasn't going right home to bed. He'd had a bad feeling about the way things were coming down since he'd seen Johanna's car pulled up at the curb with the groceries inside.

The milk in the bag was probably frozen by now. He should have taken it in for Johanna and put it in the refrigerator. Then he grimaced. Jesus Christ, the last thing he needed to worry about was her Goddamn milk.

He turned his thoughts back to the problem at hand, but he simply couldn't draw any more conclusions. So far, he'd come up against a series of dead ends. Maybe Johanna's assistant Betty could tell him something.

"Please, Mommy. I have to get up. I have to go to the bathroom," the muffled voice pleaded.

Johanna closed her eyes for a moment. "Sweetheart, I'll get you loose as soon as I can. Just let me get my hands free." It was an effort to talk around the gag, an effort to make herself back away from Kirsten and push her hands against the leg of the credenza.

Her shoulder pressed painfully into the corner of the wooden chest. By twisting so that the tape cut into her wrists, she could feel the loops on the leg with her fingers. There were a lot of layers. No wonder she hadn't been able to pull the tape off. But maybe there was another way. She would scrape the tape loose and push it down the wooden leg. Then, maybe she could press it into the fibers of the rug and off the bottom of the chest. That might work or it might not, but it was the only thing she could think of to do.

Dan managed to get down some of the burger. The fries were already cold. Mechanically, he dumped the remains of his meal into the trash. Then he went to the phone and looked up Betty's number. She wasn't home. It was a good guess she was still at the hospital. In the men's room, he peered at himself in the mirror. He needed a shave, his eyes were bloodshot, and his clothes were rumpled. The look was sexy on Don Johnson. Too bad it didn't do anything for him.

When he came out of the alcove, he stood for a minute regarding the patrons with idle curiosity: Teenagers having a good time, couples with kids. A sandy-haired man wearing corduroy slacks and a blue jacket came in the door. He looked out of place in the crowd, somehow.

Dan watched him for a moment. As if sensing he was being observed, the man ducked his head self-consciously and walked rapidly toward the counter.

Dan stood there for a moment longer, listening to the guy order milk shakes. Two chocolate and one strawberry.

Chapter 28

Slowly, painfully, Johanna scraped her nails against the tape, working it down the wooden leg. The nails on her right hand bent and broke, one by one, so she switched to her left, praying that they wouldn't give out. She had no way of knowing how long Cliff had been gone or how much time she had. Beside her, Kirsten whimpered.

"Go back to sleep, sweetheart," Johanna murmured. Then she forced herself to keep working.

It seemed to take forever, but finally the tape was pooled around the bottom of the leg. She pressed one of the loops into the rug and pulled against the bottom of the leg. It slipped under. Thank God!

Forcing herself not to tremble, she worked the others free. Five minutes later she was sitting up, her head pressed against the carved wood of the credenza. It was heavenly to stretch cramped muscles, but she only allowed herself a few moments to roll her shoulders. She wasn't free. Her hands and feet were still bound.

Johanna looked over toward the phone. Not very far if you could get up and walk, it was an eternity away if you were tied hand and foot. Even if she got over there, could she knock the receiver off the hook with her shoulder? Could she press the buttons? All she had to do was dial "O" and get the operator. Perhaps she could manage that. But could she make herself understood with the gag in her mouth? Maybe she could get it out.

Her feet were too tightly bound to walk, so she began to inch herself across the room, sliding her hips and pushing with her feet.

She had to flop her body over the step at the entrance to the kitchen. Somehow she got up it and onto the vinyl floor. From there it was easier to slide across the shiny surface. When she reached the wall, she stopped to rest again. It was hard to breathe with the gag in her mouth. After rising to a kneeling position, she rubbed her face against the edge of the kitchen counter. The Formica dug into her cheek; she was going to have a bruise. Ignoring the pain, she moved her face up and down against the corner, pushing as hard as she could against the tape. Millimeter by millimeter it slipped down, ripping against her flesh as it moved. Then her mouth was free, and the tape was around her chin.

Muriel Beckett sat rocking in the chair in the family room while Tommy fixed dinner. He'd said he was making meatloaf and green beans. Or was it peas?

A little while ago she'd heard him at the

door. She'd peered around the corner and
seen him talking to one of those policemen
who'd come to the house the other day.
Tommy hadn't let him in. He probably thought
she didn't remember. Half the time he treated
her like she was six years old. That made her
cry sometimes, and sometimes she wanted to
give him a whipping. She was the mother. He
was the little boy. There was nothing wrong
with her. Only, sometimes her thoughts got
all jumbled.

Mrs. Wilson didn't act like that. She was
nice. So was Cliff Fuller. Maybe he'd come
visit her at night like the Morgensterns.

No that wasn't right. Hadn't they been away
when he was over there dressed all in black?
Hadn't she heard glass breaking? A robber.
He'd been chasing away a robber.

Her brow wrinkled. She was confused again,
and she struggled to sort it all out. He'd been
out of uniform. He was supposed to wear his
uniform. But she supposed it was all right,
because he was always so nice.

Dan zipped up his coat and went out into
the cold again. This time his destination was
Suburban Hospital.

The woman at the information desk took
one look at his drawn face and tried to send
him to the emergency room.

He laughed hollowly, showed her his badge,
and asked where he could find Colonel Norton Jennings. She directed him to ICU.

When he got off the elevator, he found a
middle-aged woman sitting in the lounge, an

untouched cup of coffee beside her on the chipped Formica table.

"Betty Cumberland?"

"Yes."

"Hello. I'm Dan Whitmore."

For a moment his name didn't register. Then her face brightened. "Dan Whitmore. Johanna's Dan."

He sat down in one of the low-slung chairs opposite her.

"Johanna was here this morning. It was nice of you to come down."

"I have a reason, I'm afraid."

"Have you found the person who attacked Norton?"

"No. I was hoping he might know who it was."

Betty shook her head. "He had surgery early this morning. This afternoon I think he tried to tell me something, but he just couldn't—" Her voice trailed off.

"What do you think he was trying to say?"

"I don't know." Her expression became sad. "Just sounds. Mmmaaa. Or something like that."

Could it be a name or what? Dan couldn't make any sense of it now. He could tell the woman was under a lot of strain, and he hated to make it any worse, but he couldn't school his features into the detached objectivity of a cop on a routine case.

"What is it? What's wrong?" she asked.

"Mrs. Cumberland . . ."

"Call me Betty."

"Betty. Believe me I wish I wasn't having

this conversation with you, but you're the last person I know who talked to Johanna."

Betty clutched at the beads around her neck. "What's happened to her?"

Succinctly, he told her what he knew about the events since Johanna had left the hospital.

"Oh, Dan. Oh, no. Not Johanna and Kirsten, too."

The look on her face was so despairing that Dan came over and put his arm around her. He thought he was the one offering comfort to her, but as she turned and put her motherly arms around his shoulders, he knew that he wanted to be comforted, too. They held each other tightly for a moment. When he pulled back, neither one of them looked the other directly in the eye.

"If anything happens to Johanna and Kirsten—" Betty murmured.

Dan clenched his hands together so tightly that his knuckles shown white in the dimly lit room.

"Do you think Rick has them?" Betty asked.

"He was seen taking Kirsten away, but I assume Johanna didn't drive herself to the school, because her car was at the bus stop. Unfortunately, nobody saw her leave her car."

Betty nodded.

"I want to know who drove her to the school. They might be able to tell me what happened next."

"It could be someone from the neighborhood."

"Susan said she'd spent the afternoon calling around. If she'd found out anything, she would have gotten back to me. Were you expecting any clients to stop by?"

"I've been out of touch with the office for a couple of days. I suppose it could have been someone, but I don't know who. We do most of our work on the phone."

"Nobody from your current workload would be likely to come over?"

"Just Norton."

Her voice cracked, and he covered her wrinkled hand with his. "If anything else comes to mind, let me know." He got out another one of his cards and wrote his home phone number on the back.

"And if you find Johanna, call *me*."

"I will."

Before Dan left the hospital, he checked in with one of the nurses at the intensive-care monitoring station.

"Would it be possible to talk to Colonel Jennings?"

"Are you family?"

"Police." He dug out his badge again. "I'd like to ask him some questions."

"He won't be able to tell you anything, but you can have a few minutes with him."

The colonel's head was swathed in bandages, and his body was connected to a morass of tubes and monitors. Jennings's eyes fluttered halfway open when Dan came up to the bedside. The nurse hovered in the background, as if she didn't trust him not to harm her patient.

Dan drew up a chair. "I'm Detective Whitmore with the Montgomery County Police," he began.

Jennings didn't respond.

"I'm trying to get a lead on the man who attacked you." He debated whether to mention Johanna and decided not to.

"Did you see his face?" Dan asked.

Jennings's eyelids fluttered.

Yes or no? Dan wondered. Or was it just a muscle reflex?

The colonel grimaced. "Maaa—" The sound came out like a gasp.

Dan leaned closer. "Are you trying to tell me something?" Wasn't that what he'd tried to tell Betty, too?

"Maaa—"

The nurse touched his shoulder. "He's getting agitated. I'm afraid you're going to have to come back later."

Dan nodded. This wasn't getting him anywhere, and he didn't want the old guy to have a heart attack.

When Dan left the hospital a few minutes later, he was even more down than he'd been earlier. It came from a feeling of helplessness—coupled with fear. With no more evidence than he'd had a few hours ago, he was more sure than ever that Johanna was in trouble, and he couldn't do a damn thing to help her.

Tommy Beckett stared at the T.V. screen. He'd been looking forward to seeing John Wayne in *The High and the Mighty*, the granddaddy of all air-disaster movies. He knew the plot was corny, but he wasn't watching it for that. Good old macho John turned him on. But tonight, not even the Duke could hold his attention. He was feeling bad about that cop who'd come by earlier. What was his name? Whitmore.

He'd been perfectly justified in telling the guy to go to hell. Yet that didn't make the sick feeling in the pit of his stomach go away.

He wiped his hand across his clammy forehead. He kept thinking about his own daughter —Mandy. Carol had taken her and Tommy, Jr., away from him. They were living in Seattle, and he hadn't seen them in over a year. But what if Carol called up and told him that some maniac who'd raped and murdered a bunch of little girls had their daughter? What if she said a witness had information that might lead to the guy's capture—but he refused to talk to the police? He'd want to shake the information out of that guy.

Tommy closed his eyes for a minute, but he couldn't erase the image of Mandy in the clutches of some crazed killer. Getting up, he snapped off the T.V. set and began to pace around the room. Mom didn't know her ass from a hole in the ground these days. She probably couldn't tell the cops anything . . . but if he let Whitmore talk to her, he could go to bed with a clear conscience.

When he called the station, Whitmore wasn't there. He didn't give them a message, because he didn't want to leave his name.

Tommy chewed on a hangnail. Whitmore had scribbled his home number on the back of his card. He'd tried that, but the man wasn't home either. So much for good intentions.

*   *   *

With an upward push of her shoulder, Johanna tried to knock the phone off the hook. The receiver swayed, but didn't come loose. Holding back a sob in her throat, she tried again and again. Finally the receiver clattered to the floor. She could hear the dial tone, and she was concentrating so hard that she wasn't aware that the garage door had opened.

Thank God it was a touch-tone phone, she thought. She pushed the "O" button with her nose and then dropped to the floor where the receiver still rested. There was a pause, and the operator asked, "May I help you?"

"This is Johanna H—"

She gasped as the receiver was kicked away by a heavy shoe. The shoe swung back again and aimed a blow at her ear. An excruciating pain shot through her head, and Johanna saw stars. She teetered on the edge of unconsciousness. Through the haze she could hear Clifford Fuller slamming the receiver onto the hook.

With his foot, he shoved Johanna over so that she had to look up into his pale eyes. The outrage and fury she saw in them made her blood curdle.

Chapter 29

Juanita sat bolt upright in bed. Had she screamed, or was it the dark-haired woman? She put her hand to the side of her head. It throbbed as if she'd just been kicked. No, not Juanita. It was that poor woman. *El hombre muy mal* had taken her away . . . and the little girl, too.

She squinted at the clock on the bedside table. Only nine-thirty. She had to call the police.

Juanita slipped into a robe and silently tiptoed up to the front hall. At the foot of the stairs, she listened. Señor and Señora Hempsted were upstairs in bed watching T.V. *Los niños* were playing baseball on the Nintendo in the den.

In the kitchen, she dialed the emergency number, 911.

"Name and address," the dispatcher answered.

"I need to talk to the police."

"Name and address."

"It's not for me," she whispered hoarsely.

"Is this an emergency?"

"Si."

"What's the problem?"

"He kicked her. He's going to kill them."

"Who? Where?"

Juanita pressed shaky fingers against her forehead. She didn't know the woman's name. She didn't know where she was.

"I'm sorry. We can't help you unless you give us some basic information."

What could she tell them? With a little sob, she hung up. Maybe if she thought about the dream, she could figure out where the woman and the little girl were.

Cliff dropped to his knees. His fingers dug into Johanna's shoulders as he shook her. "How dare you! How dare you!"

"Cliff, please, don't do this," Johanna begged as she tried to struggle away. With her hands and legs still tied, she didn't have a chance.

He struck her with the back of his hand so hard that her teeth gouged the inside of her lip. Tears of pain and anguish streamed down her face and mingled with the blood leaking from her mouth. Even then, she thought of Kirsten. Thank God, the kitchen counter blocked her daughter's view.

When he gripped her shoulders, she braced herself for another blow. Instead there was a heart-stopping moment of total silence. Then he gently touched the tearstains on her face. "I didn't want to hurt you. But you were being very bad."

Johanna blinked, hardly able to take in the abrupt change. He had gone from furious anger to tender concern while her teeth were still chattering. He got up and ran water in the sink. When he came back, he wiped the blood away from her face with a damp paper towel. Then he pulled her to a sitting position.

"I brought dinner."

The last thing Johanna wanted to do was eat, but his mood had changed from angry to conciliatory so quickly, it could just as easily shift back. Her best chance right now, she thought, was to go along with whatever he wanted.

"That was thoughtful of you, Cliff. But how can I eat with my hands tied?"

"I'll undo them."

Hope surged in her breast.

He reached for a bag behind him. When he turned back to her, he was holding a pair of handcuffs.

Johanna cringed, but he ignored her and calmly looked around the room. His gaze settled on the kitchen table. It was a rectangle of white Formica, resting on an old-fashioned cast-iron sewing machine base. "No problem. We can cuff your leg, and you'll have your hands free."

"Before you do that, Kirsten and I both have to go to the bathroom."

"Okay."

He went back to the family room, swung Kirsten up into his arms and carried her down the hall. As they disappeared from view, Johanna's heart started to pound. She was afraid that if she moved from the spot where he'd placed her, he'd go into another rage when he came back. Her ears strained for the sound of her daughter's voice.

Finally Cliff came back, hoisted her up, and carried her out of the room. There was a small powder room in the hall.

He'd untied Kirsten. She sat on the closed toilet seat, too frightened to move.

Cliff pulled a knife from a sheath strapped to his right calf and slashed the tape that bound Johanna's ankles. As she freed her hands, she felt the cold steel of the knife-blade slide against her wrists. Then he gave her a little push toward the bathroom door. "I'll be right out here waiting."

Johanna closed the door and swept Kirsten into her arms. "Are you all right?"

"Yes, but I lost my tooth somewhere." She opened her mouth, and Johanna inspected the gap.

"Does it hurt?"

"No." Kirsten eyed her mother. "You look like the time Daddy hit you."

"I'm okay. You go ahead and go to the bathroom."

While Kirsten used the toilet, Johanna looked around the room. It had no windows. What about a weapon? Towels. Soap. A toilet brush. There was nothing she could use.

After she went to the bathroom, she didn't flush the toilet right away. Cliff would make them come out if he thought they were finished.

"Why is Mr. Fuller being so mean to us?" Kirsten whispered.

"He's very upset."

"But we didn't hurt him."

"I know, honey. It doesn't make sense, but

we've got to try extra hard not to make him angry."

"Like we used to do with Daddy?"

Johanna hugged her daughter to her chest. "Yes, just like that."

"Hurry up in there," Cliff called through the door.

"Just a minute."

She flushed the toilet. "I'm going to do everything I can to get us out of here, but right now, we have to do what Mr. Fuller says. All right?"

Kirsten nodded. "Mommy, I'm scared."

"Remember, Dan said it was okay to be scared."

"I wish he was here."

"So do I."

They washed their hands.

When Johanna opened the door, Cliff had the gun trained on them.

Neither rain, nor snow, nor gloom of night kept Baron from his evening walk, so Marian had bundled into a hooded ski jacket and fur-lined boots. Since the sidewalks were slippery from the sleet, she tried to keep the route short.

No one else was out. The night was as still as death. Marian could hear Baron's claws clicking on the sidewalk. As they walked past lighted windows, she could see people moving about in several houses. She wanted to get back inside, too.

At the corner, she debated whether to turn back. Baron pulled to the right and she let him lead her. One more block, then they'd go home.

Halfway down the block, the big dog stopped in his tracks and growled.

"What is it, boy?" she soothed. "Do you see a cat?"

She couldn't believe how skittish he'd been lately. Like that time when all the neighbors had been at the Waterfords'. And tonight— barking at poor Clifford Fuller like that. Was there some kind of pattern to what was setting him off? A particular noise? A smell? A person he didn't like?

As if the dog sensed her thoughts, he turned toward one of the houses and started to bark again. Marian peered into the darkness. It was the Goodwins'. Weren't they away? There was a light on in back. Probably on a timer, she thought.

She tugged on the leash. "Come on Baron."

The dog delivered another series of sharp barks.

"Come on, you naughty dog. I'm cold." She tugged again, and he gave in.

Johanna normally didn't mind McDonald's food. Tonight the French fries were like corrugated cardboard in her mouth, and the hamburger might as well have been a charcoal briquette.

Kirsten's face had taken on the frightened look that she used to have around Rick, as though she were waiting for someone to hit her.

"Are you going to hurt us?" she asked Cliff in a small voice.

"I just want to play with you, the way I did with my sister."

Kirsten visibly relaxed. Johanna cringed. Suddenly she knew that his sister had been a little girl with blond hair and blue eyes, like Jeanie Waterford, and Heather Morrison. Had he just wanted to play with *them*, too?

"Then why do you have me and my mommy tied up?"

"I want to make sure you stay with me," Cliff answered, giving Johanna a meaningful look.

She bent her head and pretended interest in her cold hamburger. She had choked down half her milk shake when the barking started. She saw Cliff tense. Then he got up and slipped out of the room.

It sounded like Baron out there. He'd barked at Cliff a few hours ago when she and Kirsten had been in the mail truck. Maybe he knew they were here, too. Maybe it would be like Lassie, in the movies, and he'd lead the authorities to the door. She shook her head. It wasn't going to be like in the movies.

After dinner Cliff let them sit on the sofa, with Johanna's ankles bound together. He dimmed the lights and turned the stereo on low—to a classical station. He also poured himself a generous glass of the Goodwins' bourbon.

Emotionally exhausted, Kirsten fell asleep in Johanna's lap. Their captor kept the gun he'd taken from Rick in his hand. Johanna watched his finger massage the edge of the trigger. She wanted to beg him to stop before the damn gun went off. She didn't dare. She'd noticed that stroking things seemed to help him calm down, and he'd been edgy ever since the dog had started barking.

Johanna was as wrung out as her daughter, but she fought sleep. Trying not to look at the gun, she began talking in a calm, soothing voice to the man in the armchair across from them.

"We're friends, aren't we, Cliff?"

He took a swallow of bourbon. "I want to be."

"What can I do to help you?"

He swallowed again and looked hesitant.

"Please. I want to know."

He stared off into space, and she thought he wasn't going to answer. Then he started talking in a stumbling voice, relating bits and pieces about his life. All the time, he watched closely for her reaction.

"Emily was my sister. She and I loved each other."

"Um hum."

"I mean—physically."

"Sometimes that happens."

"We weren't very old. We didn't know what we were doing."

"Of course not."

"She let me fuck her."

Johanna nodded, not trusting herself to speak. She was torn between trying to understand him and wanting to shut out the dreadful revelations. He kept talking.

The horror made her shrivel inside, but she tried to keep her features compassionate.

He described Emily, his mother's cruelty, the awful accident in the barn, and the years of retribution and isolation that had followed.

The terrified boy who'd seen his sister impaled on that bed of sharp stakes had needed psychiatric help. Instead, his mother had taken out her own inadequacies and anger on him, warping his mind, feeding his guilt, stunting the development of normal sexuality.

The revelations brought tears to Johanna's eyes.

"Why are you crying?" he demanded.

"It must have been terrible for you. Your mother was so brutal."

He sat forward. "Then you understand."

"I think I do," she murmured.

"Like I told you in the letters, you have to make everybody understand."

She nodded, even as her mind tried to take in everything he'd just said. "You mean, you want to be my client?"

"Yes!" he exclaimed. "Like that Vietnam cripple or that old fart of a colonel. Real losers. You wrote press releases about them and made everybody love them."

"I can write about you. Change your image, too." She repeated one of the phrases from the letters.

He grinned. "Momma died last year. Had a heart attack, and I didn't even call the ambulance. I sat there and watched her until she took her last breath."

The abrupt change of subject and the vindictiveness behind the revelation caught her off guard.

His voice rose to a giggle at the end of the sentence. "She said what me and Emily did was dirty. She beat the shit out of us. But now there's no one to stop me from getting back together with Emily."

The words were like an icy wind, sweeping over Johanna's skin. The past and present were all twisted up in Cliff's mind. Cliff's mother might have caused his instability, but she'd also kept him in check. The old woman had been the only thing standing between her son and the violence he'd repressed for so long.

His face became sad. "Emily's dead. But there are other little girls almost like her." His eyes darted to Kirsten, and Johanna shifted her hands as though trying to hide her daughter from his view. Cliff had done terrible things to those other little girls.

"Kirsten isn't like Emily," she said.

"She is to me."

Feeling like someone lost in a swamp, Johanna took a deep breath. One misstep and she and her daughter would both be sucked down by the quicksand of Cliff's insanity. "You're not going to hurt Kirsten."

He stared at her, considering. Then his eyes became crafty. "Not if you do what I want."

She was sure he was lying. Maybe she could buy them both some more time . . . until help came, or she figured out how to get away. "If you want me to work with you—write about you—you have to pay my price."

"That's fair. I have a lot of money saved."

"I don't want money from you."

"What do you want?"

"You have to let Kirsten go."

He licked his lips nervously. "You know I can't do that."

She hadn't really expected that he would. "I won't be able to do my best job if I'm worried about her."

Cliff stood up. "You're working for me now. We'll talk about it in the morning."

He marched Johanna upstairs at gunpoint to one of the boys' rooms.

"I bought you a nightgown. And Kirsten, too."

"We'd be more comfortable in our own clothes," she refused softly.

"All right."

He handcuffed her and Kirsten's ankles together before securing her foot to the frame of the captain's bed.

It was a bizarre setting for their captivity. The curtains and the sheets were decorated with dinosaurs. The toy shelves were full of Matchbox cars, Lego building kits, and an army of G. I. Joe action figures.

Kirsten had kept her eyes closed as Johanna carried her upstairs, but the moment Cliff left them alone in the narrow bed, she started to whimper.

"Mommy, when is he going to let us go?"

"Soon, I hope."

Kirsten looked over at the toy shelves. "I need my dolls to make me feel better."

"We'll make each other feel better."

They pulled the covers up around their

shoulders. She and Kirsten had been through some terrible times together, but this was far worse than anything that had ever happened with Rick. It was hard to keep from giving in to her own terror. Perhaps if she'd been alone, she would have started to sob. Instead, she forced herself to sound unruffled and reassuring for Kirsten.

After a lot of hugs and a long quiet talk, her daughter finally fell asleep. Johanna could not.

She was too keyed up even to close her eyes. Cliff had killed Rick. As much as she'd hated what her ex-husband was doing to her, she was revolted by the cold-blooded way Cliff had plunged that knife into him.

The reality of that made her bunch up the sheets in her fists to keep her hands from trembling so badly that she'd wake up Kirsten.

When she'd heard about Heather Morrison and Jeanie Waterford, she'd cried for those little girls. Now she knew she hadn't really comprehended the horror. You had to be there, experiencing it, to really understand.

She'd seen the way Cliff killed Rick. A little while ago he'd beat her, when he'd come in and found her trying to make that call. One more degree of rage, and he might have killed her right then.

She couldn't afford to set him off like that again; she had to protect her daughter. She knew from what he'd said, and from what he'd done to those other children, that Cliff wanted Kirsten sexually, like his sister. In a way that had been the best time in his life. He wanted that again. The implications made a wave of fear and nausea sweep over her.

If only she could tell herself that he would just let her and Kirsten go. But she knew he wasn't going to do that.

She closed her eyes and drew in a deep breath. There was such a fine line between distracting Clifford Fuller and antagonizing him, and she couldn't afford to cross it.

Her arms tightened around Kirsten. The little girl stirred in her sleep and snuggled into the warmth. Johanna gently stroked her blond hair, wishing it were dark like her own. If Kirsten hadn't looked like Emily, Cliff never would have gone after her. Somehow she had to keep her safe now.

She spent hours lying awake, desperately trying to figure out how to get away. Force wouldn't work. She was going to have to trick Cliff into giving her the opportunity to escape, or at least to get Kirsten out of there. But how? And did they have enough time before he snapped?

If only Dan knew she was missing. He had been looking for Rick, and he'd promised he'd be there for her. Would he figure out what kind of crazy twist her life had taken? She could only pray he would.

Chapter 30

Thursday, November 4

The phone rang at five A.M., and Dan reached out automatically to slap the button on the alarm. The ringing didn't stop.

"Hello?" he croaked as he fumbled for the receiver. Even though he'd been dead tired, he hadn't been able to fall asleep until after three in the morning.

"Is this Detective Whitmore?"

"Speaking."

"This is, uh, this is Tom Beckett."

Dan sat up. "Yes?"

"I've thought it over. You can talk to my mom if you still want to."

Dan tossed back the covers. "I'll be there in twenty-five minutes."

Frank Cantrell was the *Washington Post* distributor in the northern part of Montgomery County. The night before, he'd had to maneuver around a yellow compact car, almost blocking the entrance to the narrow lane that led to his house. The weather had been nasty, and he hadn't bothered to see who'd left it there.

In the early morning darkness, he peered at the vehicle. The right front fender was crumpled against the dirt bank. Maybe if he called the police, they'd have it towed away.

Rolling down the window, he shined his flashlight toward the license plate. The edge of the beam caught something down by the wheel that made him redirect the light. Tousled gray-blond hair was fanned against the dirt.

He climbed out and walked around to the hidden side of the car. The twisted body of a man was lying in a pool of frozen blood behind the abandoned vehicle. Holy shit! He'd better get the police right away.

Dan was on his way out the door when the phone rang again. He didn't want to take the time, but it was a good bet that a call at six in the morning wasn't someone selling lawn-care services.

It was Fogel. "That APB you put out last night."

"Yeah, what about it?"

"They found the car, wrecked, out in the western part of the county."

He gripped the receiver. "Anyone in it?"

"No. But there was a dead body behind it. Looks like that composite picture you put together of Hamilton. We're trying to get a positive I.D."

"Thrown from the car on impact?"

"No. Stabbed."

"Jesus!"

"The kid's school books were in the back of the car—along with three hundred K of powdered cocaine—hidden in jugs of industrial cleaner."

Dan swore again. So Hamilton had graduated from just using the stuff to selling it. Or maybe he was only a delivery boy. That was more likely. If he'd done something to make his employers angry, they might have iced him, but where did that leave Johanna and Kirsten?

This new development knocked all his theories into a cocked hat. Had Johanna and Kirsten gotten caught in the middle of a gangland execution? Christ, he hoped not, because that probably meant they were dead, too. But whoever had killed Hamilton hadn't bothered to hide the body—it would have been just as easy to leave three—and the cocaine was still there.

So there was a good chance Johanna and Kirsten were alive, he told himself. Somehow this *was* tied into Jack Daniels—and the other murders. He just had to find out how.

"You still there?" Fogel asked.

"Sorry. Just thinking. Nothing else on Hamilton's ex-wife and daughter?"

"Not yet. There were skid marks on the pavement from a second vehicle. Maybe a jeep."

"I'm on my way to check out another lead—someone who may have seen Jack Daniels. I'll be in as soon as I finish."

He hung up the receiver. Could Johanna have somehow killed Rick and gotten away? If so, where the hell was she? Hiding? Afraid to turn herself in? No. She'd call him ... wouldn't she?

He'd been telling himself that if they found Rick, this whole thing would be over. Deep down, he'd known it might not be that simple. Unable to suppress his frustration, he kicked the nearest kitchen cabinet. The wood splintered, but he didn't stop to inspect the damage.

Cliff slouched low behind the wheel of his car, a visor-cap pulled down over his face. He had already passed Marian Lewis and Baron once. Now he made a right at the cross street, turned around in a driveway, and came back for another pass.

She always walked the damn dog around six. He'd seen them a lot of times when he was out cruising the neighborhood. This morning was going to be the last time they went out.

Baron knew who he was, and it was just a matter of time before Marian Lewis realized she did, too.

When he passed them again, Marian peered inquiringly after his old Dodge. He'd better get this over with fast. She might have recognized him.

He'd wait for them where he'd grabbed Jeanie—the place where the scraggly junipers overhung the sidewalk.

Bloody hell. He wished he had a silencer, like on T.V. He'd have to get away fast after firing the shots, so he couldn't leave the car around the corner. Instead, he pulled it up onto the path where it was screened by the bushes. Climbing out, he stationed himself behind the tall evergreens.

He didn't start shaking until Baron began to bark and pull Marian right to the place where he was hiding.

He wanted to jump back in the car. That

son-of-a-bitching dog. Instead, he leaped out of his hiding place and leveled the gun.

For a frozen moment he and Marian stood there looking at each other.

"Cliff? Are you crazy?"

Then he pulled the trigger.

He wasn't prepared for the way the gun jerked his arm back, or for the loud report that shattered the early morning silence.

Marian groaned and staggered toward the ground. Yelping frantically, the dog strained at the leash, yanking it from Marian's weakened grasp.

Baron was a dark blur of motion as he lunged forward, straight at Cliff, teeth bared.

Cliff got off another shot, but it went wild as the dog knocked him backwards. Its teeth locked onto his shoulder, and he screamed.

Reflexively his fingers squeezed the trigger.

The dog yelped, and his grip loosened slightly.

Across the street, lights were going on in a couple of houses. People had heard the shots.

Cliff shoved the gun into his belt and kicked at the dog's belly even as he pried the massive jaws open. No time to go for the knife strapped to his leg and finish off Marian, but she was probably in no shape to talk. Even if she did, it would be too late. It would all be over by this afternoon, anyway.

His shoulder was throbbing as he threw himself into the car and slammed the door. Thank God he'd been wearing a heavy coat, or he might have really gotten hurt.

Chapter 31

Tommy Beckett answered the doorbell on the first ring. He looked uncomfortable as he led Dan back toward the kitchen.

His mother was sitting at the table with a cup of tea and a bowl of oatmeal. "If I'd known you were having company, Tommy, I'd have gotten dressed."

Beckett shot Dan an "I told you so" look. "Don't you remember, Mom? This is one of the police officers who came over to talk to us after the Morgensterns' house was broken into."

Her face took on a reflective look. "I know the Morgensterns. They don't like me."

Dan pulled out a chair opposite Muriel. "Mrs. Beckett, don't you remember we talked about the break-in?"

"Of course I remember! You were with that dark fellow. He was a spic or a nigra or something."

"I'm sorry," Tommy whispered, obviously very embarrassed. "She's gotten like that."

"Don't talk about me like I'm not there,"

Muriel snapped. She launched into a tirade that ended abruptly when her eyes filled with tears. Tommy handed her a tissue.

"Do you remember the night of the break-in?" Dan gently changed the subject back to the reason for his visit. "You said you'd heard breaking glass in the middle of the night."

"My, you have a good memory, young man."

"And you said you saw someone." He took out the picture of Rick. "Was it this man?"

Her brow wrinkled. "No, not him. It was Cliff."

"Who's Cliff?"

Tommy shook his head. "That's her friend, the mailman." She talks about him all the time. She's always telling me how much nicer he is to her than I am."

"Are you laughing at me?" Muriel demanded.

"No," Dan assured her. "I'd like you to think very hard about who you saw that night."

Muriel scowled at him. "Cliff. I told you it was Cliff. He wasn't wearing his uniform. Sometimes my husband doesn't wear his uniform, either."

"Mom, he's dead. Remember?"

"Cliff? Dead? Oh, no. Such a nice young man. What happened?"

"Not Cliff. Dad."

So she thought she'd seen the mailman. He was wasting his time after all.

"His name is Fuller," Muriel broke into his thoughts. "Cliff Fuller. He's so nice. And smart as a whip. He has time to chat with me."

"Satisfied?" Tommy asked.

"Thanks for letting me talk to her. It was a longshot, anyway."

His expression was grim as he made his way back to his Chevy. Damn. He'd gotten his hopes up, and now another dead end. As he opened the car door, he could hear sirens close by. The radio was dispatching available units to respond to a shooting on Orchard Hill Run.

That was almost around the corner.

Juanita had barely slept. In a way it was better not to. Every time she closed her eyes, the dreams started.

Finally she got out of bed at a little after six and went upstairs to the kitchen.

It was early, but she started fixing lunches for *los niños*. She made turkey breast and carrot sticks. They both liked that. She usually didn't want to take the time to peel carrots, but this morning she needed something to do to keep herself from worrying.

The cookie jar was low. She'd make gingersnaps. She got out the flour and the sugar and spices. But the thick molasses dripping out of the bottle made her think of blood.

Madre de Dios. She couldn't get away from the horror. She sat down and covered her face with her hands. The dark haired woman. The little girl. *El loco* had them, and he was going to kill them—today. The feeling was so strong that it made her throat constrict.

She had to go to the police. She had to tell them what she knew, no matter what. Even if it meant she got sent back to El Salvador. If she said nothing, and the bad man killed the woman and the child, it would be on her head. God would never forgive her ... and she wouldn't forgive herself.

Talking on the phone to the police hadn't worked, but if she went to the station, maybe she could make them understand.

Yes. That was the way to do it. As soon as everybody was out of the house, she'd call a taxi and have it take her to the station house on Seven Locks Road.

When Dan pulled up at the curb on Orchard Hill Run, a woman was already being loaded onto the ambulance stretcher. The uniformed officer who had arrived at the scene a few minutes earlier filled him in. "Marian Lewis. Her dog's been shot, too."

Nearby, a group of neighbors was clustered around the dog. One man had taken charge. "Got to get him to the vet right away. We need a sheet to lift him up—and a station wagon."

"Marian Lewis?" Dan asked. "The same woman who found the first little girl that was raped and murdered?"

"Yeah."

"Does she know who shot her?"

The officer shook his head. "She's in a lot of pain, so I couldn't get much out of her. Just keeps mumbling something about a cliff."

Dan stared at him. It was as if he'd suddenly stumbled on the key to a previously unbreakable code.

Muriel Beckett had tried to tell him a few minutes ago, and he'd assumed she was mixed up. Norton Jennings ... he'd struggled to get it out, too. And now Marian Lewis. They all knew the killer. Not a cliff. *Cliff*. Cliff Fuller, the mailman.

All the clues had been there, if he'd just been able to put them together.

Someone had been stalking Johanna. Someone who knew her very well. Not just her ex-husband, but someone who had been reading Rick Hamilton's letters—and imitating them. Jesus, he should have made the Goddamn connections. His fists balled into tight knots.

The killer was someone who knew when people in the neighborhood were away, so he could break into their houses.

And dammit, someone Johanna had trusted enough to get into his frigging mail truck to go after Rick.

It had to be Cliff Fuller who had taken her up to the school yesterday. They must have chased Rick to that country lane where his car was found. Fuller was the one who'd stabbed Rick, and now he had Johanna and Kirsten.

He must be pretty busy, if they were still alive.

God no! Not that. They *were* still alive.

But why had he picked *this* morning to go after Marian Lewis and Baron?

The answer made his heart start to pound. Fuller must think Marian Lewis knew that he was the murderer and where he was holding Johanna and Kirsten. Maybe she did.

Dan reached for his badge as he ran back

toward the ambulance. The attendant was just closing the door.

"Detective Whitmore, Montgomery County Police. I've got to talk to Mrs. Lewis."

"She's unconscious. She's not going to be talking to anybody for a few hours."

"Damn!"

Dan watched the ambulance pull away, siren blaring. Then he looked over toward the dog. Four men had lifted him up on a makeshift stretcher made from a folded sheet and were carrying him toward the open tailgate of a blue station wagon. Probably the dog knew where Cliff was, too, but he wasn't in any condition to lead a search party.

After climbing into his car, Dan banged his fists against the wheel. He could have figured out the mailman connection last night, if he'd been thinking straight. Then he shook his head. There just hadn't been enough evidence until now to nail it down.

Despite the early hour, by the time Dan arrived at the Rockville District Station, Fogel had assembled most of the task force. They were in the middle of a discussion about the cocaine in Rick's car.

Dan interrupted to tell them what he'd just figured out.

"Jesus. The mailman?" Fogel muttered. "Do we have enough to bring him in?"

"Not unless we get a statement from Marian Lewis—or find something incriminating at his house."

Fogel arranged for a search warrant. Someone else phoned the post office and found out Fuller had called in sick that morning. They also got a street by street description of his route—which they laid out on a county map.

"I want a picture of the guy," Fogel snapped.

When the messenger had delivered it from the post office, they studied the smiling face: sandy hair parted on the right side, light blue eyes, light eyebrows, a straight nose. Nothing about him was remarkable or particularly menacing, yet the man looked familiar to Dan. Had he noticed him around Johanna's neighborhood? He didn't remember seeing the mail truck, but he hadn't been looking for it.

The familiarity of the face was still bothering him when he went to get the Jack Daniels file. He and Greg Greenway went through the reports, correlating them with a map of the Rockville district. Every house was on Fuller's route.

"He's probably still in that area," Greenway observed. "We can try a house-to-house."

"That's going to take all day," Dan muttered.

"Not if we confine ourselves to the houses the post office knows are vacant," Fogel pointed out.

"Someone has to check Fuller's place. I'll do that," Dan volunteered.

"If you're wrong about his using a vacant house, he could be home," Fogel cautioned. "And we know he's armed and dangerous."

"If he's smart, he's not home."

"Take three men with you, just in case," Fogel ordered.

"I'd like to be one of them," Greg Greenway volunteered.

*   *   *

Fuller lived in an old farmhouse in a rural area near the Howard County line. They turned off onto a long dirt driveway that wound through stands of pines and maples. Honeysuckle vines and briars weighted down an old metal fence.

They took two cars, Dan and Greg in one, two uniformed officers following in another. Dan drove while Greenway scanned the woods.

"Real deserted back here," he remarked.

"Yeah. Maybe we'd better not advertise that we're coming." He signalled the second car, then pulled over to the side of the track and cut the engine. They climbed out and drew their guns. It was a tense quarter-mile hike.

When he heard a rustle in the woods, Dan whirled and his hand tightened on the trigger. Out of the corner of his eye he saw a frightened doe bound away. "Jesus! I almost shot a deer."

"Better watch it, Whitmore."

The house was a small wood rancher with peeling paint and an unkempt yard. There was no car in sight, no light on inside, no sound except the squawk of birds flying south for the winter. Still, they approached cautiously.

Dan and Greenway took the front door. The two uniformed officers went around back.

On the porch, Dan peered through the dirty window. The living room was unoccupied. His hand reached down and twisted the doorknob. Surprisingly, the door wasn't locked, and it creaked open on hinges that needed oiling. Dan edged inside. It took only a few minutes to determine that the place was empty.

They turned on the lights and started searching.

Dan kept picturing the man in his surroundings. Where the hell had he seen him before? He just couldn't bring the scene into focus.

Fuller had made no attempt to hide his activities. Either he was arrogant enough to think he wouldn't be found out, or he didn't care. Dan hoped it wasn't the latter. A man who didn't give a shit about getting caught was a man with nothing left to lose.

In plain sight on the dining room table was the packet containing the letters and the answering machine tape Johanna had mailed to the Rockville District Station.

Next to them were several other tapes. Greenway put one into the recorder and turned it on. It was a one-sided phone conversation in which Johanna assumed Rick was on the other end of the line. There was no answer to her request that the caller identify himself—only heavy breathing.

"She told me about that," Dan muttered. "But it wasn't Hamilton. It was Fuller."

Greenway tried one of the other two tapes. On it, a child was crying and pleading for Mr. Fuller to stop hurting her.

"Christ! That must be either the Morrison or the Waterford girl," Dan growled as he reached out to snap off a high-pitched scream.

"The sick bastard recorded it."

They had enough for an arrest warrant, but they kept looking. There was dried blood in the sink, and a wet towel lay on the drainboard.

"Maybe he washed the murder weapon," one of the uniformed officers mused. "The lab will want a sample."

They didn't find the knife.

Before they left, Dan picked up one more piece of evidence—a bag of lemon drops and several empty wrappers.

"What's that for?" Greenway asked.

"I found some of the papers up by Johanna's house—under the pine trees along the road. He must have stood there watching her and sucking on the damn things."

"Fuller's seems like a real kinky bastard," one of the uniformed officers observed. "I wonder why he's got Mrs. Hamilton and not just the kid? Do you think he wants her for sex, too?"

Dan's jaw clenched as he shook his head. He didn't know. But he remembered the press kit Fuller had sent Johanna. What weird impulse had prompted him to do that? Or was it all part of some plan the killer had logically thought out? Dan wished he knew. But more than that, he wished to hell that Clifford Fuller didn't have Johanna and Kirsten in his clutches.

Chapter 32

Nico Jackson ran his finger down the list of investigations on his schedule: three burglaries, two auto thefts, vandalism at Cold Brook Elementary School, a rape. There was enough to keep him busy all day—especially without Dan.

All hell had broken loose with the Hamilton case. In the morning briefing he'd learned that the woman's ex-husband had been found dead—with a whole shitload of cocaine in the trunk of his car. And if that wasn't enough, Dan had probably pegged the murderer of the little girls—Clifford Fuller, the mailman on Johanna Hamilton's route.

Bizarre as it sounded, it looked like Fuller had also murdered the husband and had the mother and daughter.

Dan was out at Fuller's house now, and he was going to be tied up with the case until they nailed the bastard—dead or live, it was just a matter of time. But it was going to be touch and go with the woman and the kid right up to the end.

Nico was just reaching for his jacket when

the phone rang. It was someone named Susan Randolph, calling to see if they knew anything more about Johanna and Kirsten.

"I guess they put you through to me because I'm Dan's partner," he said. "I'm sorry; he's out following a lead on the case."

"Johanna still isn't home, and I'm so worried. Has anything else happened?"

"We're not releasing anything to the press yet."

"But you know something. Oh my God— are they dead?"

"Take it easy." He told her about Rick, and she gasped.

"We have reason to believe Johanna and Kirsten have been abducted and are being held in a vacant house in the neighborhood," he added.

"Abducted? By whom?"

"I really can't say anything about that."

"But you think you know?" Susan persisted.

"We've got a strong lead."

"Is there anything I can do to help?"

He probably should have her call the task force office, he thought. But what the hell, he might as well just take care of it himself. "We're using the Post Office Department records to determine which houses in the subdivision are vacant. But we might not get them all, because some people have a neighbor take in the mail and papers."

"I know a lot of people in the neighborhood. I'll go down the P.T.A. list and call around. Maybe I can find out who's gone."

"If you come up with any possibilities, pass

them on to the task force." After hanging up, Nico put on his jacket and went downstairs. A cab was just pulling up at the front door to the station. On the way out, he passed a short, dark woman hurrying up the stairs. Her head was bent, and she was clutching the front of her coat.

He was just climbing into his car when one of the desk officers came rushing out.

"There's a lady inside babbling in Spanish. She seems pretty upset, but I can't understand what she's talking about. Think you could help me out?"

"I'll try."

It was the woman he'd passed on the way out. Now he took a closer look. She was short and just a little plump, with glossy dark hair pulled back and clasped at the neck in a tortoise-shell barrette. She looked nineteen or twenty, hardly more than a kid, he thought.

She glanced up anxiously as he came through the door. Her large, brown eyes were shadowed by dark circles. She looked as if she hadn't had a good night's sleep in weeks.

"Señorita?"

"Habla usted español?"

He nodded, and she started off again in rapid-fire Spanish.

"Whoa. Not so fast," he protested in the same language. "I'm a little rusty."

She nodded.

Her voice sounded familiar. "Did you call before?"

"Si." The syllable was so low he could barely hear it.

"Juanita? *Correcto?*"

She looked frightened. *"Si."*

"I want to help you," he said in Spanish. "Are you in some kind of trouble?"

"Not me. The dark-haired woman, and the blond little girl. The bad man has them. Even if you think I'm crazy, I have to tell you about it."

He could feel goose bumps rise on his forearms. Johanna and Kirsten Hamilton. Did she really know something?

"What woman?"

"I don't know her name, but I saw her in the grocery store yesterday."

The grocery store. Dan had told him Johanna had left a bag of groceries in the back of her car.

"Let's sit down so we can talk," he suggested quietly, and he led her over to one of the benches along the wall.

Little by little, he began to draw the story out of her. She was a maid, working for a local family. Her work permit had expired, but she had stayed in the States anyway. The family she lived with was trying to change her status, but she was terrified of being sent back to El Salvador. On the other hand, she was more terrified of what the bad man was going to do to the woman and the little girl. From what he could gather, her only knowledge of the murders and the abduction was from her dreams. She was sure he wasn't going to believe her, and it wasn't an unwarranted assumption.

"Okay, tell me the first dream."

When she began to describe the first house Jack Daniels had trashed, Nico stared at her. It was like she'd been there with him and Dan. She was accurate about the setting, down to the smell of the rotting food on the kitchen floor. But she'd seen Johanna and Kirsten Hamilton in that house, and they hadn't been there.

"Are they in there now?" he asked.

"No. Somewhere different."

"Do you know where?"

She looked distressed. "I'm not sure. Another house. I don't know where it is."

Maybe he could pull it out of her another way. "Let's go back. Did you dream about the murders?"

Her eyes watered. "*Si*. The poor little girls."

Some of the things she had to say were eerie in their accuracy. Some didn't quite fit.

He was still questioning her when Dan and Greenway walked through the front door into the lobby.

As Juanita stared at Dan, her mouth fell open. "*Madre de Dios*. He's going to kill you."

Cliff came into the bedroom with a disarming smile on his face and a doll in the crook of his arm. It was an exquisite Victorian reproduction in a long dress of lavender taffeta. Dark, shoulder-length ringlets framed her delicate face.

Forgetting for a moment that they were prisoners, Kirsten sat up and reached for it. "I saw one like this down at the Treasure Chest."

"That's where I bought it." He smoothed the silky fabric of the skirt. "It's so pretty. I got it especially for you."

Johanna's hand clutched her daughter's shoulder as she eyed Cliff warily. A doll. Why was he giving her a doll? Then she remembered: Heather Morrison and Jeanie Waterford, the little girls he'd murdered, had each been found with a doll.

Dan stared at the woman with Nico. She thought someone was going to kill him. He felt as if he'd come into the middle of an old *Twilight Zone* episode and didn't know the story. Who was she—the sister of some punk he'd busted?

"What the hell's she talking about?" he asked his partner. "Don't tell me I've got to worry about a crackpot death threat on top of everything else." Dan shifted his weight from one foot to the other.

"It doesn't make any sense to me yet either," Nico agreed. "But remember last week, I told you we got a call about the child murders?" he continued. "This is Juanita Cordero. She's the one who called."

Dan's interest suddenly picked up. "Can you report back to Fogel?" he asked Greenway. "I'll be along in a minute."

"Sure."

"I take it Fuller wasn't home," Nico observed.

"No. But he's definitely our man. The letters and the tapes were there. And tapes he made of the other little girls."

Nico swore.

Dan gestured toward Juanita. "What about her? Did she see something yesterday?"

"Only in a dream."

Dan's hopeful expression changed to one of disgust, and he started to turn away. "I don't need this."

Nico grabbed Dan's arm. "Wait a minute. I would have sent her home a half hour ago, but she does know something . . . like about there being a symbol on the girls' wrists." He looked at Juanita and pulled out his notebook. "Can you draw the mark the man left on the little girls?"

She took the notebook and a pen and drew the figure eight. Then she looked at it for a moment and turned it on its side. "No, it goes this way."

"No! You can't have the doll!" Johanna shouted as she pulled Kirsten protectively back against her.

Cliff's face went from benign to savage in the space of a heartbeat. "Don't you dare interfere."

Kirsten shrank against her mother. "I don't want your doll. I want my own dolls."

"See what you've done," Cliff raged. Lifting the lavender-clad figure over his head, he slammed it against the heavy wooden bedpost —once, twice, a third time.

Kirsten covered her face and sobbed.

Johanna couldn't turn away from the frightening display as she huddled with Kirsten on the bed. It was like yesterday when he came in and discovered her trying to get away.

Then she'd been in the middle of it. Now she was just a spectator. His anger was like a nuclear reactor, feeding on its own energy. Each burst of rage fueled a more intense explosion. The doll's head came off and flew across the room. Cliff dashed after it, stopping it with his foot. Then, with the heel of his shoe, he ground the beautiful little face into the floorboards.

Johanna hardly dared to breathe. When the madman looked up at them again, her whole body went rigid.

Dan stared at the infinity mark and grabbed Juanita's arm. "Where the hell did you see that?"

"En mis suenos."

"In her dreams," Nico translated. "That's what I was trying to tell you."

Dan looked into Juanita's huge, frightened eyes. A damn psychic. He was reduced to consulting a damn psychic. But God, maybe she did know something.

He checked back with the task force, told them what was going on, and asked if Greenway wanted to sit in on the questioning. He did.

Nico arranged to have his workload farmed out. Then they took Juanita to an empty office downstairs where they would have some privacy.

"By the way, I almost forgot; that woman from the safety committee, Susan Randolph, called to find out if you'd heard anything about Johanna," Nico told him. "She's calling around the neighborhood, trying to get a line on vacant houses the post office doesn't know about."

"I'll get back to her later," Dan answered absently. He turned back to Juanita. "Start from the beginning, and try to speak English."

It took a long time—with many questions. Dan felt as if he were slowly and painfully digging splinters out of the palm of his hand. And then she riveted his attention.

"He jumped on her. Kicked the phone out of her hand. Beat her with his fists."

"What happened? Did he kill her?" Dan demanded.

Juanita sniffed and blew her nose. "I don't know."

Dan wanted to go over and shake her. Instead, he stuffed his fists into his pockets. "Let's try something else," he suggested when he felt more in control of his emotions. He left the room and returned with two dozen photographs and composite pictures. Among them were the ones of Rick and Cliff. He spread them out on the table in front of her.

He hardly dared breathe as she picked up each one in turn and put it down again. Finally she came back to the ones of Hamilton and Fuller.

"These. Both of these." Then she began to speak rapidly in Spanish again to Nico.

"She kept seeing those two faces in the dreams and being confused," he translated. "But last night it was the blond man who was hitting Johanna and kicking her."

"Jesus! Where the hell was she?"

"In a house."

"We know that, for God's sake." He could feel the blood pounding in his temples. He forced himself to pull a chair over and sit down.

Juanita eyed him apprehensively.

"I'm sorry," he apologized. "I'm upset."

"*Comprendo*. You love her," she observed softly.

Nico looked down at his hands.

Dan didn't turn around to see what kind of expression was on Greenway's face. Love her. He hadn't put his feelings in those terms. Now was a hell of a time to come to grips with his private emotions. "I want to get her and the little girl away from him," he said instead. "Did he hurt the girl?"

"I don't know."

"Can you help us find them?" Nico asked in Spanish. "What if we drove you through the neighborhood? Would you recognize the house?" He felt like an idiot asking the next question. "Would you—uh—get any vibes?"

"I don't know the outside of the house."

"What do you know?" Dan persisted.

She bent her head and pressed her fingers over her eyes. "I saw a scene. A kitchen. They were in a kitchen. The bottom of the table is funny—like—" She gestured with her hands. "—the old treadle sewing machine my grandmother had. He—I—I think he chained her leg to it."

Dan swore. Johanna, chained to a table. He didn't want to believe that, but at least that was better than keeping her bound up in a closet.

On the other hand, the woman had gotten some things mixed up—like seeing Johanna at the Morgensterns' house. And then there was the business about the mailman killing him. He didn't buy that.

But suppose there was some kind of dream-shorthand connecting this woman with Fuller. Suppose some of the dreams were garbled. Others could still be right.

"Anything else you know about the kitchen?" Nico prompted.

Juanita's earnest brown eyes fixed on his face. "I remember thinking the tiles on the wall were pretty, a little like some things you see in my country: tiles with blue and yellow flowers, with a border around the edge. Does that help?"

"Flowered tiles on the wall? Is that real common?" Dan asked Greenway.

"Not in our income bracket."

"So maybe that's something. We could get Susan Randolph to ask around about who has them."

Chapter 33

Cliff had been restless since he'd brought them downstairs—at gunpoint. He found WTOP and paced back and forth as he listened to a summary of the news. When the broadcast was over, he started muttering under his breath. Johanna couldn't catch much of what he was saying, just phrases that rhymed, like in the letters.

There was no mention of their abduction on the news. Didn't anybody know? She fought a swell of panic in her throat. Someone must have missed her by now. Hadn't anyone found her empty car with the groceries in the back? And what about her clients? The answering machine had been on since yesterday morning; surely someone would wonder about that. If only Betty were in the office. But she was busy down at the hospital with Norton. She might not even think to call.

Johanna took a deep breath and glanced over at Kirsten, who was in the family room watching a game show—her ankles chained to a wrought iron chair. She had to stop torturing herself. Dan would know they were missing; the police had probably found Rick's body by now. They were probably withholding the information from the press.

Was that what was bothering Cliff, or was it something else? He'd been rubbing his shoulder this morning. Had he gotten hurt?

She watched apprehensively as he picked up the bottle of Jack Daniels on the kitchen counter and poured himself half a glassful. He downed the fiery liquid in a few quick swallows—as if it were water.

When he turned to stare at her, she bent quickly back over the battered portable typewriter he had sat her at that morning. Her eyes focused on the jagged edges of her nails, which she'd broken off trying to claw her way through the tape yesterday. Her fingers froze on the keys. She couldn't remember what she had been about to write. She hadn't known Cliff drank until last night. Then he'd added water and nursed his drink. Now he was chugging the stuff. He must be heavily dependent. Last night he'd tried to hide that from her, just the way he'd hidden so much all along. This morning he didn't care—another indication that their situation was deteriorating.

He stamped over to where she was sitting and ripped the paper out of the machine. She watched, trying not to tremble as he read the paragraphs she'd been sweating over all morning.

Mentally abused by his mother, Mr. Fuller nevertheless stayed home to take care of her until she died last year.

But the most influential incident in his life was the accidental death of his sister, Emily, at age eight. They had been playing in the barn together, and she fell off the edge of the loft.

"This is good. Just what I wanted everybody to know. You're doing very well. Just a little bit more . . . but you'd better finish soon, because we don't have much time."

Not much time. She closed her eyes for a minute and the words echoed in her mind like the tolling of a bell. Was she writing an obituary? And whose? Hers and Kirsten's? Or his?

Her hands clenched around the base of the typewriter. She considered throwing it at him, hitting him in the head and knocking him out. The image of his falling to the floor was so real, she had to fight to keep from picking up the machine. But she knew the chance of its working was so slim that she couldn't risk it. Not with her leg chained to the table. Not with Kristen in Cliff's reach.

She kept her voice calm. "I can't work under a deadline unless I know what it is."

"Well, you'd better. The only reason I haven't—" He stopped abruptly.

She knew the blood had drained from her face. "You haven't what?"

He walked around the table and leaned down toward her, his face so close she could smell the liquor on his breath. "*You* don't ask me questions. *You* just do what I tell you."

*   *   *

The operator interrupted Susan Randolph's line with an emergency call. It was Dan Whitmore.

"Has something happened?" she asked apprehensively.

"No. Sorry to worry you. But as long as you're making those calls, would you ask if anybody's seen a house in the development with blue and yellow tiles in the kitchen, and a table with a sewing machine base?"

"How come?"

"It's a long story, but the house Johanna and Kirsten are being held in may have them."

Johanna and Kirsten. The only way to stop from worrying herself to death, Susan thought, was to try and help the police find them. "Okay. I'll ask."

"I appreciate that," Dan told her.

She hung up. The table-base wasn't so unusual. A lot of people who were into antiques had them. But the blue and yellow tiles . . . she couldn't get them out of her mind. When he'd mentioned them, she could almost see them. Had it been in someone's house, or a magazine? Or had she just heard about them from someone else?

She closed her eyes, struggling to drag the fragment of memory into focus. It was often that way when you were trying too hard; the connection wouldn't surface. The thing to do was just let it float around in the back of her mind.

A team from the lab had been sent to go

over the truck that Clifford Fuller drove. They were back by noon with more evidence to support Dan's hypothesis that Fuller had abducted Johanna and Kirsten the night before.

On the steering wheel were traces of blood that matched Rick Hamilton's. In the back were blue wool fibers that could have come from the coat Johanna was wearing. There was also a child's baby tooth.

Dan remembered when Kirsten had proudly shown him her loose tooth. It must have come out when Fuller was hustling her into the back of the truck. Had he been rough with her, or had the tooth been hanging by a thread? Dan clamped his lips together. There was no use torturing himself by trying to imagine the scene.

Under the jump seat they'd found something else that probably didn't belong in the mail truck—a small cream-colored notepad with the crest of the Italian government at the top.

The officer who had found it didn't know what it was doing there. Dan explained that Johanna had been working closely with the staff of the Italian Embassy recently. The notepad was one more piece of evidence that placed her in the mail truck.

The most frightening thing was that Johanna didn't know from minute to minute how Cliff was going to react.

Sometimes he would mutter to himself. And then, suddenly, he would turn on her with a question or a demand.

She was in the middle of a paragraph about his views on the Post Office Department when he whirled and came across the room.

"Who was that guy who brought you home the night Kirsten saw me out the window?" he snarled.

Johanna's head jerked up. "Why—uh—someone I met at the meeting at Susan's house."

"Yeah?"

"That's the truth."

"But he came back—to dinner. And another time his car was there late at night."

"He was worried about me—because of Rick."

"Like I was worried about Rick."

"Yes."

"Rick hurt you. He was no good for you."

"You wanted to protect me from him?"

"Yes."

Thank God, Cliff had made one of his quick changes of subject.

A few minutes later, he snapped off the television set and brought Kirsten over to the table. Johanna could see her daughter cringing as he put his hands on her, but she pressed her lips together and didn't say anything. Since Cliff had smashed the doll that morning, she'd been careful—very careful—of what she said.

After he chained Kirsten to the table-base, she sat very still, her face pinched and helpless. Johanna had seen that look before, and it had taken two years of therapy to slowly erase it. God, how long would it take her to stop waking up screaming after *this* nightmare? And would there be an afterwards? Her hand started shaking so that the typewriter keys clattered. Cliff shot her a penetrating look. Her only defense was to hunch over her work and start typing again.

Cliff rummaged in the cabinet and found a box of crackers. He set them on the table.

"We don't have time for lunch, but you can eat these if you're hungry." Obediently, Johanna took a cracker. It was like Styrofoam in her mouth. Kirsten followed her mother's example, but she nibbled without enthusiasm.

For a long time Cliff's gaze rested on the little girl. "We can play together after you finish eating," he told her, his voice smooth and coaxing.

Nobody on the task force wanted to break for lunch, so they sent out to McDonald's for burgers and coffee.

Dan sat between Wes Miner and Pat Stover, both veteran detectives who usually worked out of the Bethesda District Station. Miner was a hard-bitten type with over twenty-five years on the force. Stover had come from a big-city department, Chicago or Detroit; he didn't remember which.

While they ate, Fogel gave a report from the plainclothesmen who'd been checking the vacant houses. They'd covered more than half of the list from the post office and still had not turned up any trace of Fuller or Johanna and Kirsten.

"I suppose it's possible we're operating on the wrong assumption," Pat Stover sighed. "But it's still our best shot. We know Fuller was in the neighborhood this morning when he shot Marian Lewis. He wasn't spotted on the road. And Whitmore's sure he's following the same pattern he used as Jack Daniels."

Sure, Dan thought as he scratched random designs in the side of his Styrofoam cup with his thumbnail. He wished he were sure. He hoped to hell his deductions weren't leading them down a blind alley.

It was only a matter of time before they found Fuller. It was also only a matter of time before he played out whatever twisted scenario he'd planned for Johanna and Kirsten. Fuller had only held Heather Morrison and Jeanie Waterford for twenty-four hours before killing them. If he followed his previous pattern, Johanna and Kirsten had less than six hours to live. The man was unstable, erratic: the friendly mailman and the psychotic killer, lemon drops and knives. Jack Daniels bourbon. For some reason, milk shakes popped into his mind. Two chocolate and one strawberry.

"Damn. I know where I saw the son of a bitch."

He didn't realize he'd shouted until he saw that everyone in the room was staring at him as if he'd finally cracked under the pressure.

"Fuller. Last night Fuller was at the Mc-Donald's on Rockville Pike, buying a bag of food and three milk shakes." He banged his palm against the side of his head. "Oh God, if only I'd known he was the one who had them."

Wes Miner passed the photograph of Fuller to Dan. "You're sure it was him?"

He didn't need to study the perfectly ordinary features that belied the twisted mind behind them. Fuller's face had already etched itself into his memory. "Positive. He was nervous. I wondered why."

"What was he wearing?" Fogel asked.

"A dark windbreaker. Corduroy slacks, I think. Tan maybe. I didn't see his shirt."

"He was bringing them dinner," Greenway mused.

There was a chorus of agreements around the table.

"At least we know they were alive last night," Stover added.

Chapter 34

A white-capped face swam into view.

"Can you tell me your name?"

"Marian—Lewis," she whispered.

"How are you feeling, Mrs. Lewis?" the nurse asked.

She felt groggy and terrible. Every breath was an effort. A nurse: this must be a hospital, but why was she here? What had happened, a car accident? No that wasn't right. The terrible scene leaped into her mind. Cliff had shot her. And Baron. The dog had been trying to tell her about the mailman right from the beginning.

"Baron," she managed. "How is Baron?"

"You were the only person brought in."

"My dog Baron."

"I'll try to find out how he is."

"Please—"

"Just try to rest."

"Something else—"

The nurse bent over so she could hear the low words.

"Tell the police. He was at the Goodwins' house last night."

"Who?"

"The man who killed the little girls."

The nurse leaned closer. "Mrs. Lewis, what are you talking about?"

It had taken a tremendous effort just to deliver that message. "Tell them—"

"Tell them what?"

Marian murmured a few more garbled words before she drifted off again.

The nurse stared down at her. People said a lot of strange things in the recovery room. Should she call the police, or wait and see what the patient said when she woke up again?

Susan was in the middle of dialing the next number on the P.T.A. list when the thing she'd been trying to remember finally came to her. Blue and yellow tiles. Bill Goodwin had been so proud of the hand-painted blue and yellow tiles he and Alice had shipped back from Italy last year.

The Goodwins were out of town. Their kids were too young for elementary school. That's why she hadn't come to them when she was going through the P.T.A. roster.

Susan started to phone the police station and realized she had dialed the first three digits of the Goodwins' number. My God, what was she doing? Slamming the phone down, she took a deep, steadying breath. Then, very carefully, she checked the correct number again and dialed.

"Montgomery County Police. May I help you?"

"I'd like to speak to Dan Whitmore."

"We're only putting through calls that are directly related to the murder task force."

"This *is* directly related."

Cliff Fuller's head bobbed up and down as he read the press release.

"Yes. This is good. Very good."

He put the papers on the table and let his hand trail down Kirsten's leg as he reached for the handcuff at her ankle.

Johanna had been watching apprehensively as he read her work. Now she shot him a murderous look as he touched the little girl.

Cliff saw, but he didn't care. It would all be over soon. For the three of them.

He'd have to use the knife on Kirsten, but he'd shoot himself and Johanna.

He was just starting to turn the key when the doorbell rang. The sudden, unexpected sound pierced his head like a spike. He and Johanna both jumped.

Maybe whoever it was would go away. But the bell rang again.

"Bloody hell!" He pressed his palm against his forehead. Nobody had ever rung the bell when he'd been out "visiting" before.

The roll of tape was handy on the kitchen counter. With a now-practiced hand, he slapped several lengths over Johanna's mouth and around her wrists. Then he did the same to Kirsten before slipping the gun under his loose-fitting sweater.

"If you make any noise, I'll shoot whoever's out there and then the two of you."

He could tell from the look of terror in Johanna's eyes that she believed him. He wished she didn't have to be afraid of him. He'd thought maybe the two of them could help each other. But that was a long time ago.

He ran his fingers quickly through her dark hair before he left the room, just because he wanted to, just to show her he could do anything he wanted—to her *or* Kirsten.

There was a pleasant, relaxed smile on his face as he unlocked the front door. But it came from the feel of the gun next to his skin.

"Can I help you?"

"Hello, sir, my name is Walter Tucker," the young man on the porch began, "and I'm trying to win points to get a college scholarship."

He was a kid of eighteen, maybe twenty. He had a bad complexion, but the white shirt under his blue nylon jacket was clean. Cliff recognized someone trying to make a good impression.

Salesmen didn't venture up Cliff's long, rutted drive. It took several minutes before he realized what the guy really wanted. He was selling magazines.

Cliff's smile became malicious as he twirled a lemon drop between his fingers. He'd take out some subscriptions for the Goodwins. Studying the chart Tucker handed him, he selected *Field and Stream*, *Snowmobiler's Monthly*, and *Modern Maturity*.

Walter Tucker smiled and thanked him for

the business. "Your magazines ought to start arriving in six weeks, and you'll be billed at that time."

Cliff kept up the affable homeowner act until the door closed, then he sagged back against the solid wood, a barrier between himself and the world. It had always been that way. He had wanted to be like everybody else. What in the hell had happened to him? But it was too late to turn back now. His hands were shaking so badly that he had to clasp them together in front of him. What if the police knew where he was? The Lewis woman could have told them. What if that salesman had come to spy on him. He didn't have much time now. If anybody else came to the door, he wouldn't stand around talking and smiling. He'd drill them!

He squeezed his eyes shut for a moment. Calm down, he ordered himself. The cops don't know where you are. They're not that smart.

You can't lose it now, not when you're so close to the end. He pressed his hand to his forehead. It was hard to think, hard to remember what he'd planned out so carefully. He needed another drink. No, he needed to play with Emily—the way they both liked.

Damn! He'd smashed the doll. Why had he done that? His hand started to shake again. He should have thought before he smashed that doll. Now he needed another one for Emily to hold when he laid her on the ground, like the other two little girls.

Emily? He tried to clear his aching head. No, Kirsten. It was Kirsten. But she was like Emily.

He wiped his sweaty palms on the sides of his trouser legs and took several deep breaths. Emily didn't need the doll until she went to sleep. He could get another one later. After they were both dead he wouldn't have to worry about going out and leaving them alone.

Dan took the call from Susan in the task force room. "I just remembered who has blue and yellow flowered kitchen tiles."

He sat up in his chair. Out of the corner of his eye, he saw Fogel pick up line two. Another call important enough to interrupt the meeting, he thought as he turned his attention back to Susan. "Who?"

"Bill and Alice Goodwin—at 4283 Apple Orchard Run. And they're out of town." The words came out in a rush of nervous excitement.

Dan thumbed through the papers in front of him. "Goodwin? They're not on the post office list."

"But they're gone for two weeks—on a cruise. Alice told me."

"Give me the address again. And the phone number."

He wrote them down, wondering if this was the break they'd been praying for. He didn't dare let himself believe that it was—not yet. "In case we need it, do you know the layout of the house?"

"Sort of."

"Could you keep your phone line clear?"

"Yes."

"Susan, thanks."

"Got something?" Miner asked when Dan had hung up.

"Maybe."

Fogel had also put down the receiver. "That was a nurse from the hospital where they took the Lewis woman. She said something strange when she came out of the anesthetic."

"And?"

"Is there a Goodwin house on that post office list?"

Dan stared at him, hardly able to believe what he'd just heard. "No. But Susan Randolph just called me on the other line. Guess who has blue and yellow kitchen tiles and is out of town?"

"The Goodwins," Greenway supplied.

Fogel slapped his hands together like a quarterback coming out of the huddle. "Let's go kick that bastard Fuller's ass."

Suddenly, the oppressive tension the men in the room had been under exploded into a frenzy of activity. Dan could feel adrenalin pumping into his bloodstream. Up till now they'd just been stumbling around in the dark praying for a ray of light. Finally, here it was.

Fogel called Susan Randolph back and sent a squad car to pick her up. She and Juanita could work on the floor plan together under Jackson's direction.

Next, the lieutenant put the SWAT team on alert. Then he called in Larry Innis, the man who had waited in the cold most of yesterday to notify Johanna about the stakeout.

As Fogel brought the undercover detective up to date on the recent developments, Dan got up and began to pace back and forth. He couldn't stop himself from glancing at the clock every few minutes. One-thirty-four. Fuller had had Johanna and Kirsten now for over twenty hours.

He didn't want to sit at the station while Innis went to the Goodwins. He wanted to be the one to reconnoiter. That way he could see for himself what was going on. But one wrong move could set Fuller off—make him speed up his timetable. The mailman had been at Johanna's the first night he'd brought her and Kirsten home. And then later, when Dan had come to dinner, Fuller had seen him. He'd written about it in the letters.

Fuller hadn't looked up and seen him in the hallway at McDonald's, but he might recognize him if he were snooping around the Goodwin house. It was better to let Innis scout things out. Besides, he was a specialist in undercover surveillance.

"We need to know for sure whether Fuller is holding the woman and the girl at the Goodwins," Fogel concluded. "And if he's there—what he's up to."

"But the guy is likely to be trigger-happy," Greenway added. "Got any suggestions?"

Innis ran a hand through his thinning hair. "I could pretend to be a salesman and just ring the bell," he quipped.

"Ringing the bell's too dangerous—for you and Johanna and Kirsten," Dan interjected.

"There's always the old meter-reader trick.

I have that blue-collar look. I could probably get close to the house without arousing suspicion if I dressed up in a PEPCO uniform."

Fogel agreed. "Let's go with that. If the woman and the girl are in there, I'd like to plant a transmitter."

"If I can get close enough to read the meter, I can put a bug under a window."

"We'll back you up with a van around the corner. You can report to them with a walkie talkie."

"For God's sake, be careful," Dan broke in again. "Fuller's killed two little girls, and he's already shot and wounded a woman and a dog this morning. He doesn't have any compunctions about killing. He's likely to turn on Johanna and Kirsten if he thinks we're on to him."

Fogel looked at Dan assessingly. He was a good cop, and he usually followed procedures, but he'd been pushing this investigation pretty hard right from the beginning—like yesterday when he'd gone around him to the captain.

The only way to do a job like this was to stay cool and detached, but every time someone mentioned the Hamilton woman, it was obvious that this wasn't just another case to Whitmore.

Too bad, because you could never be sure what someone who was emotionally involved was going to do, like take stupid risks that endangered the victims—and the other officers on the scene. He'd be perfectly justified in taking Whitmore off the case. On the other hand, Whitmore was the one who had connected Jack Daniels to the murders—and the one who had pegged Fuller. That counted for a lot.

"Whitmore."

"Sir?"

"You want to go with the back-up team in the van?"

Dan swallowed around the knot in his throat. "Yes, sir. And thanks."

It took forty minutes to get Innis fitted out with the equipment he needed—including a bulletproof vest.

While he was getting ready, Dan went across the hall.

"How's it going?"

Susan passed him a sketchy floor plan she and Juanita had drawn of the Goodwins' house. "This is the best we could do."

Dan studied it, wondering where Fuller was holding Johanna and Kirsten. There was a combination kitchen and family room that opened onto a patio in the backyard. A kitchen door led directly from the garage. That was pretty standard. But the house also had a downstairs wing with three bedrooms—including the master suite. The children's rooms were upstairs.

Dan rolled the paper into a tube. "I'd better get this copied."

He was just turning to leave when Juanita put her hand on his arm.

"I have to talk to you," she said slowly in English.

"I've got to go."

"You must guard against him, or he will kill you."

"Listen, I'm not even going near the place. I'll be in a van around the corner. Someone else is casing the house, and he's only going to have a look around the outside."

Juanita ignored his words. "The bad man is going to try to kill you. *Con una carta.* A letter."

"What in the hell are you talking about, kill me with a letter—a letter bomb?"

There were tears in her eyes. "I don't know. It doesn't make sense to me, either, but I saw it in a dream. A letter with wavy lines and that strange sign. Like on the little girls' wrists."

A letter with the infinity mark. He'd seen it too. Fuller had drawn it and the wavy cancel lines on the outside of the envelope he'd left in Johanna's screen door. So Juanita was mixed up again. The realization was a relief. He hadn't wanted to believe Fuller was going to get him. "Please. Please be careful."

"I will. Sure. And thanks."

Johanna watched tensely as Cliff came back into the room. Over the past eighteen hours she'd become an unwilling but very attentive student of Clifford Fuller's moods.

Also, she'd come to a terrible realization a few moments ago. She'd been struggling so hard to do what he wanted. Now that she was almost finished, there was nothing to keep him from following through with his final plans, for Kirsten. And for her.

He'd looked sick and shaky when he went

to answer the door. Now his shoulders were squared and there was a purposeful glint in his pale eyes.

She'd prayed that somehow the police were at the door. Apparently not. What had happened out there? Was there another body lying in the living room now? A shivery wave of fear swept over her body.

Cliff strode across the room and ripped the tape off her mouth.

She couldn't stifle a scream.

"Quiet!"

The fury in his eyes made Johanna's heart freeze. She tried not to betray her terror. He was losing whatever control he'd had. "Cliff, that hurt. I thought you didn't want to hurt us."

He didn't answer as he set the typewriter back on the table in front of her. "You stay here and polish up that press release. Emily and I are going out to the barn to play."

Cliff walked up behind Kirsten. For a moment his hand hovered over her head, almost like a priest delivering a benediction. Then he sunk his fingers into her blond hair and sighed with pleasure. It had taken a lot of willpower not to play with her sooner, but he'd been waiting for Johanna to finish the press release. She was almost done. He could type the last few sentences if he had to.

Kirsten had been docile all morning. Now, at the touch of Cliff's fingers in her hair, something inside her seemed to snap. She twisted around and began to hit him with her fists. "Stop touching me like that. Stop touching me."

Johanna gasped, waiting for him to lash out at the child the way he had with her.

Instead he grabbed both of Kirsten's wrists with one hand. She continued to try and struggle, but he was like a cat restraining a mouse with one firm paw. With the other, he stroked her head. "Your hair's all tangled. We'll have to comb it," he murmured.

Tears welled in Kirsten's eyes as she looked pleadingly across the table at her mother.

Johanna's fingers clenched on the edge of her chair. She knew what he wanted, but what could she do? God in heaven, how could she stop him?

Larry Innis looked down the street. The brown van he'd come in with Stover, Whitmore, and Greenway was out of sight around the corner.

Communications had fitted him out with a transmitter that looked like the new digital hand-sets used to read electric meters. He could use it to talk to the men in the van.

He drew his hand from the pocket of his khaki jacket and adjusted his visor-cap. On it was the logo of the Potomac Electric Power Company.

Just in case someone at the Goodwin place was watching, he'd already checked the meters at the first three houses on the block.

Stopping on the sidewalk, he pretended to make an entry in the notebook he was carrying as he studied the Goodwin residence.

"From out here, it looks like it matches the floor plan we've got," he murmured into the hand-set. "The shades in front are drawn. I won't be able to see anything unless I go right up and press my face against the window, and I wouldn't want to bump into Fuller right on the other side of the glass."

There were no cars in the driveway. "I'm going to check the garage."

MVA showed an Acura and a BMW registered to the Goodwins. Fuller had an old Dodge.

Johanna sat frozen in her seat, unable to take her eyes off Cliff's hand as it combed slowly through Kirsten's hair. She could hear the ragged edge of his breathing from all the way across the table.

"Oh, darn, there's no barn. But we can pretend. Right up to the end."

Johanna could feel the chair's buttons digging into her back. The barn. Right up to the end.

Cliff had told her in loving detail what he and Emily had done up in the hayloft: the same thing he'd done to Jeanie and Heather before he'd murdered them.

He bent down, his lips against Kirsten's cheek as he fumbled at the cuff that held her ankle to the table-base. "If you don't want to play, you can just go to sleep. That's all right with me," he crooned.

"Wait!" Johanna gasped.

Cliff looked up, reluctant to take his eyes off the sweet little girl trembling next to him.

"I know what you're going to do."

"So?"

"Have you ever thought about a more mature relationship?" The words practically gagged her, but if there was *any way* to keep him from touching Kirsten, she would seize it.

He tipped his head to the side. For the first time in minutes, his eyes focused directly on her face. 'What do you mean?"

"Maybe you'd like to be with an experienced woman—someone who knows how to give you what you want."

"A woman?"

"Instead of a little girl."

She could see a flicker of interest in his pale eyes and she forced herself to smile at him. She tried to remember the things he had said in the letters. He had told her he wanted to take care of her, that they needed each other. "I need you, Cliff. And you need me, too. I like you a lot. That's why I gave you a piece of chocolate cake that time."

"You like me," he repeated. His hand dropped from Kirsten's hair, and he let go of her wrists.

The child hiccuped and cringed away, but he wasn't looking at her now. A lot of times in bed at night he'd thought about being with a woman. But Momma had told him no woman would ever want him. He'd told himself she was wrong. He wanted her to be wrong. He wanted to be like everybody else. But the few times he'd tried to approach a woman that way, he'd broken out in a cold sweat. And he hadn't known what to say—except in the letters to Johanna. Now, here she was offering what he'd secretly longed for.

Johanna was so pretty. She had blue eyes like Emily. But her hair was dark. His brow wrinkled. The wrong color. He didn't know if he could love a woman with dark hair.

His gaze swung back to Kirsten.

"Please," Johanna whispered reaching toward him across the table. "I want to show you how much I like you."

The pleading gesture and the entreaty in her voice made up his mind. He liked the way it sounded. Maybe he could try it with her. See if it was everything it was cracked up to be. Then, afterwards, he could have Kirsten, too. "Yes. Show me how much you like me," he agreed.

Instead of unfastening Kirsten, he unlocked the manacle around Johanna's leg. But he couldn't take any chances, so he held the gun on her and made her walk in front of him down the hall toward the bedroom.

The metal ring on Johanna's right foot dragged silently along the thick carpet. It caught in the fibers, and she had to jerk it free. Her wrist throbbed. She wrapped her other hand tightly around it to still the ache.

She walked as slowly as she could, trying to hold off the horrible ordeal she'd brought on herself. *If he's with me, he's not with Kirsten*, she told herself over and over like a mantra. And maybe she wouldn't have to go through with it; maybe she could get away while he was aroused and vulnerable.

He directed her to the master bedroom at the end of the hall. There was a wide brass bed with a soft blue and green spread. The drapes matched. Why in the name of God was she taking in details like that? Because she didn't want to think about what was going to happen, her mind screamed the answer. Her eyes darted to the nightstand, the dresser, the writing desk. Was there anything here she could use as a weapon? On the blue blotter was a letter opener. Could she stab him with that?

An image of her plunging the letter opener into Cliff's body again and again flashed into her mind. If she killed him, he couldn't hurt her or Kirsten anymore. She closed her eyes. God, what had this man reduced her to? Never in her wildest imagination would she have considered herself capable of killing another human being. Clifford Fuller had dragged her down to that level. The sudden self-knowledge was as frightening as anything that had happened to her since she'd jumped into the mail truck and gone off in pursuit of Kirsten and Rick.

"What are you waiting for?" With his gun, he gestured toward the bed. "Lie down."

The moment of truth was rushing to meet her too quickly. She turned her head away from him as she complied.

His hand closed around her ankle. She felt her leg jerk, then the open ring on the handcuff snapped shut.

Oh God, no. He had fastened her foot to

the bed-frame. Somehow she hadn't realized he'd do that.

She watched him pull the gun out of his waistband and lay it down on the window seat. Then he slowly pulled down the shade before turning back to her.

He looked nervous, like a man with his first lover.

The room was dim, except for a sliver of light where the shade didn't quite meet the windowsill.

He walked slowly back toward her, the acrid smell of his perspiration preceding him.

Johanna pressed her shoulders into the mattress, willing herself not to roll away in revulsion.

He was close enough now for her to see a muscle twitching under his right eye. He fingered the buttons on his shirt uncertainly.

His eyes suddenly hardened as he loomed above her. "Are you sure this isn't what you did with that guy who was over at your house those times?"

She blanched. He was back to that again. "No." This wasn't what she and Dan had done at all. It had been so sweet and tender with Dan. And then another thought leaped into her mind. The night he'd brought her home from the Italian Embassy. He'd been so angry when he'd thought Rick had persuaded her to go to bed with Marty Barnette. What would he think of her now? Would he understand why she had to do this? Would he ever want her again—if she and Kirsten—

The rest of the thought and the breath

were knocked out of her as Cliff threw himself down on top of her on the bed.

Innis peeked into the dim garage through one of the rows of windows in the door. He saw two cars: one, a BMW, the other, a clunker. Maybe they'd hit the jackpot after all. Cautiously, he slipped around the side of the house.

So far, so good. The meter was around back, right next to the sliding glass door. What luck. As he pretended to get a reading, he looked into the dim interior of the house.

Blue and yellow tiles ... the kitchen. A small figure sat at the table, head cushioned on her folded arms on the Formica top: a blond-haired child, quietly crying. There was no one else in the room.

Chapter 35

Walter Tucker reached the intersection of Apple Orchard Run and Covered Bridge. Turning the corner, he hurried toward the first house on the block. When you're on a roll, keep pushing. They'd told him that in the sales meeting. He was so intent on his purpose that he didn't see the door of the brown van slide open.

A hard-faced man jumped out and faced him on the sidewalk.

Oh fuck. A stickup—out here in the suburbs. At least he wasn't carrying much cash.

"Police. Hold it right there."

Another dangerous-looking man hopped down from the van. They both flashed badges in his face. The abrupt change of the threat didn't make him relax.

"I haven't done nothin' wrong." God, did you need a license to sell magazines door to door in Montgomery County? he wondered. The company hadn't said anything about that, but they could have been shittin' him.

"Been canvassing the neighborhood?"

"Just a little bit."

"We're looking for a fugitive who might be in one of these houses." Dan brought out the picture of Fuller. "Do you recognize this man?"

"Mr. Goodwin. My best sale of the day."

"How long ago?"

"Twenty minutes."

"Was there anything unusual about him?"

Walter looked down at his toes, wishing he could get the hell out of there.

"What?"

"He was real friendly-like, but I could tell he was jumpy."

"Anything else?"

Walter shrugged.

Greenway asked him some more questions. What exactly had the man said? Had Tucker seen or heard anyone else in the house?

Dan got back in the van to warn Innis. Then he checked in with Fogel. "A magazine salesman has identified Fuller. He was at the Goodwins as of twenty minutes ago."

"I'm going to start evacuating the houses in the vicinity so the SWAT team can move in."

Johanna had turned her face away from him. Her eyes stared blindly at the crack of light coming in from under the window shade, as if it offered some sort of salvation. A ray of hope. She kept repeating the phrase in her mind.

She could feel Cliff's hand stroking up her thigh. His fingers were light—like the legs of a spider—but she didn't dare jerk away, even when they reached the edge of her panties.

She was concentrating every ounce of effort on lying still and passive—waiting until he was so engrossed in what he was doing that she could smash her fist down on the back of his neck and bring her knee up into his crotch. He was strong. Was a surprise attack enough to give her the edge in a fight? It was her only chance, and she had to take it.

His fingers stopped moving; then he shifted away from her.

Her head whipped back toward him. "Cliff? Don't you want me?"

There was bitter self-reproach in his voice. "It's just not the same. I need Emily."

Emily. He'd turned Kirsten into Emily. Panic bubbled up inside her.

"No!"

As he started to get up, she dug her fingers into his shoulders. "I won't let you have Kirsten."

"Bitch. You don't really like me. You were fooling me." He wrenched away.

With a sob of anguish, she lashed out again, raking her nails across his cheek.

"Bloody hell!"

Somehow she deflected the blow he aimed at her mouth and tried to get her knee up. But he was too fast for her—and too powerful—and she was handicapped in the desperate struggle by the leg he'd chained to the end of the bed.

He crushed her down into the mattress, the hard palms of his hands digging into her shoulders so roughly that she thought her bones might crack from the pressure. She fought back desperately.

His fingers clutched at her blouse. The fabric ripped. She hardly noticed it as she fought him.

But she wasn't any match for his maniacal strength. Finally, he tore himself free. One large hand held her down. She gasped in pain as the flat of his other hand connected with her cheek. He was panting as he slapped her again and again, the way he had with the doll. The way he had broken the doll's head.

"Bitch, witch, bitch, witch," he chanted. "Bitch, witch. Bitch, witch."

With every blow, her senses reeled. Her vision dimmed, and her body went slack. She held onto consciousness by sheer willpower.

She heard him draw in a sobbing breath.

"I don't want you. You lied to me. Bitch, witch. Bitch, witch. I want Emily. I need Emily. She's the only one who loves me. She's the only one who ever loved me."

Then his weight was shifting off the bed. Through slitted eyes she saw him pick up the gun from the window seat.

He left the room, and she knew he was running down the hall toward the kitchen . . . toward her daughter.

The minute Cliff disappeared through the door, Johanna pushed herself up and began to pull frantically on the handcuff. Her head spun, but her hands kept working. If she could have cut off her foot to get free, she would have done it.

God, please don't let him hurt Kirsten. The words were a silent prayer.

Think; you've got to think. She couldn't *pull* herself loose. Was there some other way?

Her hands closed around the smooth brass rail to which the handcuff was attached. Her heart leaped when she realized she felt the rail move up and down—just a little. The footboard wasn't one solid piece. The vertical bars must be fitted into holes drilled in the top and bottom rails. With every ounce of her strength, she pressed upward on the topmost piece of tubing with her feet and pulled down on the vertical bar with her hands. It moved again.

A little more, just a little more . . .

Johanna grunted with effort as she pushed and pulled. Metal rasped against metal. The sharp edge of the vertical tubing grated against the horizontal one. She gave one more muscle-wrenching yank and toppled backwards on the bed as the brass rod came free, clanking against the handcuff.

Regaining her balance, she clambered off the bed and sprang toward the desk where she'd seen the letter opener. She grabbed it and spun around. Then she was running full tilt down the hall after Cliff.

"Jesus Christ. I can see the kid," Innis whispered into the walkie-talkie. "She's in the kitchen. Alone."

Where were Fuller and the mother? Was Johanna Hamilton already dead?

Innis knew he should get the hell out of there. Fuller could come back into the kitchen any minute.

Just then the kid raised her head, and he saw the stark terror in her blue eyes. He knew what the mailman had done to the other little girls before killing them. And he knew that a few minutes could mean the difference between life and death for Kirsten Hamilton. He had to take the chance on trying to get her out of there.

He tested the door. Locked. If he broke the glass, Fuller would probably come running in.

He got out a tool kit and looked down intently at its contents.

From the other side of the patio door, he didn't hear footsteps on the vinyl floor. But he couldn't miss the crack of a pistol shot. In front of him, the glass exploded. An instant later, a searing pain sliced into his hip—just below his bulletproof vest. "Shit. The bastard got me."

Innis dropped the walkie-talkie. His own gun was automatically in his hand. As he went down, he fired at the figure advancing on the window, but his aim was way off.

The child started to scream, a high-pitched wail.

There was another pistol crack. A slug tore into the vest. Another hit his knee and he screamed in pain.

Dan heard the first shot. He was out of the van and sprinting down Apple Orchard Run toward the Goodwins' before Innis hit the ground.

Juanita had said Fuller was going to kill him. He shoved the warning aside.

Two shots. Three. Four. Jesus. A man's scream, and a high-pitched child's wail. Kirsten.

His mind was already considering the floor plan. Innis had gone around to the back. He and Fuller were probably shooting it out in the kitchen, and Kirsten was in there. The quality of her screams hadn't changed. She wasn't hit . . . yet. He wanted to charge around the back and pull her out of there, but that would bring him directly into Fuller's line of fire. He'd have to go in the front or the garage entrance. Every second counted now.

The front was faster. He dashed across the soggy lawn.

Something whizzed past Johanna's head as she rounded the corner into the kitchen. There was another crack.

Bullets.

She saw the shattered window—Kirsten under the table screaming.

Cliff and another man were shooting at each other. The man was on his knees, and then he fell through the ruined sliding glass door into the kitchen. Cliff leaped forward, bent over him. His attention was occupied. She could get Kirsten out of there, away from Cliff, away from the shooting.

From the corner of her eye she saw Cliff tear the gun from the man's hand and straighten up. He was turning toward her. Shifting in mid-stride, Johanna sprang for Cliff's back, stabbing the letter opener into his shoulder.

There was a wrought-iron bench and a small table on the front porch. Dan picked up the table and hurled it through the picture window. He hardly broke stride as he climbed through. Ignoring the shards of glass that tore at his clothes, he stepped over the sill and onto the sofa, his foot leaving a muddy print in the middle of the rose-colored damask as he jumped down.

There were two ways into the kitchen, through the dining room or down the hall. He moved to his right, toward the hall, gun in hand, arms extended.

Johanna was still clinging to Cliff's back as he straightened.

She heard the violent crash of shattering glass somewhere else in the house. Cliff tried to shake her off. She held grimly to his shirt.

Cursing, he slammed his body backward against the wall. The force knocked the breath out of Johanna and loosened her grip. Tears streamed down her face as she slid to the floor.

"Mommy! Mommy!"

The gun was still in Cliff's hand as he swung around to face her.

Dan rounded the corner and froze as he took in the scene: Kirsten a shivering, sobbing figure crouched under the table; Johanna on the floor, her clothes torn, her hair a tangled mat. Her face was red and swollen, but her eyes glinted with unyielding rage.

Standing above her with his finger on the trigger of a gun was the man he'd seen last night at McDonald's.

He didn't hesitate. "Fuller! Here!"

The mailman whirled. "You! You bastard." He fired. A slug nicked Dan's ear as he squeezed the trigger of his own gun—once, twice.

The bullets tore into Fuller's midsection. He looked astonished. Then, in slow motion, he doubled over. A final shot from his revolver slammed into the tiles as he slumped toward the floor.

Dan sprung across the room and kicked the gun out of the killer's hand. Fuller didn't protest; he lay gasping on the floor. Innis was sprawled on his face a few feet away, blood darkening the legs of his pants. He'd been hit, but not fatally.

Johanna pushed herself up and started crawling toward her daughter. A handcuff clanked across the floor as she moved her leg. She reached Kirsten and pulled the sobbing child into her arms.

"Johanna. Thank God you're safe. Both of you." Dan knelt down to embrace them. "Are you all right?"

She looked at him as if she couldn't believe he was really there. "Oh, Dan. God, how I prayed you'd find us. He was going to—"

"It's over."

Kirsten clung to him as well as to her mother.

Johanna reached up to touch the top of his ear. "He hurt you."

Dan put his own hand up, and was surprised to see it come away wet with blood. He'd hardly felt it. "It's nothing." He could hear police sirens outside.

He wanted to keep on holding them, absorbing the reality that they were finally safe, but he had to get help for Innis, too. With one hand, he snagged the undercover man's walkie-talkie and spoke into it. "Everything's under control, but I need an ambulance—for Innis and Fuller."

"Johanna and Kirsten?" Greenway asked.

"Roughed up. I think they're all right." His eyes focused on the handcuff that secured Kirsten to the table-base. "Jesus. What did he do to you?"

"Thank God you got here when you did."

He looked into Johanna's eyes, reading the aftermath of the horror. She couldn't talk about it yet, but they'd have time for that later. "Did you see where he put the key?"

"In his pants pocket."

"I'll get it."

It was a moment before she could let go of him.

"Don't leave us again."

"You're safe. I'll be right back."

He crossed the room and squatted down beside the lifeless form on the floor, staring at it with distaste. Such an ordinary looking man—with such an evil, twisted mind.

One of Fuller's hands was flung wide. The other was half-hidden under his body. Blood soaked the front of his shirt and his gray slacks. Dan steeled himself to thrust his hand into the wet pocket. Coins, lemon drops, a pen . . . finally his fingers closed around a small key. Before he could withdraw it, the body seemed to convulse.

In the next instant, the world turned upside down. Dan was on the floor, and Cliff Fuller was above him, a final spark of mad determination in his eyes.

One large hand held Dan's shoulder in a death grip. He tried to pull away. He couldn't. Christ, the bastard was strong.

In Fuller's other hand was a hunting knife. It was too late for Dan to remind himself that he should have checked the body before going to Johanna and Kirsten—checked to see that Fuller was really dead. The weapon flashed down toward his throat. Johanna's scream filled the room.

Dan twisted desperately. The blade missed its mark and slashed through his skin, glancing off his collarbone.

His fist slammed up into the twisted visage above him, once, twice. It felt good to strike that hated face, but there was no need to continue; the killer had used up his last surge of energy. Fuller collapsed on top of him.

Pushing the body aside, Dan sat up and pried the knife out of the now limp hand.

Something made him look at the handle.

He sucked in his breath when he saw the markings that had been carved into the dark wood. They were the same as the ones on the envelope Fuller had left in Johanna's door that night: the cancel mark, with the infinity sign instead of a postmark.

He shuddered. Juanita had said Fuller was going to kill him with a letter. She'd seen the marks, but not on a letter—on the handle of the knife. She'd almost been right.

Chapter 36

Saturday, November 6

Colonel Jennings had regained his ability to speak and was making rapid progress under Betty's loving encouragement. Marian Lewis and Baron had both come home from the hospital. Larry Innis would recover, but would probably have to take disability retirement. Clifford Fuller would never hurt anyone again.

As Dan and Johanna sat on the edge of her daughter's bed, she knew she had a lot to be thankful for.

The usual collection of dolls surrounded Kirsten—like a security force around the queen. The eight-year-old's arm clutched the latest addition to the collection—an Indian princess, wearing a soft doe-skin dress and moccasins.

Mother and daughter had gone down to the Treasure Chest that morning to pick it out. By unspoken agreement, they had selected a new doll as different as they could find from the Victorian lady Cliff had smashed.

Mr. Beckett hadn't let them pay.

"I appreciate your business," he'd said. "And I'm glad that both of you are all right."

Dan had told Johanna that Beckett's mother had been one of the people with information leading to her and Kirsten's rescue. In fact, he'd filled her in on most of what had happened during the frantic twenty-four hours that they'd been missing.

But she hadn't been able to tell *him* much. The horror was too fresh. She was grateful that he hadn't pressed her on the subject.

Kirsten pulled the covers up to her chin and looked at her mother. "And you're going to be right here in the house?"

"Of course."

Kirsten had slept in Johanna's bed the night before. Tonight she'd only put up a token protest about retiring to her own room. Privately, Johanna wondered if she'd stay there all night.

The little girl reached up to give her mother a long, clinging hug that was more than just a routine "good-night."

Then she turned to Dan and shyly held out her arms.

He embraced her warmly and then gently laid her back against the pillow. "Good night, Pumpkin."

Kirsten giggled, and the sound was like a balm to Johanna's spirit.

"Oh, I almost forgot." Dan reached into his pocket and brought out a small plastic bag.

Kirsten looked at it inquiringly. "That's my tooth!"

"Yup."

"I thought the tooth fairy wouldn't find it. How did you get it?"

"The lost and found department. Now you can put it under your pillow."

Kirsten carefully tucked the prize out of sight.

After a few more moments, the adults got up to leave.

"Close my closet door, and turn on my night-light," Kirsten instructed.

"Okay."

Johanna didn't hurry with the last small tasks. With all the media attention that had been focused on the case, she and Dan had hardly been alone together since the rescue. She wanted to trust her feelings for him, but how would he react to the things she had to tell him?

In the hall, he turned and took her in his arms.

Wordlessly, she began to tremble.

"It's all right," he murmured against her hair. Then he swung her up into his arms and carried her down the hall to her room.

"Dan—I can't."

"I just want to hold you." He sat down in the wing chair in the corner and cuddled her in his lap.

She was careful to angle her head so that it didn't press against the bandage peeking out at the collar of his shirt.

"Does it still hurt where he cut you?"

"Only when I laugh. And I haven't been doing much of that."

"Dan, you risked your life to save me and Kirsten. I can't stop thinking about that."

"I wasn't trying to be a hero. I just had to get the two of you out of there."

They didn't speak for a few moments. His hand stroked over her shoulders and her hair. At least she wanted the physical comfort he could offer her ... or was she just showing her gratitude? He hoped she'd give him some clue about what she was feeling. When she didn't, he finally asked, "What are you thinking about?"

"About whether you'll still want me."

"How could you possibly think I wouldn't?"

Her voice was strained. "I remember how angry you were about Marty Barnette."

"What does that have to do with anything?"

"I haven't told you about what happened with Cliff." She felt Dan's muscles tense and was almost afraid to go on. But it was better to get it over with. "Dan, I was willing to do anything to keep him from molesting Kirsten."

"Give me some credit for understanding that."

"I made him think I wanted him. We were in bed together. He was on top of me—"

Dan's hands clenched on her shoulders. "Did he rape you?"

She shook her head. "It didn't work. I just didn't turn him on. And when he tried to leave me and go back to Kirsten, I went crazy. I started clawing at him and trying to hold him there."

"Was that when he beat you up?"

"Yes," she whispered. "Also the day before, when I almost got away. He came back from McDonald's and found me trying to make a phone call."

Dan swore. "That bastard. It's a good thing he's dead."

"Don't you understand? I came on to him."

He tipped her back so that he could look into her eyes. He could see the anxiety—and the apprehension. Anyone would feel degraded by what had happened with Fuller, but Johanna had an additional burden—the humiliation her ex-husband had made her feel.

"Johanna, when I found out that maniac had you, I was scared out of my mind. I kept hoping you'd have the sense to do *whatever* it took to save you and Kirsten."

"But—"

"Look, the most important thing was survival—yours and Kirsten's. You saved your daughter's life. If Fuller had gotten to her, she wouldn't have had any more chance than those other two little girls."

He could feel some of the tension ease out of her.

"I was so afraid, Dan."

"I know. But you didn't go to pieces."

"I was terrified. Not just of what he was going to do. I was afraid of the way he was making me feel. I wanted to kill him."

"I did too. I *did* kill him."

She nodded slowly. "Yes."

He waited for the realization to sink in. She'd seen him kill a man. Not just any man, the maniac who had brutalized her and Kirsten.

Their eyes met and held.

"He would have killed you, and us, if you hadn't stopped him."

His arms tightened around her.

"You've made me feel a lot better," she murmured.

"Good. You're making me feel better, too."

For several moments, they simply held each other.

"You remember when we promised we'd be honest?"

She nodded.

"Well, I've been wondering if you were keeping me at arm's length because you wanted to put everything from these last few weeks out of your life."

"Most things. Not you."

His lips brushed her cheek. When she turned her face so that he could kiss her on the mouth, his embrace became more sure. She'd become part of his life, and he'd been afraid he was going to lose her.

His arms around her gave her a sense of belonging she hadn't felt in years, and his lips on hers were awakening the first stirrings of desire . . . but the greatest joy was that she knew they had a future together. A madman had dragged her into his own private hell. But she'd come back. Now she and Dan would have the time they needed. Together. She liked the way that sounded.